Sugar Creek

Sugar Creek

S.C. Karakaltsas

For my family

1

Dana

1999

There's a month to go before the predicted Y2K disaster. So they say. It's all anyone talks about, but right now, it's the last thing on my mind. A crack of thunder and a glance skywards spurs me up the hill, towards my ordinary pale blue weatherboard house, in an ordinary suburban street. Ordinary like me, Dana Janssen. That's what Daniel had said: *You're a nice ordinary girl, but …* That *but* had lingered like a bad smell. He wanted someone less white bread, more exotic – someone like Petra, a brunette with impossibly long tanned legs and big boobs.

My original plan for the new year was marriage to Daniel, a GP spot in a little suburban medical centre, and a house not far from Mum and my sister, Lily. Not that Daniel had ever popped the question, but it was understood. We'd talked many times about being married, how many kids we'd have and the house we'd buy. Or maybe I talked about it, now that I think back. It makes no difference, he didn't want me, and that was all there was to it.

Time to come up with a new plan, assuming we survive Y2K.

Walking up the timber ramp to the front door puffs me out. First on the list is to get fit, and I begin feeling better as I turn the key in the lock.

"Dana!" Lily screams. "Come and see what I've done."

My younger sister's voice is music to my ears.

"Show me."

Feigning excitement, I dump everything on my bed and rush down the hallway to the family room, where a large canvas sits on an easel. I never feel ordinary when I'm with her. Take that, Daniel.

I nod at Mum and kiss Lily on her forehead. "It's beautiful. Really … what's the word? Exquisite."

And it is.

She grins before turning back to the painting, her tongue poking over her bottom lip as she concentrates. The paintbrush is like a conductor's baton in her hands, stroking fine lines of deep purple across the canvas of lilac irises. The flowers look so real.

Lily's speech is slightly slurred, and she's lost the use of both legs, but there's a vibrancy about her that I admire. She's tough and strong and loves me no matter what.

She's the reason I went into medicine and slaved over the books for years. She had misdiagnosed meningitis when she was two. The doctors saved her, but everything changed. I was eight and can still remember her poor little body and the fear in her eyes.

In the kitchen, I grab a piece of carrot and hug Mum, still in her bank uniform and enthusiastically shredding a lettuce.

"Something smells delicious. What's for dinner?"

"A vegetarian curry," Mum says.

My mother is a saint and looks remarkably young, more so after I convinced her to have her hair cut into a stylish bob. She brought us up singlehandedly, always with a smile. I can't remember her ever yelling or nagging me. Dad left when I was nine, and I haven't seen him since. To be honest, I don't care. He sent money until I turned eighteen, but after that, his obligations ended.

I gaze at the silver photo frame on the television cabinet. It's just me, Mum, and Lily. We have the same crooked-mouthed smile and almond-shaped eyes, although Lily's are blue and mine are chocolate brown, and the same honey-blonde hair, except mine is long and wavy.

I look around the comfortably furnished room and sigh: my home and sanctuary, where I'll probably stay for at least twelve more months. I'll put that on my list for next year – a new decade, new millennium. Stay at home.

"How was your final exam?"

I shrug.

"Okay."

"After years of studying and three years of GP training, plus all those exams, you should be proud of yourself. It's over now."

"I know. I just want to get a job and help people, get them better and point them towards a healthier life."

Mum hands me the cutlery. "Any prospects yet?"

I wince. Almost twenty-nine and looking for my first job. A real job. The years selling cosmetics part-time at a large department store don't count.

My mood plummets even further. How the hell will I get a job after what happened? It was one mistake. I can still practise, they said, but until the hospital board hearing, it's doubtful anyone will hire me. How am I going to pay back all the debts I've racked up and help out Mum?

"Here," Lily calls out, holding up the painting. "For you. You can put it in your new office when it's dry."

I take it from her and place it at the end of our long wooden table. "My patients will feel calm and relaxed when they see it."

That's what I say to Lily each time she gives me a painting, even though I don't have a job, let alone office space. It's become a ritual.

I'd suggested to Mum that we hold an exhibition of Lily's work, but she wouldn't hear of it. "I'm not exposing her to public scrutiny," she'd said.

I'd tried to convince her that Lily would be accepted like anyone else, but years of battling the education system to send her to a normal school – the tears, the jibes, and the name-calling – had taken their toll.

"Can you take her smock off and wheel her to the table, love?"

I help Lily and sit her next to me. She can be quite independent at times, and I've worn the odd spoonful of food in my hair when she wants to do things her way. I guess we all want our independence. I need mine, and Mum wants me to move out and get on with life.

Get fit and find a job. Spend more time with my sister. Three things on my plan. I look at her and smile. Her mouth full, she smiles back.

I take a spoonful of curry.

"By the way," Mum says, "there's a letter for you. It looks important." Her chair screeches on the worn timber floor as she grabs a bulky manilla envelope and places it on the table in front of me. "It might be good news."

I stop chewing and swallow.

"It can't be the board. Can it? It's too soon."

"Open it and see," Mum says, picking up her fork.

I weigh the envelope and rip it open. There's a thick wad of what looks like marketing stuff and a letter signed by "Herb Hipworth, Mayor."

I read the letter, then blink and read it again. "What the hell?"

Mum looks at me expectantly.

Even Lily has stopped eating.

On the edge of tears, the words on the page are a blur. I can't quite believe it. Suddenly a dizzying future of possibility is in front of me. "I've been offered a job."

"A job?" Mum rests her fork in her bowl.

Lily claps her hands and chants, "Dana got a job!"

"They'll pay out my student debts if I stay there for three years."

Without breaking eye contact with me, Mum touches Lily's arm, and the chant stops.

"Oh, my goodness. All of our prayers have been answered."

She's been praying for me? I thought she was a practising atheist. Then I turn the page and skim-read the attachments. Hope plummets, ambushed by geography.

I look at Mum, then Lily who's scooping the last spoonful into her mouth.

"There's a catch."

"Oh?" Mum says, her hands resting in her lap.

"The job's in a country town."

"That's not so bad. We can visit."

"Yeah, good," Lily says, wiping the plate with her finger.

"It's over a thousand kilometres away, in a place called Sugar Creek. They've sent me a whole heap of stuff about the place."

I hand the papers to Mum, wanting to see her reaction. She puts on her glasses and reads.

I'd applied for quite a few jobs right before Daniel dumped me. It was a blur of applications. One by one, they all came back, declined. I must have forgotten this one. I can't leave Mum and Lily. A country town an hour away? Sure. But not a godforsaken place I've never heard of.

Mum reads aloud, and I look over her shoulder. "There are one thousand people living there. They've got a pub, a police station, a couple of cafés, a golf course, a railway station, and a grocery store. They've kept the old buildings, and it looks quite charming. 'A tourist destination surrounded by sugar plantations, lying near a World Heritage protected rainforest with pristine mountain waterfalls, and not far from the coast.'" She looks at me over the top of her glasses. "It sounds beautiful."

"It looks like a run-down relic from the thirties. I can't go. I'm not leaving you and Lily."

Mum places the papers on the table, takes off her glasses, and stares me down. That look always means business. "Going there will set you up for life. No debt, rental subsidy, and one hundred thousand dollars a year. It's too good an opportunity. You have to go."

That is a good deal.

"There's no decision here, Dana," she continues. "Lily and I don't need you. We'll get along fine. Put what's happened behind you and start afresh."

Is she talking about Daniel, the incident, or herself?

"But what about the board? Once they hear what I did, they'll take it back."

"They've probably done all of their checks already," Mum says.

She's probably right. That's the reason why all the other applications were declined. No-one wants to touch me. Damaged goods, Daniel said. I can't move forward until the board decides my fate.

"Country towns are desperate for people of your calibre. The hearing won't be for months, and it wasn't your fault anyway. You can't put your life on hold. Who knows if you'll ever get another chance like this?"

My mother, as ever, is the voice of reason, able to talk me down with her positive outlook. I pick up a brochure. Ten kilometres to a surf beach. Learn to surf. I can put that on my list, suddenly expanding with possibilities.

Mum reaches for me and plants a kiss on my cheek. "If you hate it, come back."

Lily claps her hands. "Me too?"

Mum laughs and kisses her as well.

2

Ellen

May 1948

Ellen Lambert smoothed down her dress, a pale-green floral, usually kept for Sunday best. The train slowed into the platform, and she peered at the sign: Sugar Creek. Picking up her suitcase, she stepped off the train into the humidity, her heart beating with nerves and excitement. She looked at the address on the crumpled paper for the umpteenth time and headed towards the station master.

"Excuse me."

The heavy-set man stared, his face tomato red with beads of sweat spreading across his forehead. "Yes, miss."

She held out the piece of paper. "Do you know if this address is far?"

"Well, that depends if you walk or take a taxi." He glanced at her large suitcase. "Going to be taking that with you?"

She nodded.

"Then you need a taxi."

He picked up her case and turned before she had time to protest.

She could hardly tell him she couldn't afford it, so she followed him to the front of the station where a taxi waited.

"Where to, love?" the driver asked.

She handed him the paper and climbed into the back, glancing at her watch. It was four o'clock: knock off time.

"You visiting?" the driver said, driving away from the train station.

"Ah, yes," Ellen said.

"You're not planning on staying at that address, are you?"

"Why do you ask?"

"It's a boarding house for the canecutters."

The taxi meandered around leafy suburban streets filled with neat weatherboard houses perched high off the ground on stilts and soon pulled up in front of a large building with a small verandah. He turned his head towards her. "For men only."

"Oh, I didn't know. There's someone I wanted to see."

"Cane cutter?"

"Yes," she answered with growing irritation.

"Those blokes live on the farms during the week and only come back here on the weekends. Your friend won't turn up 'til Saturday."

Ellen stared at the building. What had she been thinking?

"You got somewhere else to stay?"

Her chest tightened. "Is there anything in town?"

"There's the pub. Can I take you there?"

She nodded, not trusting herself to speak. It was Monday. What was she going to do until Saturday?

Why hadn't Billy told her? It had been a mistake to come. She'd stay the night and go back on the train in the morning.

The taxi entered the main street, and she noticed the pub immediately. The Palace Hotel was a majestic building like the ones in Brisbane with fancy fretwork and stained-glass windows.

"Here you go," the driver said placing her luggage on the footpath. "Joan'll help you out."

Ellen paid him and walked into the cool foyer of the hotel. A fume of furniture polish made her cough, and a large-breasted matronly woman in a floral apron looked up from polishing the dark-timbered counter. Her face was round, with plump cheekbones under sunken eyes, and she peered at Ellen as if expecting her.

"After a room?"

"Yes."

The woman ducked under the counter to bring out a large leather-bound book and a pencil. "How long you planning on staying?"

"One night, I think."

"Right. And what brings you to Sugar Creek?" Her head cocked to one side.

"I came to surprise my fiancé," she blurted and tittered nervously. "He's a cane cutter, but I didn't realise he lived on the farm during the week."

The woman stretched her hands across the counter and leaned forward. "Really? Where you from, dear?"

"Brisbane."

She cocked an eyebrow. "Long way to come for a surprise."

"I … I'm probably going back tomorrow."

But what was she going back to? She had no job, no place to live. She'd given them up to come here.

"The train only runs twice a week. Monday and Sunday."

"Oh." Ellen fought the swell of tears. She took a handkerchief from her handbag and blew her nose, hiding her face. "It looks like I'll be staying a bit longer, then. I don't suppose you know of any jobs going around here?"

The woman brightened. "Ever worked in a pub?"

"Yes, in Brisbane as a barmaid a couple of years ago. Why? Do you need someone?"

Her face broke into a cheerful grin. "There's a job here if you want it."

"Really? Thank you."

"I'm Joan Babcock, and I own the pub with my husband, Paul. To be honest, I'm desperate for help. The last lass left two weeks ago, and it's just me on my own. I can give you board and a small wage, and you can start in about half an hour. How does that sound?"

*

Ellen placed the cold beer on the counter, where a shaft of green light came through the stained-glass window.

"That'll be one and sixpence, thanks," she said to the man as he dug into the pocket of his brown pants.

He raised an eyebrow and made to say something. Was he going to protest at the price? Joan told her to charge him more because he wasn't a local. Something about keeping afloat. She wiped away the condensation left by the glass with a well-worn cloth.

He passed over the coins in silence, and Ellen swept them off the counter and into the till before turning away.

Joan's shrill voice rang out. "Last drinks, fellas."

The noise died down for a moment before a few patrons strolled towards the bar. According to Joan, it was even busier when the cane workers came to town.

Ellen moved down the bar. "What'll it be, Cal? Another round?"

"Thanks, love." Cal rubbed the stump of his arm before turning to two men behind him. "Like I was saying, the bastards are screwing us. If they don't sort it out, we can kiss hundreds of pounds goodbye. It'll wipe me out."

Ellen had learned quickly about the locals. The Palace Hotel was their daily meeting ground, a place to recover, learn, vent, seek solace, or just escape their responsibilities.

She sat three beers on a tray on the counter, knowing Cal wouldn't accept any help. She learned that on her first day when she'd offered to help him by taking it to the table.

"What the fuckyadoin'? Puttem' down," he'd yelled, nostrils flaring and fist clenched. "I'm not a fuckin' invalid."

Ten pairs of eyes had bored into her, and the pub fell silent as Ellen returned the tray to the counter. She hadn't been too worried. Ellen knew how to take care of herself. She'd had to defend herself plenty of times from her father and her brothers when they got bigger.

"Settle down," Joan said calmly. "It's her first day."

"Yeah, button it, mate," Bert said. "We're waiting for your round."

Cal looked sheepish. "Sorry, love."

Afterwards, Joan explained Cal had returned from the war to take control of a run-down family sugar cane farm, and his missus had gone off with a Yank who'd been stationed in the town. As if that was an excuse for his sudden flare-up.

She knew better than to watch as Cal picked up the tray with his good hand and took it to the table. Instead, she swatted a blowfly trying to escape by the stained-glass window.

"They'll agree. They won't let seven hundred thousand ton of sugar lie around," Bert argued.

Ellen noticed the stranger frown and cock his head as if listening to the conversation. His brown felt hat rested on the table, and his brown suit jacket hung on the back of his chair. There was a dirty mark on the collar of his open-necked white shirt and the edge of a tattoo below rolled-up sleeves. A lot of strangers dropped in on their way north. They never stopped for long because there wasn't anything else around.

She listened more intently to Cal and Bert as she gathered the empty glasses.

"Ya' reckon?" Cal said, the stump moving as if his entire arm were still there. "A few hundred waterside workers are holding us to ransom. What do they care? We didn't fight a dog of a war for commie bastards to wreck it all."

Bert Hipworth busied himself with cleaning and then refilling his pipe before putting a match to it. He sucked on its stem, breathing in and out until the tobacco lit up. He wasn't one of them. A farmer that is. She'd known that as soon as she saw him in a fine suit and tie on her first day.

He was married to Joan's best friend, Carolyn, and his family owned most of the town. He was in his mid-thirties and was an officer in the war, but he still worked for the army at the military base on the outskirts of town. No-one knew why it hadn't closed down. The war ended years ago, but every so often, British or American soldiers still showed up in the pub. They never said why they were there or what they were doing. It wasn't Ellen's business anyway.

Her business was Billy. She'd been in Sugar Creek for four days and couldn't wait to see his face when he came into town on Saturday.

Joan began counting out money from the till.

"Ellen, can you wipe down the tables for me?"

Wally Gillespie, a local in shorts, mismatched long socks, and thongs, who had been quiet till now, piped up. "Stop ya whining, Cal. At least you've gotta income. I'll probably have to sell up lock, stock and barrel."

The few patrons still left fell silent. Even the stranger stared at Wally.

Bert glanced at his watch.

"Better get home to the missus." He drank the last of his beer. "See ya tomorrow."

"Can you tell Carolyn I'll drop the cardigan in for her tomorrow morning?" Joan said.

"Sure."

Bert shoved on his hat and left.

That began the exodus, except for the stranger who remained quietly reading the paper. As Ellen cleared two glasses from a nearby table, she noticed an article about the waterside workers strike holding up the sugar cane and wondered if it was a coincidence. What might that mean for Billy and their future? Would he be out of work again?

"See ya, ladies," yelled out another local, interrupting her thoughts.

She worked to clear the rest of the tables, washed and dried the glasses, and then put them away. Only one glass left. The stranger, still sipping his beer, wrote something in a notepad.

Joan slung a tea towel over her shoulder. "The bar'll be closing in a couple of minutes, but you're welcome in the lounge if you want. There's a room available too if you're interested."

The stranger turned painstakingly towards them, a cigarette hanging from his bottom lip. He removed it with a bony-edged hand and gave a slight nod before turning back to his drink and downing it in one gulp. "I'll have a room tomorrow night."

Then, hat perched on his head, jacket over his shoulder, and newspaper under his arm, he strode out. Ellen watched him leave in his dust-covered, brown pick-up truck.

3

Dana

February 2000

The sodden heat sinks into me as I step off the air-conditioned train and onto the platform at Sugar Creek. The air smells tropical, almost sweet, and every pore across my body prickles with sweat. I wheel my case towards the exit, grateful for the breeze, and look around for the mayor. But there are only a couple of backpackers and a tall, well-built man in board shorts and a tattered, wide-brimmed straw hat coming towards me.

"Dr Janssen?" he says, peering at me through aviator sunglasses.

"Yes."

He moves to pick up my suitcase.

"Mr Hipworth couldn't make it?" I ask.

He straightens up and stares at me; my reflection mirrored in his sunglasses. "Sorry, I should have said. I'm Herb Hipworth."

"Oh?" From our phone calls, I'd expected short, bald, and dumpy. "Nice to meet you."

When he picks up my suitcase, his biceps bulge under the short-sleeve Hawaiian shirt. It's hard to tell how old he is beneath the hat and sunglasses, but his strides are long, and his legs are muscly and tanned.

"This way," he says.

There's a late-model Ford Ute parked in the small bitumen car park. Opposite are weatherboard Queenslanders – houses with broad verandahs that sit majestically above wide timber staircases. The gardens are filled with tropical flowers and trees that you can only find this far north.

The windows of the ute are already down, and Herb lifts the canvas canopy, throwing my things into the back. When we get in, he drops his hat on the ledge behind, and I'm surprised by the tumble of thick black hair that falls to his collar. He's younger than I thought, maybe late twenties or very early thirties.

I pull my skirt under my legs to protect them from the baked leather. He starts the engine and backs out of the station car park, his head turned over his shoulder, and then we're on the highway. The wind flicks strands of hair across my face until I manage to wrestle it into a ponytail.

"You'll be staying for a few days at The Palace," he says.

A conversation starter I can deal with. "What's The Palace?"

"The pub. Your place is still being fixed up but should be ready next week. The surgery's fine, though, so you can start setting it up how you want tomorrow."

"Has it been long since you've had a permanent GP here?"

Cane fields stretch in both directions. Herb lifts a finger to wave at a truck coming the other way. There's no wedding ring, I notice.

"Five years or so. We're pretty desperate. Just had locums and sometimes the Flying Doctor service. Townsville and Cairns are too far."

"I'm looking forward to it."

I can't tell him that I wonder if I can even do this job and win the trust of the townspeople who are putting their faith in me. I slow my breathing. I have to set up the surgery, order supplies, and get organised. My to-do list is several pages long, and it's daunting. There's no nurse or other doctor, so I'm expected to do everything – take blood, do immunisations, and even perform the occasional surgery. My GP mates tell me I'll be fine, but my self-doubt almost overwhelms me.

The drive into town is short. We pass primary school children in maroon-coloured shorts and t-shirts parading noisily out of a white weatherboard building on stilts. The main street is a corridor of restored heritage buildings, divided down the middle by a procession of tall palms. The pamphlet doesn't do this town justice.

"That's The Palace." Herb points.

The building sits at the corner of the next intersection, dominating the street like only a Queensland pub in its prime can. Lace fretwork around the top verandah sits like the collar of an old Victorian dress.

"It's magnificent. Newly renovated?"

"Yeah, after a fire a while back. Tourists come now."

He parks at an angle. I get out of the ute, and a pleasantly cool breeze is fragrant from the frangipani growing in large pots under the verandah. Little tables and chairs, even a couch and armchairs, are on the wide paved footpath. I can see myself enjoying a cocktail there, taking in the distant hills and the palms dotted along the streetscape. I instantly feel at ease.

"So, this is Main Street, and that one is Hipworth Street," I say, orienting myself. I turn around and look at him. "As in your last name, Hipworth?"

He pulls out my luggage. "Yep. Named after my grandfather.

Family's been here a long time." He drops the suitcase on the ground with a grunt, and I grab my overnight bag.

Hipworth Street is more of a side street, but even so, the buildings are all old. The town looks untouched by the modern era, and there's something nostalgic and beautiful about it.

"We'll get you into your room, and then I'll take you to the surgery. That okay with you?"

"Sure."

We walk into the cool of a large foyer. There's a polished wooden reception, complete with a brass bell on the counter, and a large staircase with a floral carpeted runner. I'm dying to see the next level.

Herb thumps the bell, and the ring echoes around the foyer. "Crystal?"

A young woman with black spikey hair appears. She has rings on almost every finger and one through her nose. She stops chewing her gum and beams at Herb.

"Herbie. How ya goin?"

She's flirting, but Herb seems oblivious.

"This is Dr Janssen," Herb says. "Her room ready?"

Crystal resumes chewing and pushes a piece of paper towards me. I glimpse another piece of metal on her tongue.

Herb frowns. "She doesn't need to register. We know who she is. Just get the key."

She raises her eyebrows, pulls the paper back, and hands me a key. "You're the boss. Room 201. Our corner suite, Dr Janssen. Enjoy your stay."

"Thank you."

She shoots Herb a "was that more satisfactory?" look.

"Afraid there's no lift," he says to me, ignoring Crystal and lifting my bags with a grunt.

I regret packing so many medical books. I should have sent them with the rest of my things, but he seems to be coping as we climb the stairs. I'm eager to see the room and the rest of the place.

By the top of the stairs, I'm puffing. Herb is the fitter of us. Five weeks into the new year, and I'm yet to start my fitness regime. I'll start jogging tomorrow.

The door opens into an expansive corner room with French doors leading to a wide verandah.

The large four-poster bed with a cream quilted bedspread and mosquito net is imposing.

I walk around the air-conditioned room while Herb dumps my suitcase by the bed. There's an ensuite, a desk, and an armchair. I peek through the French doors. There are two cane chairs on the verandah and a view of the nearby mountains.

"It's beautiful. It really is."

"Okay then, I'll leave you to sort yourself out. Meet you downstairs in the bar in, say, half an hour?"

"Okay. I could do with a drink."

"It's three-thirty," he says.

"A cup of tea, I mean."

He nods and walks out.

Once he's gone, I throw myself on the bed and release a deep breath while admiring the pressed-metal ceiling indented with a floral design. My nerves and worries have dissipated a little. For the first time, I feel that I might have done the right thing, although I'm still worried about Mum and Lily. I ring and leave a message telling them I've arrived.

I leave the unpacking and head down to the bar where Crystal stands behind a walnut L-shaped counter. Behind her, two shelves of spirits are reflected in a mirror lit with downlights.

"G'day," I say. "Do you think I could order a cup of tea?"

"Sure. Take a seat, and I'll bring it over."

I find a walnut coffee table by a stunning stained-glass window. A cane armchair plumped with large, blue floral cushions sits beside it. The carpet is royal blue and unsullied by stains like most pubs. It looks as though a lot of money has been poured into this place, and I'm the only one here.

Crystal brings me loose-leaf tea in a red pot with a matching red teacup. "Our own tea," she says.

"Oh, really?"

"There's a plantation up in the hills."

"It's a beautiful hotel. Have you worked here long?"

"A couple of years. I started as the cleaner and worked my way up. Mel's family owns it, you know."

"Mel?"

Crystal giggles. "My pet name for Herb behind his back."

I wonder what she's talking about, and my expression must have given me away.

"I reckon he looks like Mel Gibson. Don't you think?"

"I don't know. I haven't really noticed." He doesn't strike me as that good-looking, but I keep that to myself. Crystal seems to have an infatuation.

"Anyway, I was travelling and stopped here and never left. It's grown on me."

I nod as I pour the tea, and she props herself on the arm of the chair opposite. She doesn't seem to be in any hurry.

"It's a nice town with nice people, and we're trying to get it on the tourist map. Well, Mel is."

Herb strides in behind her, sunglasses on his head.

Crystal follows my gaze and quickly stands up. "Well, I hope you enjoy the tea."

"I will," I say, smiling. "Thank you."

Herb flops into the other chair and throws his hat on the floor. "Settled in?"

I get a good look at his face. Blue eyes and a strong freckled nose that I hope has been covered with sunscreen. There's a slight Mel Gibson resemblance, and I stifle a chuckle.

"Do you want a cup?" I ask.

"Nah, never touch the stuff." He drums his fingers on the chair's arm.

I try to down the tea, suddenly conscious that I've probably taken up too much of his time.

"No need to rush."

He doesn't seem to miss much. I breathe out, cooling my scalding mouth, then put the cup down and stand up. "It's okay. I've had enough. Let's go."

Herb and I walk down Main Street, past a café with two old dears sitting at an outside table with tea and scones. They stare and give me the once over, then nod, slight smiles drifting over their faces before turning back to each other. We pass a pharmacy. I'll need to introduce myself as I'll have a lot to do with them. Across the road is a fish and chip shop – good to know – a fishing tackle shop, a real estate agency with five posters in the window, a second-hand place with knick-knacks in the window, and an art gallery. Then it's down another street, away from the main shopping area. A sign next to a charming old teahouse in a manicured tropical garden reads "Sugar Creek Medical Surgery."

I'm disappointed. The building looks more like an outhouse than a doctor's surgery. I was hoping for one of those heritage buildings, but this fibrocement relic from the seventies is a real let-down.

"That's it?"

"I know it's not much from the outside, but we've fixed it up inside."

I say nothing. Let's hope so.

"Next door is where you'll be living from next week, hopefully."

He points towards a hedge of trees on the other side of the surgery. I can't see much and hope it's better than this place. I should be grateful that I'm getting cheap accommodation, but if it's crawling with anything, I'll be reviewing my options.

"Come on," Herb says. "I'll show you the surgery."

I walk straight into a spider's web and brush it away, hoping like hell that the critter is elsewhere. We walk up a timber ramp with a railing – good for the oldies – and then through a wide doorway into a spacious room. The place is spotless. The beige lino floor is dotted with new blue vinyl chairs and a grey reception desk. It's basic but not glamorous, fairly standard for a doctor's surgery, and I'm not disappointed. It will do. The freshly painted white walls will be perfect for displaying Lily's fabulous paintings, and a plant or two will do wonders.

"So, who's the receptionist?" I ask.

"We placed an ad in the paper a couple of days ago. Council's HR department will send through some candidates so you can select who you want."

My heart sinks; another thing to worry about. I hope whoever's controlling the recruitment process knows what they're doing. The last thing I need is someone who doesn't know their way around a doctor's practice. Hopefully, they'll at least know the townspeople.

I follow Herb. There are two rooms off the waiting area, and both are decked out with patient beds, scales, and a notepad and manilla folder on a desk.

"We thought you might use both rooms or if there's a visiting nurse or specialist, they could use the other one."

I guess the "we" he's referring to is the council. I turn to him and smile. "You've really thought of everything. Thank you."

He grins for the first time. Perhaps he was nervous too.

"Tell me if you need anything, and I'll sort it out." He looks at his watch. "I better get going. I've got a fence to put up."

"Of course." Must be a farmer then when he's not mayor. "I've taken up too much of your time. Thank you for everything."

"It's me who should be thanking you, coming all this way and taking us on. We're all grateful. Anyway, here's the keys. It's all yours. I'll leave you to it."

I check out one of the offices. I sing "It's My Life" by Bon Jovi and begin swaying using the scales as my stage.

As I screech the high notes, I'm startled by a knock and turn around. Herb is leaning against the door frame and looks bemused.

"Jesus," I say. "You gave me such a fright."

"Sorry, but I forgot to give you the mobile phone."

I can feel myself flush red as I quickly step off the scales and compose myself. "Need to check if they're accurate. And I'm pleased to report that they are."

He grins and hands me the phone. "Good song."

I'm not sure if he's making fun of me or reconsidering his hiring choices. "Yes. It is."

"I better go."

"Yes, bye."

I watch him walk out, probably wondering if he's hired a lunatic.

I go back to my inspection. Without singing. There's a toilet –

spotless – and a kitchenette – also spotless – and another small room with a bank of filing cabinets. Patient files, probably.

I choose the back office for myself, which has a view of what looks to be a nature park. There's a welcome note on the desk with numbers for the chemist, ambulance, and police station, plus other useful information. I get out my to-do list and ring the pharmacist to make a time to meet. Then it's phone calls to the local police – only one policeman – and the nearest ambulance station. Next, I order my doctor's bag and some supplies like bandages, iodine, and syringes, then start organising the office how I want it.

Before I realise it, it's dark, and my stomach is rumbling. It's seven o'clock. One last thing before I go to the pub and grab some dinner. Ring Mum.

4

Ellen

1948

Ellen locked the front door as Joan counted the till. "Is there anything else you'd like me to do before I go?"

Joan looked around and jerked her head towards a table in the corner. "That ashtray's still full."

Ellen quickly retrieved it, annoyed with herself. "Sorry, I must have missed it."

"Is your fella coming to town tomorrow?"

"I hope so."

"Remember, he can't come to your room."

Ellen nodded; Joan had already lectured her about having male guests.

"Off you go then. Rest up. It'll be busy tomorrow when the canecutters get in."

*

Before he left, Billy gave Ellen a journal as his going-away gift. "So, you don't forget me," he'd said, laughing. "As if I could," she'd replied.

She wrote in it after dinner.

Day Five in Sugar Creek. 14th May 1948.

Tropical rainstorms come and go in minutes, refreshing at first and then hot and humid. I've been caught out at least twice since I got here. I walked in a different direction this morning and found a place on the outskirts of town. It was surrounded by a high wire fence covered in Keep Out signs. I peeked through, but all I saw was bush. Joan says it's a military base. I'm sure Billy will be interested to see it if he hasn't already. On the way back, I saw a house I like, and when Billy comes, we'll need to talk about where we'll live when we get married. I can't wait to see him.

*

That night, Ellen lay awake, listening to the distant cicadas and frogs. She should have been exhausted from being on her feet all day, but she was anxious and excited. What would Billy say when he saw her? How would he take the news? Hopefully, he'll be pleased. She pushed away the thought that he might not be. Instead, she imagined his face, the taste of his lips, his adoring eyes.

It was so hot. She moved her legs across the bed, searching for somewhere cool, and reached for her alarm clock – one o'clock. Climbing out of bed, she flung open the French doors and welcomed the cool night air against her skin. She leaned against the iron railing and could almost reach out and touch the fronds of the tallest palm tree she'd ever seen. If only she could drag her mattress out here.

She'd never get any sleep with the chorus of cicadas that had just started outside her window. Then she heard another sound: footsteps. She'd forgotten there were other bedrooms off the verandah, and at the far end was the unmistakable glow of a cigarette. She clutched the neck of her nightgown and abruptly returned to her room, closing and locking the doors.

The next morning, Ellen woke up and scratched her arm; she'd forgotten to pull the mosquito net around the bed. She took her towel and clothes down to the communal bathroom just as the stranger from the other day appeared. As she stepped aside for him to pass, he stopped and stared at her with dark eyes. Below a pencil-thin moustache, trimmed to perfection, his thin lips parted as if to say something. His gaze drifted to her chest and lingered a moment too long, then he turned and went downstairs.

Ellen wondered if it had been him smoking on the verandah, but there was no time to dwell on it. She was already late. What if she missed Billy before she got to see him?

She washed her face and changed before heading to the boarding house. Heart thumping, she smoothed down her mauve floral dress, Billy's favourite, pinched her cheeks, took a deep breath, and knocked. A stern-faced woman, cigarette hanging from the corner of her mouth, opened the door.

"I'm here to see Billy Nolan."

The woman rolled her eyes and put her hand on her hip. "He's not here yet." Then she mumbled something and slammed the door.

Ellen blinked, wondering why the woman had been so rude. What was she to do now? She wasn't leaving until she saw Billy. She looked around for somewhere to sit out of the sun, but there was nothing. She settled on the timber steps of the boarding house to wait.

Using the paper with the address as a fan, hardly helped. Feeling nauseous, she wished her throat wasn't so dry. She wiped her face with her handkerchief, reassuring herself that Billy couldn't be too much longer.

An hour went by before a sturdy-looking woman in a pale pink dress, a handbag hanging from the crook of her arm, stopped and peered at her from under a wide-brimmed hat.

"You know you're sitting on the steps of the men's boarding house. The women's are in the next street."

Ellen stood up, suddenly woozy, and reached for the railing. "Oh, I know. My fiancé is a cane cutter, and I'm waiting for him."

"Did you knock?"

"Yes, I did."

"Didn't Beryl let you in?"

Ellen shook her head. "Um, no."

"Tchk. That'd be right. Well, you can't sit there, dear. It's unseemly. Besides, it's too damn hot. Come to my place. I'm across the road, just there," she pointed, "and we'll have a glass of orangeade."

"Thank you," Ellen said, hoping she wouldn't pass out.

"I'm Mrs Phyllis Laurel."

"Ellen Lambert."

The house, a majestic Queenslander perched high on stilts with a wide verandah, was surrounded by a garden of flowers bursting with colour and tropical palms shading the brick path. "Mrs Laurel, your garden is beautiful." The perfumed scent revived her like smelling salts. "You even have roses."

She paused and looked at Ellen. "Those are bush roses. Pretty, aren't they? I spend an hour a day trying to wrestle control from the climbers. And please, call me Phyllis."

Ellen followed Phyllis up the wide timber stairs and through a wood-panelled corridor, grateful for the coolness. Phyllis put her handbag on the timber kitchen table, unpinned her hat, and hung it on the kitchen door.

"I've probably flattened all the curls the hairdresser spent hours on." Phyllis laughed as she patted her tightly curled hair into place. "It'll do. Now how about some orangeade?"

Ellen smiled encouragingly and nodded, then licked her dry lips as Phyllis poured. She was beginning to feel better and looked around the kitchen and through the windows to the rainforest beyond.

"You have such a large house."

"My husband and I bought it when we married. Met him when I was stationed here with AWAS. He insisted on a large house, believing we'd have a brood of children."

Ellen looked around for children, but there was no sign of anyone else in the house.

"Come on," Phyllis said, "let's go out to the front verandah. It's cooler, and you can watch for your fiancé."

They sat on two large cane chairs, and Ellen sipped her drink, while keeping an eye out for Billy. "This is delicious. Did you make it?"

Phyllis smiled, looking pleased. "I certainly did."

"And AWAS? Was that the army?"

"Yes," Phyllis said, setting her glass down. "The Australian Women's Army Service. We did some very important work, but everyone's forgotten about us. I was in signalling and met my husband, Edward at the military base just outside of town."

Ellen nodded. "Yes, I've seen it. Well, not seen it exactly. I saw the wire fence."

"Then he was sent to New Guinea and was killed. So, there you have it. I'm thirty-four with a big house, no brood and no inclination to replace him."

"Oh," Ellen said. "I'm very sorry to hear that." She couldn't imagine a future without Billy.

Phyllis topped up their glasses. "Bit of a conversation killer, isn't it? And what about you, Ellen?"

Ellen wondered how much she should tell her. She seemed nice enough.

"I just arrived from Brisbane on Monday, and my boyfriend – I mean fiancé – came up four weeks ago to do cane cutting. He heard it was good money, and we're saving to get married."

"Good on you."

Ellen hesitated. "I thought I'd come up and surprise him."

Phyllis raised her eyebrows. "So, he doesn't know you're here?"

"No, he doesn't."

Phyllis leaned back in her seat and glanced at her watch. "Well, the boys usually get in at twelve. They do an early morning shift, then knock off at eleven. After washing and whatnot, they go straight to the pub. They shouldn't be far away."

Ellen peered down the street, hoping to see Billy materialise. "That doesn't give me much time. I've got a job at the pub and have to start at twelve thirty."

"Joan gave you a job? That was good of her. Are you staying there too?"

Ellen nodded.

"Well, you look like a capable and smart girl. If you ever need a room, you can always lodge here if you like."

"Thank you for the offer. I'll keep it in mind."

"No boyfriends allowed, but fiancés can visit." Phyllis winked.

They heard the men shouting, laughing, and cheering before they saw them.

"Here come some of them now," Phyllis said, pointing.

Like a swarm of locusts, dozens of men on bicycles and on foot came towards them.

Ellen jumped up and craned her neck to see. "I guess I better get going. I don't want to miss him. Thanks for the drink and the shade."

"Nice to have some company. Drop by again."

"Thanks, I will."

Ellen waved as she left, then pinched her cheeks as she walked across the street to wait for Billy.

5

Dana

2000

The grunt of a truck changing gears startles me awake as a crack of light forces its way around the edge of the curtain. I squint at my watch and another truck rumbles through town. It's six thirty. I stretch, yawn, and think of all the things to be done today. In the shower, I imagine where Lily's paintings will go in the waiting room; the bright colours will cheer the place up. My mind wanders thinking of all the possibilities – perhaps an art exhibition in the town. I'll introduce her at a packed opening, and of course, there'll be champagne and lots of red "sold" stickers.

Back to reality, I slip a sleeveless floral dress over my head, buckle up my sandals, and grab my ever-growing list. Stepping into the growing heat of Main Street, another logging truck, its tray empty, roars down the street.

I duck into the café I'd passed the afternoon before and order a coffee and raisin toast. The woman in the café smiles. Nice day for it, she says. It is, I reply, although I'm not sure what it's nice for. Perhaps she thinks I'm a tourist.

On the way out, I sip the coffee. It's surprisingly good, tick. A mother and child pass me. The mother nods, and I nod back. Friendly people, tick. I'm anonymous for now and wonder what people will make of the new doctor. Suddenly, my body ripples with nerves, and I hurry towards the surgery, not yet ready to reveal myself.

Hannah, my best friend and medical researcher, warned me that country townsfolk are conservative, right-wing types who prefer crotchety old doctors. I wanted to disown her on the spot, but I guess I needed to hear it. She said it would cushion the blows when they came, but it's not like I've never had negative feedback. Old Mr Fletcher objected to having his "nether regions touched by a pretty young woman." Daniel, my supervisor at the time, laughed when I told him. He came with me and explained to Mr Fletcher what I needed to do and stayed while I examined him. After that, the old boy was fine. If some prefer to travel the hour and a half to the next town for a crotchety, old doctor, that's their choice. I can't really boast that I was dux three years in a row, but I can tell them I'm very qualified.

And only one slip-up.

There it is. My mood plummets, and my stomach churns. One tiny mistake – well, not so tiny – where I now wait on judgement by the hospital board. If it ends my career … I can't bear to think about it right now.

There's hammering from next door as I fumble for the surgery keys. A quick peek can't hurt. I head back up the footpath towards my new home, hoping it will look better than the surgery. It is. The freshly-painted white weatherboard is stunning, and a set of central stairs leads to the front entrance behind an old-fashioned flyscreen. The steep corrugated-iron roof hangs over the verandah where a bougainvillea smothered in purple flowers wraps itself along the latticework. An enormous frangipani tree covered in pink flowers shades one end of the house, and several mango trees adorn the fence line. It's better than I could have hoped for; it's picture-perfect. My spirits soar as I race up the stairs to the wide-open front door. I knock loudly, and the hammering stops.

"Out the back," a man yells.

The newly polished wooden hallway floor smells faintly of lacquer. I sticky-beak into two bedrooms, tastefully furnished with white bedspreads on king-size beds and French doors leading onto the verandah. Then past a large loungeroom with two couches and an armchair. It looks like something from a *Home Beautiful* magazine. Surely, this can't be just for me?

"Hello?" I call out.

A man with shoulder-length blonde hair and a cheeky grin gets up from the other side of the island bench. "G'day."

"Hi. I'm Dana Janssen. I'm moving in here soon."

He stands up, a full six foot five, give or take an inch. I know this because it's one of my nerdy interests to guess peoples' heights, and I'm usually spot on. His face is suntanned and friendly.

"It's nearly ready for ya, doc," he says, wiping his hand on his shorts before holding it out. "Jack Babcock, builder."

He has a nice, strong handshake, but not enough to crush my hand like some men's.

"Have you done all of this?"

He laughs, showing off the crow's feet at the edge of his eyes. "Shit, no. I've just been fixing up bits and pieces. I renovated it back in '95 for Herb and his missus."

God, Herb's given me his own house. "I can't take his house. Where's he going to live?"

"He's not homeless, ya know. He just doesn't like being so close to town. Being the mayor and all, everyone just tends to drop in with their gripes. He's got a bigger place farther out."

I don't feel so bad. "It's a beautiful house."

"You should've been in by now, but the hot water went on the blink, and I'm waiting on a new one. They reckon next week."

I place my empty coffee cup on the bench and look around the room. It's a modern white kitchen with a grey pressed-metal splashback. Unusual, although it does match the ceiling. There's a meals area with a round wooden table.

"Do you want a tour?" Jack asks.

"That'd be great. Thanks."

"Well, this here is the kitchen with all the mod cons. Dishwasher there."

I stay where I am as I don't feel it's my place yet to start opening cupboards and drawers.

"There's pots and pans and cutlery and plates and stuff, but if you need anything else, just tell Herb since he's your landlord."

I follow Jack into the adjoining family room with a comfy cream couch and TV. Double doors open onto a back verandah overlooking lush vegetation beyond the fence line.

"Beautiful," I exclaim.

"That's part of our World Heritage tropical forest. There are heaps of walking tracks, but make sure you stick to them, or we'll never find ya." He grins.

We wander into the hallway.

"This one is your room," Jack says, pointing to the larger of the two bedrooms.

I wonder if someone else will be taking the second smaller bedroom. I'd already decided it would be perfect for Mum and Lily or even Hannah. He's not the one to ask but I'd assumed that I'd be living alone, but since this town virtually owns me, I don't have much of a say. I make a mental note to ask Herb when I see him.

"It has an ensuite and walk-in robe."

I walk through it amazed. "It's more than big enough for all of my stuff."

"Thought you'd need a lot of hanging space as a girl."

I tilt my head and frown at him.

"I mean …" he stammers. "I didn't mean that the way it sounded. It's just that … sorry."

I take pity on him. "It all looks wonderful."

He seems relieved.

I glance at my watch. "I better get going and leave you to it."

"No worries, doc."

Heading to the front door, I suddenly remember my empty cup. I turn and run straight into Jack. I put my hand up to his hard chest to steady myself.

"Sorry," I say, utterly flustered as I spring back from him. "I was just going back to get my cup."

He steps aside, grinning, and sweeps his hand towards the kitchen. I hope he can't tell how embarrassed I am.

I grab my cup and head outside. He's at his truck and gives me a quick wave. I hurry past and make my way to the surgery. My raisin toast is cold and soggy, but I don't care. I'm so happy that I do a ballerina's pirouette around the surgery. I have a great job and a beautiful house, and I push the anxiety about my mistake and the hospital board deep down into the pit of my stomach.

Then it's back to work on my list.

By mid-afternoon, I'm satisfied with the number of things I've crossed off. The phone has had a beating. I haven't even stopped to eat lunch, but someone has thoughtfully put some tea, coffee, and a carton of milk in the small kitchenette. It's like a fairy has been through the place and thought of everything. Herb's wife, I'll bet. I should get her a small gift for her thoughtfulness.

Putting the milk back in the fridge, I notice something lodged between it and the wall. I can just reach it. It's a medicine bottle covered in dust and cobwebs. I brush the dirt from the label and read it, "Eamon Dunlop, use for severe pain relief."

In the filing room, I look for his file. There isn't one. Flipping through a few more files, I notice they are quite thin. There's one for Crystal Anderson, the woman at the pub. She'd come for birth control pills a year ago, and Eamon Dunlop was the treating doctor. I examine the pill bottle again and see that it was filled twelve months ago.

Didn't Herb say they hadn't had a doctor for five years? Perhaps Dr Dunlop was a locum and was too sick to continue working. Then I begin wondering why it's taken so long to get someone. Something else to ask Herb.

6

Ellen

1948

A pale, thin woman stood at the gate of the boarding house, her brown hair curled back from her perfectly made-up face. Swatting away a fly, she turned slowly and looked Ellen up and down. "They're comin'," she croaked before slipping a cigarette between her red-painted lips.

They turned their heads towards the sound of laughter, yelling, and whooping. Ellen shaded her eyes and squinted at the sea of men. Tall and short, dark and fair, riding their bikes or running like marauding bulls towards the three boarding houses all in a row. Shifting nervously from one foot to the other as the first of the cyclists arrived, Ellen watched for the familiar outline of Billy.

One man grinned at her, and another whistled, his eyes roving. "How are ya, darlin'?"

She ignored them, searching the worn soot-smeared faces and immediately recognised the tall, barrel-chested man in a blue singlet and navy shorts. She broke into a sprint and bound up to him, almost knocking him over.

He tipped back his suntanned face, mouth open, white teeth gleaming.

"What on earth?" Billy exclaimed.

Ellen wrapped her arms around his neck, smothering him in kisses, breathing in sweat, dirt, and a hint of sweetness.

The words tumbled out. "I couldn't bear to be away another second. I didn't know you were at the farm and—"

Billy kissed her hard, his beard stubble prickling the edge of her mouth. Someone wolf-whistled. Suddenly remembering where she was, she dropped her arms and stepped back, wiping her tears with the back of her hand, conscious of the other men's stares.

Grinning, Billy took her hand. "This is my girl, Ellen," he said proudly to three men who doffed their caps and continued into the boarding house.

He put his arm around her waist and pulled her to him. "You're here! Will you wait while I get washed up? I've got this afternoon and tomorrow off. We can have lunch. I can show you around and—"

She pulled away.

"I can't," she said, glancing at her watch.

He looked disappointed. "You're going back to Brisbane?"

"No," she said, not meeting his eyes.

He placed his hands on her shoulders. "Why are you here?"

"I've got a job," she said, trying to keep her voice steady.

"A job?" He lifted her chin gently. "What's going on?"

She couldn't tell if he was pleased or not. "I'm staying, Billy Nolan, so don't think about sending me back. I quit that factory job and got a job as a barmaid at The Palace Hotel. Don't you want me to stay?" she said softly, lowering her eyes.

"I do. I'm just trying to think." He glanced at the boarding house. "You can't stay there. It's for men only."

"I've got board at the pub. But I thought we could get a place together."

"But I live out at the farm during the week. We'd only see each other on the weekend and, well, it wouldn't be proper to—"

"We'll talk about this later. I have to go," Ellen said, looking at her watch again.

"I'll come to the pub then."

"No," she said abruptly. "I mean, you can come, but I can't talk to you while I'm working."

He nodded. "I've got to clean up and do a few things. See you at closing time?"

"Yes." She kissed Billy quickly on the cheek and walked towards Main Street. The tears fell freely now. It hadn't gone the way it should have, the way she'd hoped.

She'd met Billy at a dance in Brisbane eight months ago. They'd danced, his hand gentle on her back, and afterwards, they'd talked. He'd made her laugh, and when he leaned in to kiss her goodnight, he took her breath away. She'd quickly suggested a movie the next day. He smiled, his perfect teeth white in the moonlight, and he replied yes, I was just thinking the same thing. It felt right.

Ellen counted herself lucky that she'd met such a lovable, gentle-natured man. He wasn't a smoker or much of a drinker, the complete opposite of her father. Billy was someone reliable who'd take care of her and their family. That night she knew their children would have a better life than hers. Seven months later, he suggested they get married. And four weeks ago, he landed this job to save enough to get married.

She blew her nose and dried her eyes as she walked to The Palace Hotel. Now she wasn't so sure. She couldn't go back.

The factory job was boring, and she'd hated it. The foreman told her off for talking and giggling, her feet hurt, and the boss tried to kiss her when she went to get her pay packet. She shuddered, thinking about the man's foul breath and sweaty hands.

The bar was clogged with smoke and packed with the booming voices of canecutters. There was hardly a moment to herself, but she looked out for Billy, just in case he came in early. There were women, too, in the Ladies' Lounge, who gossiped, smoked, and drank their shandies or gin and tonics.

At closing time, as Joan ushered the last one out of the door, Ellen slumped against the bar, lifting one foot out of her shoe and stretching her toes. "Is it always like that?"

"A usual Saturday arvo crowd, love. You were a terrific help. I don't know what I'd have done without you. Mr. Babcock," Joan lowered her voice, "isn't so good behind the bar."

Ellen glanced over the far side of the room and saw Paul Babcock sweeping. He was a pleasant man but seemed to be in another world. He'd had a bad time in the war, Joan said, and she let him do the maintenance and cleaning while she ran the pub.

"Did you see your fella?"

Ellen nodded. "I did, but not for long. He's meeting me here, and we're going out to dinner."

Joan wiped the countertop. "Is that him out there?"

Ellen looked through the stained-glass door. Billy, clean-shaven and dressed in long pants, short-sleeve shirt and tie, paced up and down the street. She nodded.

"He looks nice," Joan said. "Handsome too. Where did he serve?"

"In Malaysia and New Guinea."

"And he's … he's all right?"

Ellen stared at Joan, puzzled. "Why wouldn't he be?"

Joan crooked her head in Paul's direction where he was humming as he lifted a chair. She understood then.

"Yes, he's fine."

"That's good. I'll finish up. Why don't you head off?"

"Are you sure?"

Joan nodded and smiled. She was a good boss, understanding and caring. Ellen trusted her, and well, if things didn't work out, she felt Joan would be on her side.

Ellen didn't waste time. She removed her apron while running up the stairs, two at a time, to her room to change. She checked her hair and pinched her cheeks. It was time to find out how much Billy really loved her.

He gave a low whistle before planting a quick kiss on her cheek. "You're a sight for sore eyes."

She smiled. They'd already embarrassed themselves in public, so she understood the kiss on the cheek. "Let's go to the Chinese place across the road."

"If you're game, I'm game," he said, holding her hand.

They crossed the road and entered the restaurant. They were the only people there.

"I've never had Chinese food before," Billy said. "I steered clear of it in Malaysia."

"We don't have to eat here."

"No, I was a chicken. I think I should give it a go."

The waiter came up with menus.

"I had some the other night, and it was delicious. You'll like it. I'll order, all right?"

Billy glanced at the menu and shrugged. "I'm in your hands."

Ellen ordered fried rice and sweet and sour chicken. Then she turned to him. "You don't seem happy to see me."

He raised his eyebrows. "I am happy. I can't tell you how much I've missed you. It's just that, well, we can't live together, and I haven't saved enough yet to get married. I'm worried about you, that's all."

"I know, but I have a little bit saved, and the job at the pub, and—"

"I don't know if I like the idea of you working in a pub with all those fellas leering at you."

She pouted. "I like the job. It's better than the factory, and so is the pay. And no-one's leering."

He took her hand across the table. "I don't know. I want to marry you so much and have our own place, but this wasn't the plan. I can't even afford to buy you a ring yet."

"I don't care about any of that."

"You agreed that I would come here, we'd save some money, then in six months, I'd be back, and we'd marry and settle down in Brisbane. Why the sudden change?"

The food arrived, and the waiter served the rice in little china bowls. "Chopsticks?" he asked.

"Ah, no, knives and forks, please," Ellen said. "I haven't worked out how to use them yet."

"Very easy for you. I show you?" the waiter said, placing the cutlery on the table.

"Maybe next time," Ellen said, smiling.

The waiter bowed and left them.

"Gee, this is a bit of alright," Billy said as he worked his way through the meal. "You were right. It's delicious."

Ellen smiled. "See, I told you you'd like it."

He looked at her. "You're not eating?"

She placed her hands in front of her on the table; the nails chewed to the quick in nervous anticipation.

"I'm not that hungry."

He stopped eating and stared at her. "I'm worried. Has something happened?"

She shook her head. It suddenly seemed hard to breathe. "I don't care about a ring."

"But I do," he said. "You deserve a ring with diamonds. It's proper."

"I'd rather be married to you and have our own place." She hesitated. "Especially now that there's a baby on the way."

There they were, the words she'd held for so long spilled out across the table to him.

Billy's eyes widened, and his hand froze in the air. "Did you … did you say a baby? You're going to have a baby?"

He dropped his fork, and a smile spread across his face.

"I'm only eight, wait, nine weeks now. And before you ask, I'm sure. I went to a doctor in Brisbane. We're going to have a baby."

He leaned across the table and kissed her.

"Billy, please. We're in public."

She looked around. They were still the only people in the restaurant besides the waiter at the doorway.

"What? I can't kiss my future wife, mother of my son?"

"Or daughter." Relieved, she smiled.

"I'm so happy right now. We have to change our plans."

"I think we should."

He reached for her left hand and rubbed her fingers. "We'll get married next week, next Saturday. And you're going to have a ring."

"All I need to keep me respectable is a wedding ring."

"You'll have an engagement ring and a wedding ring."

"But nothing expensive."

"This is a nice place to raise a kid. We can rent a room—"

"Or a house?"

"A house might be too expensive, but yeah, a house."

"You leave it up to me. I'll find us something," she said.

He let go of her hand and leaned back in his chair. "I'm the luckiest bloke in the world."

"So next Saturday?"

"You betcha. Next Saturday, we'll get hitched."

Billy paid the bill, and they walked out of the restaurant, hand in hand, Ellen's sore feet entirely forgotten.

7

Dana

2000

Back at my desk, I examine the bottle, wondering if I'd got it wrong. There's been so much on my mind; perhaps this was a detail I'd missed. A knock on my office door jolts me out of my thoughts, and Herb's head pokes around the corner.

"G'day. Hope I'm not disturbing you."

I'm genuinely glad to see him and offer up a beaming smile. "Hi. Come in. I'm glad you're here." No return smile, I note, and he stays put in the doorway. "You might be able to solve something for me. I just found this medicine bottle down the side of the fridge. It seems it was for a Dr Dunlop who was here last year, according to the records."

He looks at me like I'm an idiot. "Yeah?"

"I thought there hadn't been a doctor here in five years."

He takes a couple of steps towards me. "We had visiting doctors from Townsville a couple of days a week. You're the first full-time one. And as the town grows, I'm hoping we can expand the surgery to a full-service clinic."

"Ah." I feel foolish and put the bottle aside.

"Anyway, I dropped in with your new car and wondered if you wanted a quick tour of the town."

"A new car?"

"Not new, exactly."

I'm puzzled, and it must have shown. I don't have a poker face, so I'm told.

"You'll need some wheels to do house calls, won't you? The car was included in the contract."

"Oh, yes." I'd completely forgotten. He must think I'm a total idiot.

"Have you got time?"

"Sure."

I follow him outside to a silver Mitsubishi Magna station wagon.

"It's about four years old," he says.

"No Audi?" I say, smiling.

He doesn't seem to get the joke, and he hands me the keys, his face stern.

"I was joking," I say.

"Mmm," he says. "You *can* drive, can't you?"

I'm a little irritated. He's as humourless as a tree stump. "Yes, I can."

"Good. Shall we head off?" Herb strides towards an actual black Audi.

Not the Ford Ute, then? No wonder he didn't get my joke. He must keep the shiny new Audi for touring, but I don't say this out loud and merely follow, vowing to keep my jokes to myself.

We drive around the town, up and down each street. He proudly explains how the grid pattern makes it easy not to get lost, but my mind is on the to-do list.

"I don't think I'll get lost, Herb."

With one hand on the wheel and the other hanging out the open window, he points. "That's the primary school. You'll have to talk to the principal about a vaccination program."

I've already spoken to the principal. I bite my tongue, wondering why he's wasting my time and his.

Perhaps I should be grateful that he's so accommodating and thoughtful. Nothing wrong with a good old bit of country hospitality. I'll get used to it.

"Thank you for the mountain of work you've done getting everything ready for me. Your house is beautiful, and I'd love to thank your wife for attending to all the small details. It really is much more than I expected."

His jaw clenches. "There's no wife."

Judging from his tone, I've touched a raw nerve. "My mistake."

We get back to the surgery, and he pulls into the curb, then looks at me, his eyes stern. "You think men aren't capable of putting a house together?"

My mouth is dry as I realise how sexist I'd been. I need to get this right. "No. I'm sorry. I shouldn't have made such an assumption. You have great taste."

His face relaxes, and there's an edge of a smile.

I get out of the car. "Thanks again for the tour … and for everything."

He nods, then backs out and speeds down the street. Perhaps he has something to prove, but it leaves me a little unsettled. I'm just not sure about him.

*

The wine is good, and I feel myself relaxing in the pub lounge. It's been a long day, and I have a candidate to interview for the receptionist job in the morning. Hopefully, she'll be ideal and can start immediately. Five days to set up a surgery, place orders, and sort out everything was ambitious, but I feel I'm almost there.

There are a few people in the lounge, and I notice two elderly ladies staring at me. Good on them for being out. I nod and smile, and they seem to take that as an invitation to come over. So much for my peaceful glass of wine to unwind.

A heavy-set woman with a full head of beautifully coiffed grey hair smiles at me. "Hello, dear. I was just saying to Mavis that you must be the new doctor. Am I right?" Her voice is deep and hoarse, like a smoker's.

I do my best to smile. "Yes, I am. Dr Dana Janssen. So very pleased to meet you." I wave my hand, inviting them to sit in the comfy armchairs opposite.

"We were just on our way home," she says.

"Yes, on our way," the other woman says. She's short and slight and has a soft, weak voice – presbyphonia is my guess, a common effect of aging.

"I'm Joan Babcock, and this is Mavis Gillespie."

Joan's surname seems familiar.

"My legs aren't as good as they used to be," Joan says.

I'm not surprised, given Joan's frame. Looks like I'm about to be asked for a diagnosis. Her legs appear swollen, with large purple veins snaking along her calf. Varicose veins, no doubt.

"Nice to meet you, doctor," Mavis says. "We don't want to interrupt but thought we should say hello." Mavis raises her eyebrows at Joan, who's already settled into her chair.

"We've never had a lady doctor before," Joan says.

Mavis drops heavily into the other armchair.

"Oh, really?" I say.

"You know, it's been too long since we had a doctor. We oldies struggle to drive all the way to Townsville."

"We don't always like the locums," Mavis pipes in, her lively eyes flitting towards Joan. "We never know who we'll get."

"So, we're very happy you're here. I hope Herb has been looking after you," Joan says.

"Oh, yes. He's been fantastic. Everyone has."

"And you're staying here?"

"Only until the house next door is ready. Next week, I've been told."

Joan nodded. "Herb's old place. You might have met my grandson, Jack."

No wonder the surname was familiar. "Yes, I did. He seems very nice."

Joan puffs out her ample sagging chest. "He's a very good builder."

"So nice to have a lady doctor," Mavis says, grinning. "It's such a pity what happened to the last one."

"The last one?" I ask. "What happened?"

Joan looks sharply at Mavis.

"It's been so long, I can't even remember."

Mavis is quick. "He died. Cancer. Poor man."

"That's right," Joan says. "Well, we should leave you in peace now. Come on, Mavis. We better get you home."

Mavis seems surprised that Joan's on her feet already. "Dr Dunlop was nice, but he was so sick. I'm glad old Dr Cummins is gone, though. He'd been here for too long and just didn't have it in the end. Don't you think, Joan?"

"Come now, Mavis," Joan says a little louder.

Mavis heaves herself out of the chair. "I hope you don't get sick like the others, dear. Nice to meet you."

Joan rolls her eyes and shakes her head as if saying Mavis isn't all there.

"Lovely to meet you both," I say, "and I hope to see you again very soon."

"Too many people getting sick, don't you think Joan?" Mavis says as they waddle away.

I finish my wine and head up to my room. Two sick doctors, one of whom died? I wonder what happened to Dunlop. I'm confused but much too tired to think more about it.

8

Ellen

1948

Ellen met with the Anglican minister on Monday while Billy was at the cane farm. She'd squirmed when he looked at her as if he knew why she needed to marry in a hurry, yet he never brought it up. He couldn't marry them until 29 May, a fortnight later. She hid her disappointment as she calculated that she'd be almost three months gone. She sent a note to let Billy know.

On Tuesday she found an outfit at a charity shop – a cream suit with a little pillbox hat. She gazed at herself in the mirror. The fit was perfect. She ran her hand down the jacket and noticed a mark on the lapel. The woman behind the counter gave her a discount, claiming it could be hidden with a brooch, and promised to keep it for her until payday on Thursday.

The next thing was to talk to Joan. She'd started work an hour early, and cleaning the cupboards under the bar gave her something to do while anxiously waiting. She knew Joan wouldn't be happy and prayed she'd understand. Paul hummed while pulling out chairs, inspecting them, for what she didn't know, before pushing them back in again, a daily ritual before opening. Ellen glanced at her watch. Ten minutes. Where was Joan?

Paul grabbed a rag and rubbed an imaginary spot on a table. His humming began to annoy Ellen. Finally, the back door opened, and Joan swept in. Paul stopped humming and stared at his wife, waiting to be told what to do.

"Right," Joan said, glancing around the bar before opening the till. "Are we ready?"

Paul nodded.

"In there?" Joan said, pointing to the Ladies' Lounge.

Paul frowned. He slung the rag over his shoulder and disappeared into the lounge. The sound of chairs scraping backwards and forwards drifted through the closed door.

"Ah, I wonder if I could have a word with you, please?" Ellen said. "Before we open?"

"Make it quick, love." Joan pulled notes from her apron pocket and placed them in the till.

"I was wondering if I could have Saturday week off?" Ellen broke out in a sweat.

Joan frowned. "I don't know. It's the busiest day of the week. It'll put us under a lot of pressure. What on earth do you need the day off for?"

"I'm getting married."

Joan slammed the till shut and turned to Ellen. "Married? To your fella?"

Ellen nodded and shifted from one foot to the other. "I'm sorry, but that's the only day available for the minister."

Joan's face creased into a smile. "Well, that sounds like a good enough reason. Don't worry. We'll manage."

Ellen exhaled and grabbed a glass to polish. "Thank you."

"Less than a fortnight away? That's quick."

The murmur of voices outside drew Ellen's attention. Through the stained-glass window were the shadowy figures of the patiently waiting regulars.

"Any reason?" Joan continued.

Ellen's reply stuck in her throat.

"Don't answer. None of my business." Joan glanced at the clock. "Better open the door, love."

Ellen couldn't tell if Joan had guessed. During the war, a quick wedding had been normal, even encouraged. After the war, there was only one reason why a girl married suddenly. Well, that was just too bad. Joan was right; it was none of her business.

She smiled and opened the door to let Cal, Wally, and Harold in. They were deep in conversation about the merits of cane toad racing.

"Hello," she said.

"G'day, love," Cal said.

Wally nodded. "Race the bastards," he said as he perched himself on a stool. "Then use the losers for target practice."

The jagged cut from a barbed wire fence on Cal's arm was healing, Harold's eye was bruised and shadowed with yellow tinges from the weekend's footy match, and Wally, as usual, had his mismatched socks pushed into his thongs.

"That's one way to get rid of 'em," Harold said.

"It's the only way," Wally said, downing his beer before wiping away the froth with the back of his hand.

The week flew by, and soon it was Saturday, one week before the wedding. The bar was hectic as usual, filled with canecutters. Billy came in for a beer with his mate, Hector. There was no chance to talk, just the occasional wink.

From the corner of her eye, she noticed the man in the brown suit was back, chatting with Jonno, a man Billy had introduced her to. When she collected the empty glasses, Bob, another cane cutter, was talking to the man. Bob got up, and they shook hands. Throughout the afternoon, there was always somebody different sitting with him, even Billy. She wondered what was going on.

After closing time, Billy was waiting outside.

He smiled and held up a bundle wrapped in newspaper. "Fish and chips in the park?"

She nodded and grabbed his arm, pulling him close. "God, I'm starving. And in just over a week, I'll be cooking for you in our very own kitchen!"

He stopped walking and turned to look at her with a cocked eyebrow.

"I got a place across the road from your boarding house." she said. "Remember I told you that I met Phyllis Laurel while I was waiting for you last week? She offered us a room. Anyway, it's got a kitchen."

He grinned. "There's no doubt about you. You sure get things done."

"Let's hurry. I've got lots to tell you, and if I don't eat, I'll faint."

They walked briskly and found a picnic table under a streetlight surrounded by a merry-go-round of moths.

Billy swatted a mosquito from his arm and slapped his leg. "Buggers."

"One more week, and we can eat inside."

He ripped open the paper, and the smell of hot salty chips made her mouth water. She plunged her hand in and grabbed one. "Ooh, these are so good."

"Now, just wait a minute. Unwrap more of the paper so you can get to the fish."

She licked her fingers and tore more of the paper. A small red box fell out.

"What's this?" she said, staring at him.

Smiling, he got down on one knee and opened the box. Inside was a gold ring with a tiny ruby. "Will you marry me?"

Ellen gasped. "Oh, my. How did you …? We can't afford this. I said I didn't need a ring."

He took the ring out. "You haven't answered me, Ellen Lambert."

"Yes, yes, and yes!" she yelled, then leaned over and kissed him so hard they toppled over and sprawled on the grass, laughing. "You know I will."

"We have to do things properly. After all, we need to tell the right story to our little one."

She laughed as they both sat up. "But not the whole story, huh?" She slipped the ring onto her finger and tilted it towards the streetlight.

"How did you afford it?"

"I got it from the second-hand shop. It's not fancy, I know. But it's real gold."

"I love it, and I love you."

The chips lay forgotten as they hugged and kissed again.

She suddenly remembered where they were. "Goodness, what must we look like? Come on, help me up."

He sprang to his feet and pulled her up. "Who cares?"

"But seriously, Billy, how can you afford it?"

"Well, I met a bloke today in the pub."

"The man in the brown suit? Thin moustache?"

"Yep, that's the bloke."

"I've seen him a few times. Who is he?"

"Mr Taylor, I think. He's some sort of recruiter for the military.

There's a base on the outskirts of town. Don't know if you've noticed it."

Ellen nodded as she wiped a chip on the paper for extra salt. "There's a big, barbed wire fence, isn't there?"

He nodded. "Anyway, the base never closed down, and the fella was looking for ex-soldiers to do a job for twenty quid. Heaps of the other blokes are doing it, so I said yes, and he gave me ten quid upfront."

He leaned back on the bench, stretched out his arms and legs and patted his stomach. "Best fish and chips ever, don't you reckon?"

She kissed him again. "Twenty quid's a lot. What do you have to do? You don't have to go back into the army again?"

"Nah," he said, pulling her close and wrapping his arms around her. "Apparently, all we gotta do is show up and try out this new topical ointment. Then I just gotta wait around all afternoon and chat with the other blokes. Twenty quid of the easiest money I'll ever make. I told him to count me in if there's any more work like that. Then we'll really be set."

"That's all? It seems too good to be true." She tried to hide her uneasiness. "And it's safe?"

"Why wouldn't it be?"

"And you promise they're not making you join up?"

"No! It's just a one-off job. Don't worry." He turned her chin and kissed her tenderly on the lips. "I've no intention of going back into the army again. I've done more than my bit and have the scars to show for it."

She thought of the shrapnel scars on his arm and back; he was lucky to be alive. "When do you have to go to the base?"

He dug into his trouser pocket and pulled out a scrap of paper. "One o'clock tomorrow arvo."

She sat up. "Then you've got time to see Mrs Laurel's house after church and before I go to work. After that, I won't see you until the wedding."

"Tell me more about the place."

Her uneasiness gave way to excitement as she told him about their new home.

9

Dana

The clouds are heavy, and it's going to rain, so I break into something between a trot and a fast walk, which is difficult since I'm carrying a coffee. I'm anxious to get to the surgery, not just because I want to stay dry. I'm interviewing for a receptionist, and she's the only candidate.

My handbag slips down to my elbow as I unlock the surgery door. I yank my arm up and spray coffee across my new silk top. "Bugger."

In the surgery, I clean myself up as best as I can and finish what's left of the coffee. I straighten one of Lily's paintings in the waiting room. There's a knock on the door.

A mass of black curls pokes through.

"I know I'm a bit early, but I'm Linda Saxby."

The rest of her comes in, and I'm already taken with her wide smile and crinkling eyes.

I shake her hand and lead her into my office.

"Thanks for seeing me," she says.

I'd read her well-presented and comprehensive resume and was already impressed. "Tell me a bit about yourself."

"Well, I grew up here, but I've been living in Townsville for twenty years and the last ten as a single mum. The kids are off my hands, and I've been trying to get back here to keep an eye on my mother." She waves her hands around for emphasis. "I don't know if you know her. Of course, you wouldn't. You've only been here two minutes. And well, I hope you don't mind, but she heard you needed someone, and well, I just jumped at the chance. I worked with Dr Wolff and Dr Maddison in Townsville for years, and they're only too happy to provide you with references. I also know how hard it can be to start something from scratch, and well, I reckon I can be a valuable asset to you."

When she pauses, she places her hands on her lap and takes a deep breath. "Sorry, I can't believe I said all that so fast." She rolls her eyes. "I'm a little nervous."

"Me too," I say, and we both break out in laughter.

She has experience and seems well organised based on her resume.

"When can you start?" I blurt out.

Linda breaks into a smile showing off a smudge of pink lipstick on her perfectly straight teeth. "Don't you want to ring my referees?"

"Ah, yes, subject to your referees giving you a glowing report," I add hastily.

I haven't done this right. You're meant to do a full interview, get references, and then offer the job. But I trust my gut, although I don't know why since it let me down with Daniel, the snake.

"Who's your mother?" I ask.

"Mavis Gillespie. I use my married name."

"Mavis? Yes, I think I met her at the pub a couple of nights ago."

"Probably with Joan?"

"Yeah, that's right."

"Joan looks out for her. She thinks Mum might have early onset dementia, so I really need to be here."

From what little I remember of Mavis, it didn't strike me that she had dementia. Some testing would tell. "I fully understand."

"I'd like her to see you at some stage if that's all right."

"Of course, I'd be happy to. Now, can you start tomorrow by any small chance?"

She looks upset. "I can't, I'm afraid. I'm moving on Monday, and I've already booked the removalists." Then she brightens up. "I can start on Tuesday, though."

We talk about salary and hours, the appointment system and fees, the town, her kids, my sister – it's like we're old chums. Afterwards, I call her referees, who rave about how they hadn't wanted her to leave and that I was very lucky.

I look at my dwindling to-do list and cross off "get a receptionist," feeling very pleased with myself.

My Friday and Saturday are filled with unpacking deliveries, installing an answering machine, and taking appointments now that the phone's been reconnected. I take Sunday off and head for the beach, where I take a well-deserved dip, read the book I started months ago, and sunbake, slathered with sunscreen. I feel strangely calm as I stare out at the blue water, seagulls, and swaying palms. I'm a world away from Daniel and the pain he caused me, away from the hospital board and what might happen. But no amount of scenery can take away the niggle of guilt about my mistake. That's with me constantly, gnawing away.

*

I'm bright and early this Monday morning, as I want to double-check everything before my first appointment at eight. As I round the corner, two middle-aged people are already waiting: a thickset man and a slim woman. It's not even seven. So much for double-checking everything.

"G'day, doc," the man says, smiling apologetically. "We're a bit early."

"Sorry," says the woman, her face lined with worry.

I struggle to find the keys in my enormous handbag, wondering why it's a such a cavernous black hole. Then I realise these two are expecting a reply.

"Um. Yes. You are keen. Give me a moment, and I'll see what I can do."

I unlock the door and close it, leaving them outside. I guess I could have let them in, but I'm flustered. Instead, I throw my handbag into the kitchenette, down my coffee, and re-open the door.

"Come in."

I slip behind the counter and open the exercise book I've set up as an appointment schedule, hoping to hell that Linda knows how to do it on the computer. Then I realise I hadn't asked if she had any computer skills. My day is already deteriorating.

"Bob and Shirl Harper," the man says. "We haven't got an appointment."

I look up. "Oh?"

The woman looks embarrassed. "We thought we might squeeze in ahead of the others if that's okay. We won't be long."

I close the book and look at my watch. I can't even remember what I'd planned to do before the first patient, but they seem worried. "Please, come into my office, and I'll get your files."

I show them in, then hurry to the bank of filing cabinets. Inside their files are notes from an appointment with Dr Dunlop six months ago and nothing else.

"What can I do for you?"

"We've got a heap of bruises," Bob says lifting the sleeve of his t-shirt. A dark blue bruise covers his bicep.

"We've had these for a few months," Shirl says, lifting her cotton skirt to reveal a two large bruises. "and I can't seem to get rid of these sores." She opens her mouth wide for inspection.

I check her mouth then examine her inner arms and legs, which are covered in bruises.

"Are you sleeping?" I ask.

"Like a rock because I feel so exhausted all the time. Aren't I, love?" She looks at Bob, whose face is deadpan, but he nods. "He's the same, aren't you?"

He nods again.

Next, I examine Bob. He has a slightly enlarged spleen and enlarged lymph glands in his neck and armpits. He has bruises all over his back, and he winces when I touch his stomach.

"We saw a doc," Bob says, getting up off the examination table. "He said to come back if the bruises persisted."

"But we wanted to wait to see a permanent doctor." Shirl is picking at a hangnail.

"I thought they'd go away, but there seems to be more," Bob says.

"And when was this?" I ask, writing rapidly.

They look at each other. "Six months ago, at least."

My heart sinks; I've got to get this right. It could be chronic B-cell leukaemia, and if it is, the progress will be slow.

"And you're feeling worse?"

Shirl frowns. "I'm okay, but Bob … he can barely get out of bed some mornings."

Bob hitches up his shorts and does up his belt.

"Whaddya think, doc?"

"To be honest, I'm not sure, so I'll need you to have some further tests. Then we'll have a clearer picture. Are you okay to do that?"

They nod, and Bob rubs a hand through his thinning grey hair.

I see them out then call a courier to urgently take the blood samples to pathology and listen out for the jingle of the door. It's not long until my next patient arrives. Throughout the day, more patients turn up just to see if they can be squeezed in.

At seven thirty, it's already dark and I switch off the lights and lock the door, exhausted. No lunch. My mouth is parched from talking about aches and pains, blood pressure, diabetes, and skin complaints. It's all a bit overwhelming on my own.

My biggest worry is Bob and Shirl. The notes from their last visit said to come back if the symptoms persisted. Why the hell didn't Dr Dunlop organise tests back then?

Rubbing my neck, I stretch as I walk down the ramp, hoping they don't have what I suspect is the problem.

A man's voice calls out.

"How was your first day?"

I peer into the dark and make my way to the footpath.

"Working a bit late?"

It's Herb, and he's smiling, probably thinking he's getting his money's worth. Is he checking up on me?

"Yeah. There's a lot to do. What are you doing out this way?"

"Just out for a run."

I squint at him under the streetlight. He's in running gear and is sweaty.

"It's cooler at this time of the night," he says.

"I prefer the early morning myself."

I finally began running two days ago, but never at night. Mum's nagging about it being too dangerous has been embedded into me, despite my arguments that I have the right to go wherever, whenever I like.

"The hot water unit arrived this afternoon, and the boys will install it tomorrow. You should be able to move in tomorrow night. I'll drop the keys off sometime in the afternoon."

"That'd be great. Thanks."

"Then you won't have to go so far to get home." He smiles and seems to be trying hard to make a joke, but it comes across awkwardly.

"Yeah," I say. "Well, I better leave you to it. See you tomorrow, then."

"Yep," he says.

I turn and head back to The Palace Hotel.

*

The next day, I meet Linda at seven thirty.

"I've brought a sandwich for you," she says. "I know you doctors tend to skip lunch."

How did she know?

"You didn't have to do that. But thank you so much."

"It's not fancy. Just salad."

"It's perfect."

She's glancing at the exercise book. "I'll set up all the appointments in your diary for you; that way, you'll know who's next. I gather the files are out the back?"

I lead her to the filing cabinets and hand her the key. She unlocks one and glances into the open drawer before opening a file and shuffling through the papers.

"They're a little skinny. Bits of paper, different handwriting, and they don't seem to go back very far."

"I haven't had much of a chance to look. So, they're a bit of a mess?"

"I'll sort it all out. Leave everything to me."

I walk into my office, quietly relieved that Linda is in charge.

After a busy morning, she shoos me out of the office at one o'clock to eat and get some air.

"Your next appointment isn't for forty minutes," she says.

Even though it's sticky and hot, I take the sandwich and walk around the block, ending up at my house. Jack's ute is in the driveway. He must be putting the hot water unit in.

I'm sitting on the shady step, eating my sandwich, when the thud of work boots comes along the hallway and onto the verandah.

"You know you can sit on the furniture?"

Brushing crumbs from my mouth, I twist around. There's a man I haven't seen before in brown shorts, t-shirt, and hi-vis vest. I quickly stand and shade my eyes to look at him. He's tanned, and his dark curly hair is unruly.

"I know, but I prefer the step. I wasn't planning on staying."

He starts down the stairs towards me, his tool belt slung low on his hips.

"I'm Doctor Dana Janssen," I say.

He squints. "Yeah, I know. I saw you in the pub the other day."

"Oh?"

"I reckon everyone knows who you are."

I'm a talking point. Understandable, although not comforting. I wonder what they're saying. "And you are?"

"Steve. I work for Jack Babcock."

"Are you putting in my hot water unit?"

"Hopefully."

"I'm supposed to be moving in tonight."

He looks at his watch. "I'm tryin' to get it fixed by three so I can catch the next boomer." He starts down again, and I stand aside to let him by, but he stops, and we're face to face. He's not that tall, and his face is marked with old acne.

"Boomer?"

"A large wave. Ideal conditions for surfin' this arvo." He lifts his chin and slips on the sunglasses from the top of his head. "Maybe you wanna come along one afternoon, doc?"

I'm against the rail. Sweat wafts from him. "I'm not really a surfer. Well, nice meeting you. I better get back."

"Maybe I can teach ya. Happy to give the doc a freebie."

He looks cocky as he leans against the railing.

"I don't think so."

I should have put him in his place, but, as usual, my most perfect comebacks always come later.

I head towards the surgery, not sure what to make of surfer Steve.

When I get back to my office, two messages are on my desk – one about Bob and Shirl's tests and the other to ring the hospital board. My hands are clammy, and I pick up the phone.

10

Ellen

Ellen was startled when Phyllis – who must have been waiting by the window – opened the front door and grabbed Billy in a hug.

"You just have to be Billy. I've heard such a lot about you," Phyllis said.

Billy blushed. "I hope it was all good, Mrs Laurel."

Phyllis laughed. "Naturally. Now, come in, get out of the heat, and for goodness' sake, call me Phyllis."

"It's very good of you to let us board with you," Billy said as they walked down the hallway.

"I'm thankful for the company if the truth be told. I just rattle around this big old house." Phyllis waved her arms about. "It won't feel so lonely knowing that there's someone downstairs."

In the kitchen, Phyllis reached for the kettle.

Ellen looked at Billy and then at Phyllis. "We don't know too many people in town, and well, we wondered if you'd like to come to our wedding. It's next Saturday. Just a small one."

Phyllis dropped the kettle in the sink, turned, and clapped her hands. "My goodness. I'd love to come. Thank you. I'm very touched. I haven't been to a wedding for a long time." She pursed her lips and lowered her eyes. "Well, come to think of it, not since my own."

In an instant, Phyllis's face transformed into a tight smile. "Anyway, why don't you show your young man the place, and I'll put the kettle on. You will stay for a cup of tea?"

"Thanks, Phyllis. That'd be nice," Billy said.

"We won't be too long."

Ellen grabbed Billy's hand and pulled him onto the back verandah and down the stairs. She showed him the kitchenette, the tiny bathroom, and the large four-poster bed with a floral bedspread.

"Isn't it wonderful?" she said.

"It's nice and cool," Billy said.

"And it's private."

Billy sat on the bed, pressing on the mattress with his hand. "This will do nicely," he said, grinning, before pulling Ellen down on top of him and flopping backwards.

"Shh. You cheeky bugger. She might hear."

She quickly got up and smoothed her dress and bedspread to remove any wrinkles.

"She's gonna hear a lot more than that with a pair of newlyweds," he said, chuckling. "I can't wait to marry you."

"I can't wait either."

He grabbed her around the waist and kissed her hard.

"And soon, we'll have our little family."

She smiled. "Yes, we will. I know it's not what we planned, but it can't be helped."

"I don't care. Now I've got this money coming in and the promise of more, we'll soon be able to afford our own house."

He ran his hand over her tummy and tucked her hair behind her ears. "I'm the luckiest man in the world."

A weight seemed to have lifted off her now that all her dreams were coming true – a job, a husband, a home, and soon, a baby.

"And you've made me the happiest woman in the world."

They both burst out laughing.

Billy kissed her again. "Listen to us. We sound like stars on the silver screen."

"I guess we better see Phyllis. Otherwise, she'll be wondering what on earth we're doing down here."

"I can think of a few things." Billy grinned before grabbing her again and putting his arms around her.

"One last proper kiss before a cuppa and you going off to work."

They kissed again.

"I won't see you again until our wedding. Six more days," she said. "Your shirt's come out."

Billy tucked the tail of his blue-checked shirt back into his pants, and Ellen tidied her hair.

They had a cup of tea with Phyllis, and then it was time for Ellen to leave. Billy walked her to the pub and pecked her on the cheek before she went inside.

"Six more days," he said, staring at her. "Just memorising your face."

"You look very happy," Joan said when Ellen grabbed the apron and went behind the bar.

"I am," Ellen said. "Won't be long and I'll be Mrs Billy Nolan."

"I'm very happy for you, love. Why didn't he come in for a beer? I'd like to congratulate him."

"He's got a job out at the old military base this afternoon, and then he heads off afterwards for the cane farm."

Joan raised her eyebrows. "I heard some of the blokes were doing something out there. A couple of Brits are in town, so something big must be going on. Maybe they're worried about the Russians. Could you imagine another war? I don't think I could stand it."

Ellen's mood flattened. Would they want Billy to join up?

"You know, during the war, this town was filled with Yanks and Brits, and our own, of course. Jeeps and army trucks were going back and forwards, up and down the main street."

Ellen picked up a tea towel and tried to keep her voice even. "It must have been exciting."

"Oh, it was. The Palace was packed every night. The Yanks knew how to splash their money."

Joan's sharp eyes roved around the bar and stopped at the glass door to the Ladies' Lounge.

"Love, I've just seen Mavis and Carolyn come in. Can you serve them for me?"

Ellen nodded and headed out of the bar and into the Ladies' Lounge. Both women looked to be in their mid to late twenties.

She couldn't help but stare at the beauty of the dark-haired woman who pulled off her white gloves and removed her hat.

"God, I don't know why we have to wear these damn things to church in this heat."

Her friend's mouth fell open. "Mavis, I'm surprised at you. Hat and gloves off? Whatever will you do next?"

"But you're okay with the blaspheming? Anyway, I've done nothing wrong. I'm hot." Mavis giggled.

Ellen was alarmed until she saw the smile on the other woman's face. "Can I get you anything?" she asked.

"A shandy, thanks," Mavis said.

The other woman's blonde hair was swept into a bun under a

green floral hat. Ellen admired her expensive-looking, pale-green pencil skirt and blouse. The woman tilted her head and regarded Ellen with clear blue eyes. "New in town?"

"Yes," Ellen said, keen to get back to the bar. The doors had just opened, and Joan was on her own.

"I'm Carolyn Hipworth," she said. "And this is Mavis Akina."

Carolyn eyed her until Ellen remembered her manners. "Ellen Lambert," she said, smiling.

"Welcome to our little town. If Mavis can have a shandy, then so will I. A very cold one, as I shan't be removing my gloves. Thank you, Ellen."

"I'll be right back with your drinks."

Ellen was on Mavis's side, not that she owned a pair of gloves. It was hard not to stare at her. Petite, with jet-black hair and bright blue eyes, she was the most beautiful woman Ellen had ever seen. She wondered why she wasn't a movie star. In contrast, Carolyn, tall and blonde, seemed quite plain.

Ellen returned to the bar. Half-a-dozen men were already seated at tables with their drinks.

"Do you think it'll be as busy as yesterday?" Ellen asked Joan.

Joan was putting coins into the till. "Could be, since the brass are now in town. Watch yourself. They like anything in a skirt. If they come in, they'll talk to those two." She jerked her head in the direction of the Ladies' Lounge. "Carolyn will send them packing, telling them who her husband is. She's got quite a sharp tongue when needed."

Ellen lifted a tray of glasses from the sink behind her. "They both seem nice. Not that I had a chance to talk to them."

Joan closed the cash register. "Carolyn is the nicest woman and one of my best friends. They both are." She lowered her voice. "She's been trying to have kids for years, but no luck there."

"Who, Carolyn?"

"Yes. It's very sad, but not to be."

Ellen, her back to Joan, grazed her stomach with her fingers, grateful that wasn't her problem. She headed to the sink and rinsed out the cloth.

"You know she's married to Bert Hipworth," Joan said. "You remember him?"

Ellen nodded.

"And Mavis, such a love even if her stock is a bit mixed if you know what I mean."

Ellen shot Joan a look, confused.

Joan, her tea towel-covered hand shoved into a beer jug, moved closer and lowered her voice. "Her grandfather came from the islands to work the cane fields in the late eighteen hundreds." She pulled away and tittered. "Although we don't hold that against our Mavis."

Ellen wondered if Joan did, in fact, look down her nose at Mavis.

"But she has got beautiful olive skin. I'll give her that much. And married the best-looking man in Sugar Creek, though I don't for the life of me know why she went back to her maiden name. Another one we lost." Joan sighed and stared at the stained-glass window filtering the sunlight from outside. "But a word of warning. Don't mention anything about the war while she's around. She's still very teary about what happened."

"Maybe she'll remarry and start again?"

"Mavis? No, she swore there was no-one else for her. I don't blame her. If you've had the best, how could anyone else measure up? Anyway, it's not like she has to marry. He left her with a nice little pension, so she's set up to grieve for the rest of her life."

"Do you have kids, Joan?"

"Two boys, fifteen and seventeen. Charlie and Ronnie. They're at boarding school." She stopped putting the glasses away and giggled. "Had the oldest when I was twenty. I would've liked a little girl, but the war put that to rest."

"You were left with two kids and a hotel to run by yourself?"

"Yep. Mr Babcock went off and saw the world, leaving me behind." Joan picked up the cash and looked at Ellen. "Don't look so shocked. He had a good time with a cushy admin job and saw no action because of his gammy leg. Had polio as a kid."

"Oh?" Ellen said. She'd assumed he'd been affected by the war in some way.

"You probably noticed that he's a bit … slow. He got a bad knock on the head when a Yank started a fight in the bar. He came between a flying chair and a table, poor love. It's slowed him down, but that's all."

It wasn't any of Ellen's business, but she wondered why Joan was telling her all of this. Not that she wasn't interested. She was, of course. It helped her understand the town, the pub, and the people just that little bit more.

"Your fella seems nice," Joan said.

"He is. I hope what he's doing out at the military base will be okay."

Joan looked at her sharply and frowned. "Why do you say that?"

"I dunno. I'm not sure about it."

"What does he have to do?"

"He's helping with some medical experiments. A topical cream, he said. But … I'm terrified he might be called up again," she blurted.

Should she have said anything? Billy hadn't asked her to keep it secret, and she felt comfortable confiding in Joan.

"No-one's been called up," Joan said. "Why would they? It's 1948, and the war is well and truly over. There is Russia … No, I'm sure there won't be another war. No wonder it's quiet in here. That must be where everyone is today."

Ellen nodded, feeling foolish. Still, she wanted the next six days to fly.

11

Dana

"Doctor Janssen?"

Tearing my eyes from the words on the page, I keep a firm grip on the pen. "Yes?"

Linda moves towards me, her long curly fringe held off her face with a red-glitter bobby pin.

"Are you all right?" she says softly. "I've been knocking."

I nod. "I'm fine. Sorry. Deep in concentration. The next patient's here?"

"Yes. Here's the file."

I slip the paper I'd been writing on into the desk drawer and take the file. "Thanks."

She's still studying me, so I force a smile and push a strand of hair from my face. "Really, I'm fine."

It's nice how she's taken on a mother hen role. She just seems to know when I need help, such as now, but I can't tell her what's on my mind. It's not that sort of thing.

"Do you want me to send him in?"

"Yes, that would be great. Thanks. Oh, and can you please call Bob and Shirl Harper and tell them to come in tomorrow? Just let them know their tests are back, and I'd like to talk it through with them."

Linda raises her eyebrows. "Not good?"

"Not great."

She nods, and perhaps she thinks that's what's upset me. The pathology report was as I dreaded: leukaemia.

The afternoon goes quickly, making me forget, for a time, about my own problems.

Linda pokes her head in the door after I've seen the last patient out. "I'm off. Do you need anything?"

I look up, puzzled.

"It's 5:30," she says.

"Is it? Hell." I look at my watch. "You go, and I'll see you in the morning."

Linda looks concerned. "I've made fewer appointments for you tomorrow. You should pace yourself a bit. This town's waited months for a doctor, so a day or two isn't going to hurt."

I nod and smile wearily. "I know. It's my first week, and everyone's waited long enough. When it settles down, I'll work out when I can take an afternoon off."

Linda doesn't look so convinced.

"By the way," she says, "I've tried sorting out the files, but there's nothing before 1995. It's like all the files have been shipped off somewhere and whoever was here just started again."

"Oh?"

"They must be archived, somewhere."

"That seems odd."

"I vaguely remember Mum telling me that when the previous doc left, they were going to close the surgery. I can check with Mum. She's bound to know."

"It would be great to have everybody's full medical history."

"Anyway, I'll keep digging and let you know."

After she's gone, I go back to my desk and open the drawer.

The hospital board want another statement. I shut the drawer as if closing off the words will make it all disappear. But it doesn't.

I open the drawer again and spread the second statement on the desk. It's much like my first.

I was working night shift in emergency on the day in question.

Daniel, my supervisor, was on, too.

It was an unusually quiet Saturday night. A few drunks, one with a broken leg, another with a cut hand; a baby presenting with a high fever; a suspicious faint and one heart attack.

I pick up my pen and twirl it between my fingers. What I can't tell them is that Daniel was my boyfriend at the time and that I'd confronted him about another woman just before seeing Mrs Kaluski.

I wasn't concentrating.

I chew the end of the pen. I should have taken a minute to compose myself. How could I have missed it?

And I was in a hurry. My supervisor handed over the patient to me. It was busy.

Is that how I remember it?

I didn't check when I authorised the dose of penicillin.

I can't tell them I was in a state of shock after finding an anonymous note in my pigeonhole.

I should have double-checked. I'm normally very thorough. The fever was too high. It was clearly an infection. Penicillin was the appropriate drug to use. I didn't have to refer to my supervisor.

I couldn't face him anyway, and I can't tell them why.

It was just a casual comment before I saw Mrs Kaluski.

*

I'd laughed when I saw Daniel and said, "I can't believe how some people try to cause trouble."

"What do you mean?" He'd leaned over and planted a kiss on my mouth before picking up a handful of files.

"Someone left this in my pigeonhole." I fumbled for the crumpled piece of paper in my pocket. "It's nasty, don't you think?" I said, forcing myself to sound casual.

I held out the note: *Daniel is fucking Petra.*

I knew and liked Petra. I either didn't believe it or didn't want to believe it. People can be malicious sometimes, and Daniel would never do that to me. We were getting married and going to buy a house when I got my new job. It was all planned.

I knew as soon as his eyes flickered across the page, his face wooden, his lips hard.

He turned his back on me and walked towards the ward. I followed.

"So, it's true?" My heart was thumping, my mind in a crazed whirl.

He stared straight ahead. He couldn't, or wouldn't, look at me. "We'll talk about this later. Mrs Kaluski's waiting. She's got a nasty infection from a cut on her leg. Clean it up, and give her a shot."

I'd expected him to laugh and deny it, not want a discussion. But he'd walked off, expecting me to follow, and I did, totally confused.

Why didn't he just deny it?

Daniel led me to the patient's bed. "Mrs Kaluski, this is Doctor Janssen. I'll leave you in her capable hands."

Then he strode off to the far end of the ward.

And those hands of mine trembled as I examined my patient. I cleaned up the gash and drained the pus. Routine. The nurse looked bored. I organised the penicillin and injected her.

Daniel wandered past without glancing at me, but I noticed him wink at the nurse. So intent was I on tackling Daniel again, I stepped away, not noticing the patient's eyes bulging or her arms waving until the nurse yelled out.

Anaphylactic shock.

I worked to revive her, and she was transferred to Intensive Care.

I found him in the corridor outside the ward.

He pulled me into his office. "What the fuck happened?"

"Where were you?" I said. "I paged you."

He cracked one of his fingers. "I'm going to have to report this."

"You haven't answered my question."

"What question?" he snarled.

"Two, actually." I folded my arms. "Where were you? I had to deal with everything on my own."

"And you fucked it up. It was a simple process, and because of your incompetence, I have to report it. I can tell you right now I'm not taking the rap on this one. It's a simple job to review for allergies. Any moron could do it."

"But …" My anger fell away. What had I done?

"There's no way I'm jeopardising my career; you're on your own. I want your report on my desk before you leave. And don't be surprised if they throw the book at you. You'll probably never practice again."

I couldn't speak. The words were stuck, and my legs were like jelly as I walked out of his office.

He was right. I should have checked if she had any allergies and not relied on the "No allergies" box she'd ticked on the form. I should have checked her GP's letter. She nearly died.

I deserved to lose my licence.

*

I push myself from the desk; I can't do this tonight. My heart is heavy, my mind weary, my body drained. I glance out the window into the darkness towards my house, then remember I still don't have the keys. Herb must have forgotten unless Linda left them on the front desk. I check, but there's nothing there. I'm too tired to move in tonight anyway. What's another night living out of a suitcase?

I trudge down to the pub, get something to eat, arrange to stay another night, and call Mum from my room.

"Try not to worry about the board, love," she says.

"How can I not, Mum? It's not helpful telling me not to worry. The family think it's my fault. I should have double-checked."

"I'm sure Daniel's statement will help, too. He knows how diligent you are. He'll stick by you."

She doesn't know what he did to me. He won't do anything but protect himself. I blink back tears and try to control the pressure building in my throat.

"I should have delved deeper, crosschecked everything."

"Dana, you can't keep going over and over this. It happens sometimes, you said it yourself. And the patient didn't die. You weren't to know she had a rare condition. She didn't know herself."

What she said was right. At the time, the Medical Registrar hadn't been too concerned. She said there were more issues with the patient, and the reaction to the penicillin didn't kill her. She said also it was lucky I was there to revive her in time.

"The family don't agree with you, Mum. My career could be over before the year is out."

"I'm sure you're wrong. Hell, if every doctor were struck off each time they made a mistake, we'd have no-one in the medical profession."

She has to say that. My mother is my rock, and I miss her. She keeps me sane when I catastrophise things. I wipe away the tears.

"How's Lily?" I ask.

"You can talk to her yourself. Here she is, and I'll talk to you tomorrow, my love."

I sniffle, feeling sorry for myself. "Okay, and thanks, Mum."

Lily's funny story about her latest painting class and her classmates distracts me. By the time I'm ready for bed, I'm calm enough to fall into a deep, exhausted sleep.

12

Ellen

Sunday, May 23

The afternoon dragged until Cal and Wally wandered in around three, talking about sugar cane and tonnage, fires, rain and drought. Ellen liked listening, although a lot went over her head. She could tell from the amount he drank Cal was a tormented man.

"Don't be surprised if there's another war," Cal declared.

Ellen looked at him sharply. Is there a ruse to force the men to join up?

"Mate, no-one can afford another war," Wally said.

"Listen, the Yanks are telling everyone that atomic weapons are gonna be banned. But I reckon that's so they'll be the only ones with 'em. They're making sure the commies don't get too big for their boots. I tell you, it's still anybody's game. It ain't over yet."

"I reckon you've had too many beers, mate," Wally said, grinning.

Cal struck a match and brought the flame to the cigarette hanging out of his mouth.

"Wonder where Bertie boy is? Carolyn's here. Not like him to not pop in on a Sunday arvo."

"Betcha he agrees with me. He works out there and knows what's going on." Cal downed his beer and signalled to Ellen to bring him another. "You can't explain why the Brits and the Yanks have turned up again, can ya'?"

She placed the beer in front of Cal.

"Probably to close the place down. Take their stuff and get the hell out, is what I reckon. Glad to see the back of them bastards," Wally said.

Cal wrapped his fingers around the glass, his cigarette hanging limply. "And the other thing. Why is Bert Hipworth still working out there? It's been nearly three years." Cal waved his glass in the air, spilling some of the beer. "Listen, mate. The Yanks are building bases, not closing 'em."

Ellen's grabbed a mop. She'd forgotten that Bert Hipworth worked at the base.

"Why do ya reckon there's no-one in here, mate?" Cal moved for Ellen and her mop. "It's because that bloke who was in here last week tricked half the fellas into re-enlisting."

Ellen's chest tightened; she was right. Even Cal had said so.

"Thanks, love," Cal said, sitting again.

Wally stubbed out his cigarette and then looked at his watch. "They're just there to get a few extra dollars for testing some bloody cream, mate. Bloody hell, you gotta calm down. I reckon you've had enough. Time to go home."

"Since when are ya' my mother? I'm still drinking, and I aim to have another."

"Suit yourself," Wally said. "I'm off."

Ellen put the mop and bucket away and cleaned the glasses. She'd lost three brothers to the war, all when they were sixteen years old. The oldest, Danny, had been tricked into joining up in 1940. He never came back. She was twelve, motherless, and her father was a drunk. She and Mack had to keep the family going until he enlisted in 1941. He hadn't come back, either. She'd stayed until little Marty left in 1944, and he, too, never returned. Her father had taken it out on her with his drunken rages, and his beatings. She left two years ago. She didn't care if he was dead or alive; it made no difference.

She cleared the glasses from the table.

"Thanks, love," Cal said, flicking a dead match into the ashtray.

She moved into the Ladies' Lounge to collect the empty glasses and wipe the tables. Carolyn was still there with Mavis. An hour to closing time.

Carolyn looked up and smiled. "Has Bert arrived yet, Ellen?"

She shook her head.

Carolyn sighed. "I'll have to go home on my own. I really don't know why he had to work on a Sunday. Be a love and get me one more shandy, please. And then I better go."

Ellen nodded. "Would you like another, Mavis?"

"No," Mavis said, looking at her watch.

"Mavis, are you coming tonight or not?" Carolyn said. "I've got a roast on, and we're having some of the top brass over for dinner tonight. I don't know why Bert insists on entertaining them. But some of the Yanks are nice." Carolyn leaned over and took out her cigarettes.

Mavis laughed. "You've got a roast on? You mean your maid has the roast on, and you will get the credit. I don't think you've cooked since the beginning of the war."

Carolyn folded her arms and cocked her head. "I don't think that's strictly true. But I know my strengths. So, what if cooking isn't one of them?"

"Yes, you should stay out of the kitchen."

Carolyn put a cigarette to her red-painted lips and struck a match before throwing it at the ashtray. She missed, and it slid across the table. "Why don't you come, Mavis? You might meet someone. Please, it'll be a bore otherwise."

"How many times do I have to tell you? There'll never be anyone for me again," Mavis retorted. "I'm happy to grow old and single. Besides, I'm busy."

"Pff. Busy washing your hair. I never heard such drivel. You're not even twenty-six yet," Carolyn said, a slight slur in her words.

Mavis stubbed out her cigarette and picked up her handbag. "I don't know how you can be so insensitive. I just don't want to. I've got to go."

Carolyn shrugged. "What about you, Ellen? Would you like to come?"

Ellen swung around. "Who me?"

"Yes, you. Would you like to come to dinner at my place tonight? You're new in town, and I'd like to get to know you. Besides, I need another woman to keep me company now that Mavis has bowed out." Carolyn looked sideways at Mavis. "What about it?"

"Enjoy your evening," Mavis said, waving as she left.

What else did she have to do other than write in her diary? Why not? She might be able to ask Bert if the men were re-enlisting.

"Thank you," Ellen said. "That would be nice."

13

Dana

Shirl is twisting the folds of her skirt, and Bob is drumming his fingers on the side of his thigh. I'm nervous for them. It's not like I haven't done this before, but since the stuff-up in the hospital, I'm super vigilant, probably to the point of zealousness. I've double-checked the blood tests and spoken again to the pathologist, who, understandably, got a bit testy. I don't want to get this wrong.

Twirling my pen, I take a deep breath.

"There is some abnormality with the blood tests, and I need to refer you both to a haematologist, Dr Jeffries, in Townsville, who will conduct further tests."

Shirl covers her mouth and closes her eyes. Bob hunches over, hands clutching his knees, and says nothing.

I give them a moment and glance down at the results just to make sure. Again.

"That's cancer, isn't it?" Bob says. "You go to a haematologist for cancer."

"The tests are not conclusive. A bone marrow biopsy should be done before making a final diagnosis."

"Jesus," he mutters. His chin has dropped so low it's almost touching his chest.

Shirl opens her eyes and stares at Bob. "Me too?"

"I recommend you also go to the specialist, as there is a slight abnormality in your results as well."

She sniffs and pulls a tissue out of her battered handbag.

Bob lifts his face and stares at me with red eyes like he's daring me not to say anymore.

But I have to.

"I've made an appointment for you both. I hope that's okay, but I think it's prudent to deal with this as soon as possible." I hand them the referral and gently push the tissue box forwards. Shirl leans over, grabs another, and dabs at the tears edging down her cheeks.

It's not my place to say what I fear they have – acute myeloid leukaemia or chronic B-cell leukaemia. They need to get treatment now, particularly for Bob. My voice is almost monotone, spilling out the information they'll need for the appointment, but they're only focused on one word – cancer.

The air-conditioner whirs, and the faint sound of voices filters in from the waiting room.

Bob leans back in his chair and folds his arms. "How long, doc?"

Shirl flinches, then shifts nervously in her chair. Her composure has long gone, and she sobs uncontrollably.

"We have to be pragmatic, Bob. More tests are needed before treatment options can be discussed," I say hopefully, trying to delay what I think he really wants to know.

"If I have cancer, how long have I got? Days? Weeks? What?"

Shirl's red eyes flit from him to me.

"Dr Jeffries will be the best one to guide you."

Shirl holds her crumpled-up tissue and touches Bob gently on the arm. "Just like the Jamieson's," she says, almost in a whisper.

He throws her a look of sudden realisation.

"The Jamieson's?" I ask.

"They were our next-door neighbours or had been for more than twenty years. They both died last year from cancer. The year before that, our other neighbours died of cancer." Shirl sniffs. "And now us."

Bob suddenly gets up. He looks like he's about to sprint off running blocks. "Come on, love. We've taken too much of the doc's time."

Shirl looks bewildered. "Should we make another appointment?"

I stand and move to the side. I'm not sure why, but my legs feel wobbly, and I rest my hand on the desk to steady myself.

"Yes, after you've seen the specialist."

"Thanks, doctor," Shirl says as Bob pulls her out the door.

Patients react in all sorts of ways. I hope I'm wrong, but I suspect Bob is in the advanced stage and will be in hospital within a week.

"Linda, can you find me these files." I pass her a note with the files I'm after. "There should be at least two." I screw up my face in apology.

"Not sure of the Christian names."

Linda suppresses any curiosity and nods.

The waiting room is finally empty, and Linda tells me she's going.

"Sorry, but I didn't get a chance to find those files you were after. I had poor Shirl on the phone in tears making another appointment. Bob wouldn't let her make it when they were here. Poor things."

I rub my neck and sigh. "One of the worst things about this job."

Linda looks sad. "I don't know how you do it."

I shrug.

"See you," she says.

I yawn and stretch, trying to loosen the day's tightness, then stare at the name on my desk pad: Jamieson. Suddenly, pushing my chair and knocking it into the wall behind me, I walk to the back room and find their file under J-K. Both husband and wife had acute myeloid leukaemia: advanced stage. There's something else in the doctor's notes, "same as the Thompsons."

I throw down the files and go to the drawer marked S-T. There it is: Thompson. Files for Prue and John, both with the same cancer. All three couples live close to each other on Old Goanna Creek Road.

According to the map of Sugar Creek, which is plastered to the wall, the road is out of town, five kilometres away. Why did they all get the same type of cancer within two or three years of each other? Perhaps it's just a coincidence. In a big city, maybe. A small country town?

Maybe not.

The men were in their sixties and died within six months of diagnosis. No history of previous chemotherapy, which could have explained the cancer. One smoked, but not for years, and the others didn't. There's no history of any other blood disorders, and nothing in their family histories, either. The only thing I can't dismiss is their exposure to a chemical, like benzene. The men all worked on sugar cane plantations back in the seventies. Perhaps there's a connection. Or maybe it's all just a coincidence. But what about the women? All housewives.

I hear a knock.

Still holding the folders, I open the front door letting the humidity and Herb slip through.

"Got your keys to the house," he says. "The hot water is on, and everything is good to go."

I murmur my thanks and drop the keys onto the reception counter.

"You alright?"

My mind is on those patients. "Uh?"

"You look a bit pale."

"Sorry, long day."

"I haven't had dinner, and I bet you haven't, either. Want to grab a bite at the pub, and I'll help you with your stuff?"

I glance at my watch and am suddenly hungry. "Okay."

14

Ellen

The room smelled spotless, like freshly waxed furniture. Ellen perched herself on the edge of a seat and steadied her jiggling knee. Her best floral dress seemed drab next to Carolyn's royal-blue pencil skirt and grey silk blouse.

Carolyn walked across the floral carpet to the mahogany drinks trolley.

"You'll join me in a gin and tonic, won't you?"

Ellen didn't drink. Despite working as a barmaid, she only served it and already regretted accepting Carolyn's invitation. "Um, no. But thank you."

"Nonsense," Carolyn said, her cigarette holder clenched firmly in her mouth. "I can't drink alone." She poured two glasses of gin and tonic.

Ellen took the expensive crystal glass, terrified of dropping it, and watched Carolyn settle into the armchair opposite. She copied and crossed her legs to the side, too.

"Cheers," Carolyn said. "Here's to you, Ellen. We hope you enjoy living in Sugar Creek."

Ellen held up her glass. "Yes, cheers. And thank you." The bitterness of the liquid stuck in her throat.

"Joan told me you're getting married" – Carolyn settled her glass on the coffee table, then puffed on her cigarette— "to a cane cutter."

Ellen was hardly surprised that Carolyn knew and had prepared for the questions. "Yes, next week."

"Why so soon?"

"Why wait, hey?" Ellen coughed as the burn settled from too big a gulp.

Carolyn's eyes were on Ellen, her cigarette teetering from the end of its silver holder. "I agree. He's been up here a few weeks, I heard. Though I do wonder why you didn't get married in Brisbane. You came from there, didn't you? You could have come up here with him."

"Oh, well. It was just one of those things." Ellen's knee jiggled.

"Marriage, my dear, isn't just one of those things," Carolyn said, not taking her eyes off her.

"Mrs Hipworth, are you ready to eat?"

Ellen was drawn to a thin, young woman in a faded floral dress and freshly stained white apron standing in the doorway. She was relieved by the interruption.

"Goodness, I'd quite forgotten about dinner. We were having such a nice time." Carolyn looked at her watch and frowned. "They should have been here half an hour ago. The lamb is going to be spoiled. I'll ring and find out, Jess."

Jess nodded and walked away while Carolyn made her way to the phone just outside the loungeroom in the corridor.

"Hello? This is Carolyn Hipworth calling. Is my husband there?"

Ellen drank another mouthful and began to relax.

"Oh? Thank you."

Carolyn returned and drained her glass. "He's running late and asked that we start. Apparently, the other gentlemen aren't coming after all. I don't know about you, but I'm starving. I hope you like lamb. Goodness, I didn't even ask you."

Ellen nodded and smiled. "I love lamb."

Carolyn rested her hand on the doorframe. "I'll go and let Jess know. She'll scream blue murder since she prepared for six, and now it's just three. Thank goodness you're here."

Once alone, Ellen leaned back into the cushion, her stomach queasy. Should she say she wasn't feeling well and apologise? It had been such a mistake to come. She looked at the expensive carpet, furniture, crystal cabinet, all the things she'd never be able to afford. Carolyn knew what to say, what to do, and even had someone to cook for her. Why on earth does she want someone like me in her home, she wondered.

Carolyn bobbed her head around the door. "Come on. Dinner won't be long. Bring your drink into the dining room." Carolyn led the way into a spacious room with a polished dining table large enough for ten people. Six places were set with gleaming silverware.

Maybe she's lonely, Ellen thought. Or perhaps it's the way country people are – hospitable.

"Now, you sit over there, Ellen."

Jess placed an oval platter in the centre of the table. On it was a large leg of lamb surrounded by crisp potatoes, green beans, and baked pumpkin.

"We'll serve ourselves, Jess." Carolyn held out a bottle of red wine. "Have a glass with dinner?"

Ellen stared at the food and giggled. "No, thank you. I think the gin and tonic has gone to my head a bit."

"You must be hungry. Alcohol on an empty stomach can do that.

Naturally, I'm used to it, so it doesn't affect me." Carolyn laughed. "It's so nice that you're here. Bert is often at work, Mavis has been avoiding me lately, and Joan is run off her feet at the pub. I guess your cane cutter has gone back to the farm?"

"Yes, he has."

Carolyn raised her glass. "And here we are. Here's to us."

Ellen held up a glass of water instead. "Thank you for inviting me."

"Let's eat."

Ellen served herself what she thought was enough to not appear greedy, despite being ravenous.

Carolyn served herself a tiny portion.

"So, what's it like working for Joan? She can be a battle-axe sometimes. You know she's thirty-six but hardly looks it, don't you think?"

Ellen gulped down a tough morsel of gristle. "She's very nice, and I enjoy working for her. It's a really interesting job." She quickly removed her elbows from resting on the table. How could she forget her manners?

Carolyn glanced up. "How so? What's so interesting about it?"

"The people, for one. I love listening to their stories and getting to know them. Like you, for example."

Carolyn smiled. "That's so nice of you to say, but I don't have much of a story. Born and raised in Townsville, met Bert at a dance in the middle of the war, married, and moved here so he could work at the base as a scientist." She looked at her watch. "He shouldn't have had to work on a Sunday, but who am I to tell him?"

"No children?" Ellen asked.

Carolyn drained the last of her wine. "Nope," she said, stabbing a potato with her fork. "Not yet."

The chime of the mantel clock echoed the time throughout the house – eight o'clock. Ellen then remembered that Joan said Carolyn couldn't have children.

"I suppose you must get all sorts of gossip, listening in to the fellas?" Carolyn said.

Ellen wiped a smear of gravy from her lips with a crisp white serviette. Had she been invited to spread gossip? Is that why she was here?

"Not really. A lot of talk about sugar cane mostly."

Carolyn looked disappointed as she poured herself another glass. "I suppose you see Wally and Cal in there a lot?"

"Yes, they're regulars."

"Poor Cal. His wife up and left him when he came back from Papua New Guinea with only one arm. He's quite attractive, though, don't you think?"

"He seems sad to me." And angry, she thought, but didn't want to say.

Carolyn pushed her plate away, pieces of meat and potato uneaten. "He should be since he had an affair before enlisting."

Ellen raised her eyebrows. "Really?"

"Ha!" Carolyn laughed. "I thought that would get you interested. Not really. I was just pulling your leg. He's a war hero."

Ellen hardly knew what to make of this woman. Then she heard a key in the lock, the front door open, and the heavy thud of footsteps. Carolyn's face quickly transformed as she pushed her chair back and snarled.

"About bloody time. Dinner is basically ruined, and … Bert, what's happened? You look awful," Carolyn said.

Ellen gaped at the pale, exhausted face of Bert Hipworth. His hair unruly, his eyes bloodshot, his face drawn and worried.

"Nothing," Bert said, tossing his hat onto the other end of the table. He peered at Ellen. "I didn't know we had company. Hello."

Carolyn raised her eyebrows. "We were meant to have those officers to dinner, remember? And Ellen was at a loose end, so I invited her and Mavis to make up the numbers. Then Mavis decided not to come, and now it's just three of us and all this food."

Bert held up his hand as he slumped into the chair and filled a glass with wine. "Don't start. I've had one hell of a day. If anything could go wrong, it did."

Carolyn folded her arms. "You shouldn't have been working today, anyway."

"Well, I had to." He turned to Ellen. "Glad you could join us. I'm sorry that I was so late. Don't stop eating on my account."

He drained his glass while Carolyn took his plate and served up a generous helping.

Ellen's appetite had gone. She sipped her water, wondering when might be the right time to leave.

"Ellen here is getting married next week," Carolyn said.

"Is that so? Who's the lucky bloke?" Bert said, his mouth full.

"I don't think you'd know him. He's a cane cutter, but you might have seen him at the base today," Ellen said.

Bert stopped eating and stared at her. "Today?"

Ellen thought she saw something in his eyes. Fright?

"He was one of the men doing the experiments with the topical cream."

Bert took a sudden breath before quickly composing himself and cutting the meat on his plate. "And what's his name?"

"Billy Nolan."

The fork clattered against the gold-rimmed plate. Bert stopped chewing, then swallowed, his Adam's apple dancing up and down.

"Sorry. So clumsy." He picked up the fork, fingers trembling, yet he seemed calm and composed as he vigorously sawed another piece of lamb. "I can't say I can place the chap."

Ellen seized her chance. "The men today, they weren't going to the base to be called up, were they?"

Bert looked up in surprise. "Of course not. What gave you that idea?"

"I just heard talk about war with Russia and, well, I just wondered."

Carolyn laughed. "War? We just got out of one. Goodness, Ellen, you have a wild imagination."

Ellen's face burned.

Bert pushed back his chair and grabbed his wine glass. "If you'll excuse me, I've got some paperwork to do. Congratulations on the wedding."

"Bert! You haven't finished your dinner."

"Not hungry. And tell Jess to get a better cut of meat next time. Too much gristle."

Carolyn watched him leave and shook her head. "Sorry, he's normally very hospitable. He must have had a very bad day. I've never seen him like this."

Ellen sucked a bit of meat from her teeth and finished the water. At least Billy wasn't going to be called up. Yet why did she still feel uneasy?

"Thank you for a lovely dinner, Carolyn. It was delicious. But I think I'd better be going now. It's quite late."

"Already?"

"Yes."

Carolyn rested her elbow on the table and sank her chin into her hand. "I forgot you're a working girl. Now listen, if you want any help with the wedding, let me know. We didn't get to talk about it enough. Maybe I'll come into The Palace later in the week. Mavis and I, we're a good team. We can help you."

She reached over and poured the rest of the wine into her glass, and Ellen saw herself out.

15

Dana

Herb is more talkative than usual over dinner. Or maybe I'm quieter. I can hardly focus; my mind has been wandering since he started on the history of the sugarcane industry.

"Your family owned a lot of sugarcane farms around here?" I ask. His personal history interests me more, especially now that the food, or maybe the wine, has revived me.

"Yeah, they did. We had hundreds of acres that needed a big labour force."

"There were slaves here, too, weren't there?"

From the look on his face, I seem to have touched a raw nerve.

"Don't believe everything you read in the newspapers." He drums his fingers on the table. "There are some who'd like to believe that story, but it's not true. Islanders who came here were indentured, and my family treated them well."

His defensiveness annoys me. I've read wider than newspapers. Little does he know that I did a paper on this in high school. "Indentured? That's just a nice way of saying slaves."

"Rubbish! Many Islanders stayed on here. Look at Mavis. Her

family goes back a long way, and they're highly respected members of our community." He drains his wine glass. "How did we get onto this?"

"I think you were giving me a history lesson." I try a smile. Perhaps that's a topic to debate another time.

He grins. "Sorry, I should have known you'd be a well-read doctor. Probably researched all our ailments before you got here."

"Not exactly, but I do try to make sure I'm up to date with tropical health issues."

"And have you seen many?"

"Not tropical conditions, although I've had a few surprises." I rub my head.

"What sort of surprises?"

I've said too much. "I can't break patient confidentiality. You know that."

"I'm not asking you to. I just meant what sort of things have surprised you?"

His blue eyes look into mine. He's genuinely interested. I stifle a yawn.

"You're tired," he says, picking up his wallet. "Maybe another time."

He's right. I haven't the energy to talk to him, but he's given me an idea. I should do some research into Sugar Creek.

Herb springs up from his chair. "How about we get moving so you can sleep in your new bed?"

"Good idea," I say wearily. If I could lie down here and sleep, I would.

"I'll pay and meet you upstairs."

"But …" I draw out my purse. "I can't let you pay for me."

He half turns as he strides to the bar. "Your shout next time."

I wonder at his presumption and shrug. Perhaps that's how they do things in the country. I drag myself up to my room and am packing away my toiletries when I hear the knock.

"Come in," I yell.

"Shall I take this one?" Herb calls back.

When I come out, he's carrying my large suitcase. "Yes, thanks."

"It's a hell of a lot lighter than when you arrived."

I grin. "That would be because I've removed my medical books."

He rolls his eyes and shakes his head. He has a very cute smile when he's relaxed.

"Ready?"

I glance around the room. "Let's go."

*

The next day, in between patients, I ring Dr Jeffries.

"Hello, Dr Jeffries. I spoke to you the other day about my patients, the Harpers."

"Yes," he says.

"There were four other cases of the same cancer from the same street."

Silence, then, "So?"

I'm floundering. His attitude puts me off, but I persist.

"I'm wondering if you know of any cancer issues in Sugar Creek. It seems odd, don't you think? Is there something that I should look out for? I'd really appreciate your guidance."

"I don't take any notice of the geographical location of my patients, Dr Janssen. It's not my concern. I'll send a written account of my findings once I've seen your patients. Is that all?"

I hang up, completely dissatisfied. Then I ring Hannah, who works in the medical research department of my old university, and ask her to find out if there's been a spate of cancers in the Sugar Creek region.

Afterwards, I see two more patients with the same symptoms as the Harpers, and my heart sinks. I send off the bloods, hoping desperately that I'm wrong, but I've got a bad feeling.

I jump when the phone on my desk rings.

"G'day. Back again," Hannah says.

"That was quick."

"You piqued my interest."

"So?"

"I reckon you gotta cancer cluster up there."

"Shit," I say.

"I've only looked at stats from 1990 to 1995 so far. Seventy people died from various cancers, at least ten times the state average, and very high given the population."

"In Sugar Creek?"

"Yep. I had to look it up for each town."

"That's a lot."

"It sure is," she says.

"They haven't had a permanent doctor since 1995. The reporting is based on where the patients live, right? But nothing after '95?"

"Not that I can see."

"The reporting must have come from wherever the patients went for treatment. From what I can gather, they might have closed the surgery in '95 because there are no files before then."

"It certainly warrants more investigation. There are various types of cancers, such as bladder, breast, chronic B-cell leukaemia, Hodgkin's disease … Were pesticides used in the area? Maybe overzealous spraying by crop dusters or the like?"

"It's a large, rural community. They grow sugar cane and have done for most of the century." Now I was glad of Herb's history lesson. "And they have a timber industry. It wouldn't be any different to other rural areas."

"Yeah, true."

"Leave it with me, and I'll dig around a bit more." I'm more concerned than alarmed … at this stage.

"Okay, but if you need anything, sing out. It doesn't sound like nothing. Good luck."

16

Ellen

For a Tuesday, the bar was quiet, a rare moment without customers. Joan was checking the till, and Ellen could think about her wedding while she polished glasses. She'd sent a note to Billy, letting him know that the minister had changed the time to ten o'clock. She hoped he'd be able to get the morning off. Surely getting married was a good enough reason.

Carolyn poked her head through the Ladies' Lounge door. "Joan, we need to borrow Ellen. That okay?"

Joan nodded. "It's not busy, love. Go and have a break."

It was eleven o'clock, and there were Carolyn and Mavis, cigarettes in one hand, a gin and tonic in the other.

"Come and join us. We want to talk about the wedding."

When Carolyn had told her she'd help with the wedding, Ellen thought she was just being nice to make up for Bert's rudeness. But here she was.

"Cigarette?" Mavis pushed a pack towards Ellen as she sat down.

Ellen shook her head; the smell of smoke these days turned her stomach.

"She doesn't smoke, Mavis. Now, let's get down to business. I've thought long and hard and, well, you're all alone and don't know this town. We're going to help make this a fabulous wedding. It wasn't so long ago that we planned our own weddings, so we're well qualified, aren't we, Mavis?"

Mavis nodded glumly. "1943 for me."

"And 1944 for me. Four or five years is not so long."

Ellen opened her mouth to say something.

"No ifs and buts, Ellen. First of all, you'll need a photographer."

Mavis perked up. "Exactly! In this day and age, you need to have some nice photos."

Ellen blinked. She'd only had three photos taken of her, ever. "I can't afford a photographer. It doesn't really matter."

"Ridiculous. Of course, it matters." Carolyn stubbed out her cigarette. "Lucky for you, I have a camera and will take all the photos." She sat back in her chair. "So that's settled."

Ellen nodded. "I don't know what to say. How can I repay you?"

"Repay? It's my pleasure. Bert bought me the camera for my birthday, and I've been dying to use it on something worthwhile. I'll pick out the best photos, and that will be our wedding present to you."

"Really?" Ellen said. "It's –

"It's nothing, is what it is. Good, so that's settled. Next?" Carolyn looked at Mavis.

"You'll need something borrowed." Mavis fumbled in her handbag.

"Do I?" Ellen said. She'd never been to a wedding before.

"Yes, you do!" Carolyn said.

Mavis brought out a blue velvet box. "I wore these on my wedding day and haven't since. And, well…" Mavis pushed the box across the table. "I thought this was an occasion where they could be put to good use."

Ellen didn't know what to say as she stared at the long rectangular box in front of her. It looked expensive; she dared not touch it.

"Go on, open it," Carolyn said, watching her closely.

Ellen cleared her throat and reached out to touch the soft velvet. She tugged at the silver clasp.

"Here, let me. I've got longer nails," Carolyn said, grabbing the box.

Mavis stared at the box, ignoring Carolyn, and as the pearl necklace spilled out onto the table, she put her hand to her mouth. "I haven't looked at them since my wedding day." A tear slid down her cheek.

Ellen leaned over and patted her on the arm. "It's so thoughtful and generous of you, but I can't take these."

"Oh, Ellen." Carolyn picked up the pearls and held them against Ellen's neck. "They'll look beautiful on you. And Mavis wants you to borrow them. Don't you?"

Mavis stared at Ellen and then at the pearls. "They do look good against your fair hair. Yes, they should be put to good use." She blew her nose. "Don't mind me. I'm just a bit of a sook sometimes. I was twenty when we married, and we knew he'd be shipped off sometime. Still, we were lucky to get six months. And then he was gone." She sighed. "Now it's your turn. You've no war to worry about, just a long, happy life together. I want you to wear them. It would mean a lot to me. Please?"

"What if I lost them? I'd never forgive myself. They look so expensive and well… I… I just couldn't."

Carolyn's face softened, and she lay the pearls in the box. "You won't lose them. Besides, Mavis and I will be right with you to make sure. Won't we, Mavis?"

"If it makes you feel any better," Mavis said, "you can return them right after the reception."

"The reception?" Ellen said.

Her head was in a whirl.

"But we only have Phyllis and Hector coming."

"Don't be ridiculous. We'll be there too. You must have a reception," Carolyn said.

"We can't afford a reception."

"We'll see about that. Mavis, take the pearls for safekeeping. We'll bring them on Saturday. Oh good, here comes Joan."

Joan pushed through the double doors, and Ellen got up.

"It's okay, sit down," Joan said, as she slid into another chair. "You're still on your break."

All three women were smiling and bursting with excitement as if they had planned it all.

"I'd like to put on a small wedding breakfast for you," Joan said. "The ceremony is at ten o'clock, so we'll have a little reception right here in the lounge. Would that be all right?"

"I'm overwhelmed, really. You would do that?"

"Of course, that's what we country people do for each other. Paul will look after the bar, and I'll slip out just after the ceremony and get things ready. It won't be fancy, mind. Just some scones, cakes, and sandwiches. And it'll be all over by the lunchtime rush. It's our wedding present. That's okay, isn't it?"

Ellen blinked. "I can't thank you enough. All of you. I … I just … you are all just the nicest people I've ever met. Thank you."

"I better get back in there," Joan said. "Some of the fellas are coming in."

"I should be going too," Ellen said.

Carolyn put her hand on Ellen's arm, anchoring her to the chair. "There's one more thing. I asked Bert if he'd walk you down the aisle."

Ellen stared at Carolyn. "Really, that's not necessary."

"Good, because he can't anyway. He has to work. Again. Any other ideas?"

Ellen decided to take back control. "I prefer not to have anyone walk me down the aisle. It's a personal thing."

"Why on earth not?" Mavis butted out her cigarette more firmly than needed. "I've never heard of anything so—"

"I just don't feel it's necessary. Really, I prefer it." There, she said it. Her own father, a drunkard, would have been an embarrassment. Not that she'd told him she was getting married. And for some reason, Carolyn and Mavis never asked about him. "Actually, I insist."

"Okay, then," Carolyn said. "You don't have to. It happened often enough during the war, and no-one batted an eyelid."

"But—" Mavis said.

"No," Carolyn said, nodding. "It'll be fine."

Ellen shifted about on her chair. "I really should go. And thank you so much for everything. I don't know what I would have done without you."

"We're glad to help. Aren't we, Mavis?"

Mavis looked morose.

*

Ellen stared at the mirror. Her belly seemed to have popped out since she'd bought her wedding outfit. The skirt was tight, and she smoothed the fabric over her stomach, trying to flatten her once flat-as-a-board tummy. She turned side on. Would anyone notice? The jacket would surely hide it.

She looked at her watch. In less than an hour, she'd be walking down the aisle of the St Francis Anglican Church. She took a deep breath and looked at her stomach again. Why did it have to poke out now?

Picking up the silver brooch – the only thing left of her long-dead mother – she pinned it over the stain above her left breast. Then, a knock.

"Yoo-hoo. Are you ready?" Carolyn's voice was loud through the door. "Open up and let us in."

Ellen quickly popped on her heels. Carolyn and Mavis wore expensive, colourful dresses that contrasted with Ellen's yellowing, once-cream-coloured suit.

Mavis put her hand to her mouth. "You look really nice. Doesn't she?"

Carolyn beamed. "You do. Gorgeous. Can we come in?"

Ellen stepped back. Maybe she did look good. Or maybe they just said it to make her feel as if she truly was.

"Now for the pearls." Mavis took the box out of her bag. "Let me put them on you."

Carolyn smiled and brought the camera up to her face. Click.

Mavis's eyes filled, and she pulled Ellen to her. Their faces pressed together; Ellen smelled the perfume – freshly picked roses – and the waft of gin; she felt the brittleness of her body.

"Those pearls look magnificent. Much better on you than me," Mavis murmured before quickly letting her go. She left the box on the table.

Then it was back to business.

"Where's Joan?" Mavis said, looking around the room.

"Joan?" Ellen asked.

"She's coming up with a bottle of sherry," Carolyn said, winking. "Settle your nerves. And to get the party started."

Sherry was the last thing Ellen wanted. Her stomach was already swirling with nerves and anticipation.

"How's the bride?" Joan sang out from the corridor before entering.

Carolyn put her hands on her hips. "About time." Then she took the glasses from the tray and handed them around. "Here's to a beautiful wedding. The first one we've had in town since … since when, Joan?"

Joan sipped her sherry. "Mmm …"

"Since I don't know when," Mavis said, waving her glass as she sat on the end of the bed and giggled.

Ellen stood in front of the mirror, fingering the necklace but staring at her stomach.

"Looks like you two started the celebrations a few hours ago," Joan said.

"We had one gin and tonic for breakfast. What's wrong with that?" Carolyn said, sitting next to Mavis. "It's a special day. Now hop out of the way. I need to take a picture."

"Are you sure you know how to use that thing?" Mavis said, giggling again.

Another knock. It was Paul, with a small bunch of flowers.

"Paul! Who on earth is looking after things downstairs?" Joan said.

"I had a delivery from Phyllis Laurel. Here, love. She wanted you to have them. From her garden."

"Phyllis Laurel?" Carolyn looked at Ellen. "I didn't know you knew her."

"We're going to be living with her. She has rooms under her house."

Carolyn nodded. "That's why your room looks so empty. Spending your wedding night there, I take it?"

"Thanks, Paul," Ellen said, taking the bouquet and ignoring Carolyn. She sniffed them and gently placed them on the dresser. "They're beautiful, and the perfume is better than out of a bottle."

One hand on her hip, Joan glared at her husband. "Off you go."

"I'm going," he said. "Congratulations, Ellen."

"Yes, the flowers are nice." Carolyn half lay on the bed, sipping her sherry, one shoe slipping onto the floor.

"And how are you faring, love? Nervous?" Joan said, rubbing Ellen's arm.

"A little bit."

"Okay, drink up. Let her finish getting ready," Joan said. "We'll wait for you downstairs so we can walk you to the church. Is that okay with you?"

"That'd be nice," Ellen said.

Joan glanced at her watch. "It's almost time, but then again, the bride should be late."

"Not too late, hey." Carolyn and Mavis screamed with laughter and rolled around on the bed.

Joan frowned. "What's so funny?"

Carolyn sat up. "We don't know." Then she burst into laughter again. "Sorry."

"For goodness' sake, get up. You're like two schoolgirls," Joan said.

"Wish we still were." Mavis sat up and wiped her eyes. "Guess we needed a laugh." She drained her glass.

Joan's gaze was on the bed. "There, see what you've done. You've squashed her hat."

The pillbox hat was flat. Ellen let out a groan.

"It's okay. It can be fixed." Carolyn punched it out, then glanced at the inside rim before giving it to Ellen.

Then they all left, and Ellen was alone, hat in hand. She looked inside the rim. There was a thin layer of grime and a torn label, clearly second-hand.

She pinned on the hat, went out to the verandah, and tossed the sherry over the railing into the garden. Then she took a deep breath. This was it. It was time to go.

17

Dana

It's the sound of church bells that needles me out of sleep. I squint at the clock on my bedside table and shut my eyes to block out the sun that blazes around the edges of the blinds. I roll over and shove my head under the pillow.

Perhaps the windows at the pub were soundproofed, or maybe it's just that I live closer to the church now. I've passed the white timber St Francis Anglican Church many times on my early morning jogs.

I wait for the bells to stop, but they persist, nudging me to get up.

Pulling on shorts, runners, and a singlet top, I take off into the side streets. The footpaths are shaded by a canopy of eucalyptus trees that front the manicured gardens of newly renovated Queensland weatherboard houses. During the week, these streets are jammed with trucks, and tradesmen crawl over old houses, hammering, sawing, and cursing. Today, there are just a few children playing outside.

It's nine thirty by the time I get back and shower. Plenty of time to enjoy a boiled egg on toast with a cup of tea and read the Sunday paper before my meeting with Linda's dad at eleven.

I'd decided to learn more about Sugar Creek and its history, so a couple of days ago, I asked Linda if there was a historical society.

"In Sugar Creek?" Linda said.

"Yeah. I want to get a feel for the history, and I thought that might be the best place to start."

"I'm pretty sure we don't, although you'd think we would since the historic buildings are being flogged in the tourist brochures now. You could talk to Joan and Mum. They've lived here on and off since the war."

"What about some of the sugar cane farmers? Anyone you know?"

Linda's eyes widen. "You should definitely talk to Dad."

"I thought your mum lived on her own. Isn't that why you came back?"

"She does, but her health isn't great. They divorced when I was young, but live here now. Dad had a sugar cane farm until after the war. You can get the town's history from a male and female point of view."

"That sounds good. Do you think I could meet your dad first?"

"Most days, he's at the pub with his mates. I'll organise something. How about Sunday morning?"

*

"I'll leave you two in peace," Linda says. "I've got a few errands to run. Okay, Dad?"

Wally Gillespie nods from the armchair opposite. He's a trim man sporting a grey moustache, a blue Hawaiian shirt tucked into brown cargo shorts, and knee-high socks, one blue and one grey.

"That's my trademark," Wally says, grinning. "It gets all the nice young ladies in."

"Oh? I'm not sure what you mean."

Already I'm wondering if Linda should have left me alone with him.

"My socks; I noticed you staring at them. It's a fashion statement." He bends down to pull them up. "It'll catch on one day. Mismatched socks are everywhere, yet we spend too much time trying to make a match that's, quite frankly, not meant to be. I mean, if couples aren't matched, they divorce and move on. Not everything has to go together."

Now I'm lost and wonder if I'll get anything worthwhile from him. Luckily, Crystal interrupts his ramblings and sets down a coffee for me and a beer for him.

"Nectar of the gods," he says, raising his glass. "Secret to a long life, I reckon. One in the morning, one in the afternoon, and a whisky before bed."

He looks at me, and suddenly his smile fades. "Perhaps I shouldn't have said that to a doctor. I know you people like to lecture on alcohol consumption."

I hold my cup aloft. "No judgement, Wally. You look fit and healthy to me."

He grins and sips his beer before putting it gently on the small round table between us. "So, Linda tells me you want a bit of history about the place."

"She told me you had a sugar cane farm before the war."

"Yep. Handed down to me from my dad. A hundred acres. But it was tough trying to make a living, even for him. Even worse when I went and joined up. Ended up in New Guinea and copped a bit of shrapnel in my leg." He rolls down the sock on his left leg and shows me a faded jagged scar. "Then I went off to Korea in '51 with the United Nations. Got a bit of frostbite on the lungs there. And then

Vietnam in '65. Got injured in my second month and decided my luck had run out."

"Remarkable. I don't think I've ever met anyone who's been in three wars. Why did you—"

"Keep going? Yes, many have asked me that. After New Guinea, I came back to a sugar cane farm that needed a lot of work. The bottom fell out of the price of sugar, and I guess my heart wasn't in it. I only stayed because of a girl." He grins and brings the glass up to his lips.

"Linda's mum?"

"She told you, did she?"

"I've met Mavis."

He looks downcast. "She never could work with mismatched socks." Then he perks up and scratches the side of his face. "Anyway, we've got off track. Couldn't make much of a go of farming, and I ended up in freight. The things I could tell you. Not so many oldies like me left now." He looks around the room. "Even though there should be."

"What do you mean?"

"See that old bloke over there on the oxygen?"

There's a man hunched over in a wheelchair, a tube running from an oxygen cylinder to his nose, his fingers around a glass of beer.

"That's Cyril. How old do you reckon he is?"

"Maybe eighty?"

"He's fifty-two."

I gasp and stare, hardly believing he's that young.

Wally leans forward and lowers his voice. "Got sprayed with Agent Orange."

"In Vietnam?"

"Here!" He picks up his glass.

My body prickles with goosebumps. "Here?"

"Yep. Poor bugger. He's got cancer of the oesophagus, stomach, and lungs. His son was born with a deformed lung, and his daughter has a skin problem."

"I don't understand. I thought that Agent Orange was only sprayed in Vietnam."

His eyes flicker around the room before resting on me as if he's weighing up what he should tell me. "I've probably said too much. I complained to the authorities, but they denied it. Had to, didn't they? They were that damn cagey; it made my blood boil. Got us nowhere. But I reckon, as the town's doctor, you should know what you're up against. Lot of people have moved away, but the problem's still here."

"How did it happen?"

He sighs and drains the glass. "They bought up a few cane farms in the early fifties, including mine, and sprayed some of the stuff there."

He then tells me all about his cane farm again, how big it was, how long it had been in the family, and how hard it was on the land. "Should have kept it. Sugar cane is this town's lifeblood."

I glance at my watch as he begins a detailed history of the sugar cane industry.

At the first pause, I jump in. "And you think it was Agent Orange that they sprayed on your farm?"

He looks at me, incredulous. "Too right they did. At first, they sprayed by hand, and everything died. But mostly they sprayed in the forest. Then they started flying over and spraying. It wipes out all the vegetation. We'd see it and not think anything at the time. Of course, now we know how dangerous it was. I reckon it's in the water table, and the run-off is probably in the town's water supply. That's why I stick to beer."

He sits back in his chair, and I follow his eyes to my cup of tea, hardly touched.

"You see, it stays in the soil for decades and leaches into the water table each time it rains. Just look at what's still happening in Vietnam. There's plenty of evidence."

It all sounds very far-fetched. "How do you know it was Agent Orange? It could have been anything."

He looks at me with his piercing green eyes. "I saw barrels with 'Dioxin TCDD' written on the side. That's the chemical name for it."

I lean forward in my seat. "Surely, they cleaned it up after your complaints. There's no way that we're all drinking contaminated water."

He scoffs. "There was no clean-up. They ignored our complaints. Said it never happened; said it was crop dusting. But crop dusting doesn't kill everything on the land. Go out past Old Goanna Creek Road for about five kilometres, and you'll see. It's barren and has been like that since the mid-sixties. The only thing they did was stop the spraying."

"Old Goanna Creek Road?" That's where the Harpers, Thompsons, and Jamieson's live.

He studies my face. "Some of us were enticed out there to be human guinea pigs. To be sprayed. Not me. I stayed here. Not Paul, either. He had to work in the pub. But blokes like Herb's dad and his grandpa, Bert, old Cyril and his dad … they were all there, standing right under the spray like idiots."

Slumped in the armchair, I try to process what he's told me, and more questions swirl through my head. Do I believe this eccentric old man or not?

Linda approaches, smiling.

"G'day, you two. Hope you've had a nice talk. Dad, I think it's time to have lunch."

"We've had a lovely chat. Thanks, Wally." Does she know about what's happened?

Linda helps Wally out of his seat. "We're going next door into the beer garden. You're welcome to join us if you like."

"Thanks, but I better get going. Got a few things to do, and the day is flying."

Mum is expecting me to call at twelve thirty for our regular Sunday catch-up. Then there's the washing, the dishes in the sink, and the ironing.

That's the thing with working six days a week. There's not much time to do anything.

Wally holds out his hand. "If you want to chat again, you know where you can find me. I'm in here most days."

His hand is large and warm in mine.

"Thank you. I'd like that."

18

Ellen

Ellen walked slowly down the staircase, the floral carpet runner soft under her pumps, the curved mahogany banister smooth in her hand.

Carolyn and Mavis were staring at the curtain of rain spilling off the verandah roof. Ellen stopped on the bottom step and stared as well.

Carolyn turned first. "There you are. We'll have to go in my car."

A thunderclap made Ellen jump.

"God, it's getting heavier," Mavis said, wringing her hands. "We'll have to make a run for it."

Ellen looked at her watch – just after ten o'clock. "Where's your car?"

"Just around the corner in Hipworth St. There's still plenty of time."

And just as suddenly, the rain stopped, and the street burst into sunshine.

Carolyn looked around. "Right, let's go. Where's Joan? Mavis, get Joan, and we'll meet you at the car. Hurry up."

Mavis looked startled and nodded. "Be right with you."

Ellen took a deep breath and followed Carolyn out, stepping over the flooded gutter and ignoring Carolyn's chatter. Her stomach was in knots, and her hands were clammy as she slid into the scorching front seat of the late-model Holden sedan. Carolyn slammed the door shut.

Something felt wrong to Ellen as if she had forgotten something, although she couldn't think what. She opened the door.

"Here they are," Carolyn said, getting into the driver's seat. "Come on."

Ellen stayed where she was and pulled the door closed, her hands clasped around the bouquet on her lap, trapped in the sticky, stifling heat.

Joan and Mavis piled in the back, and the rain started again.

"Right, let's get this girl to the church."

Carolyn turned the ignition, and the car jerked forward and stalled.

"You haven't flooded the engine, have you?" Joan said.

Carolyn turned the ignition again and pumped the accelerator. "It's a bit temperamental, that's all." The engine roared. "See?"

More rain hit the windshield; the wipers flung from side to side.

"Why does it have to rain right now?" Mavis whined. "Let's hope it stops."

They turned left and sped up Main Street.

"Slow down," Joan said.

"This isn't fast." Carolyn laughed. "Do you really want me to put my foot on it?"

"NO!" they all yelled.

Ellen gripped her flowers with one hand and the edge of the seat with the other as they turned left into Griffiths Street.

"Jesus," Mavis muttered.

"You have passengers back here, Carolyn," Joan said.

They turned right into Westover Street. The weatherboard church loomed ahead, and the car slowed.

Carolyn looked sideways at Ellen. "You all right? You're awfully quiet."

She blinked, forcing a smile. "Bit nervous." And frightened.

"Everyone's bloody nervous with this maniac behind the wheel," Mavis muttered.

"It'll be over before you know it, and then you'll be eating the best scones in Far North Queensland," Joan said, patting her on the shoulder from behind.

"We're not that late, are we?" Carolyn parked the car at an angle in front of the church.

"Why aren't you driving up to the door?" Mavis said. "It's still raining."

Carolyn jerked the car into reverse. "For goodness' sake, it's only a light drizzle."

"Watch out," Joan yelled.

Carolyn steered the car up and over the footpath, just missing the gate. She braked suddenly in front of the church steps and turned the ignition off.

"Safe and sound, and only fifteen minutes late. The rain has stopped, and the sun is out. It's an omen for a wonderful day."

"Right. This is it," Ellen said, getting out of the car. She wasn't sure if her legs wobbled from the ride or her nerves.

"We'll race on inside," Carolyn said grabbing her camera. "See you in a minute."

Joan gave her a quick hug. "Do you want me to walk in with you?"

Ellen nodded, and Joan held her hand. She'd said she didn't need anyone, but she did. She couldn't walk down that aisle alone.

Together, they walked into the cool dim of the large church and waited. As her eyes grew accustomed to the subdued light, she looked for Billy. Carolyn and Mavis clustered near the white-robed minister; their voices muffled.

Carolyn waved her hands around; Mavis stood with her arms folded. The minister's head was lowered.

Ellen wondered why they weren't in their seats next to Phyllis, who wore a large black hat.

Joan's hand tightened in hers, and she pulled Ellen down the aisle, not waiting for the organ to start. Ellen scanned the church for Billy. Was he out the back with Hector? She turned to Joan for answers, but her eyes were riveted to the front. Getting closer, she could make out what was being said.

"What do you mean you don't know?" Carolyn said to the minister.

They turned and looked at Ellen, their sombre faces saying it all: pity and worry. The minister didn't look at her at all.

She let go of Joan's hand. "What's happened?" Ellen asked.

The minister slowly raised his eyes. "Your fella hasn't arrived yet."

Ellen blinked. "Are you sure?"

The minister looked surprised. "Yes."

"Maybe he's waiting out the back?" Carolyn said.

The minister's expression changed as if it hadn't occurred to him. "I'm not sure."

"Well, do you think you might like to go and get him?" Carolyn said.

The minister nodded and left.

"He'll be out there," Carolyn said softly. "For sure."

Ellen put her hand to her chest to stop the rising panic. Her heart thumped; her face prickled with heat.

The minister returned looking grim. "He's not there."

The strength seemed to leach from her body, but she held herself rigid. "He's just late, that's all. He'll be here."

A hand touched her arm. "Love, it's after ten thirty," Joan whispered.

"Maybe the boss didn't let him off this morning," Carolyn said. "You know what these cane farmers are like."

Ellen turned, latching onto the idea. "Yes, that'll be it."

She remembered the note she'd scrawled to Billy, telling him about the time change. Not one o'clock, she'd written, ten o'clock.

The minister coughed. "I can only wait until eleven."

"Have a heart," Joan said. "The cutters don't knock off until eleven, and then they have to get back to town and clean up. If he's working, he can't get here until at least twelve thirty."

The minister shook his head. "I have the Dawson christening at eleven thirty and the Jamieson child at one. That's why I changed the time. I'm sorry, but if he's had to work, you'll need to come back next week."

The room seemed to tilt, and everyone's faces were a blur. She might be showing more by then.

Ellen ran her finger down the stem of a rose and pressed down hard on a stray thorn, the pain jolting her. She cleared her throat.

"We'll come back next Saturday. Same time?"

The minister nodded and smiled thinly. "That's a very sensible plan."

Carolyn and Mavis, silent on either side of her, walked her out of the church into the bright sunshine. Spirals of steam lifted from the road, and Ellen had a sudden urge to run. Instead, she closed her eyes and breathed deeply.

"I think I'd like to walk back to Phyllis's if you don't mind," Ellen said. "I'm living there from now anyway, and it's only in the next street."

Phyllis, who stood a little way from her, nodded.

Carolyn stroked her back as if she were a sick child.

"Are you sure?" Joan said.

Mavis lit a cigarette. "What about all the food back at the pub?"

"It's got to be eaten," Joan said.

Ellen wished Carolyn would stop, and she ran her finger over the thorn again. "I'm not really hungry."

"Okay, then. When you're ready." Carolyn dropped her hand and opened the car door.

"Phyllis, won't you come back for a bite?" Joan asked.

"I'll come by a bit later, thanks. I'll accompany Ellen."

Joan nodded.

Mavis opened the front passenger door. "Good idea. You shouldn't be alone after a catastrophe like this."

Catastrophe.

The word shocked Ellen. These women thought she'd been jilted, left at the altar, abandoned. She clenched her hands around the bouquet, pain searing into her fingers, petals dropping.

"It's not a catastrophe," she snapped. "Billy had to work. I'll see him shortly, and then I'll come in for the afternoon rush. And get married next week."

Mavis raised her eyebrows, and Ellen dared not look at the others. She wouldn't let these women feel sorry for her for no reason.

"She can't go to work," Carolyn said to Joan.

"No, of course not. Listen, when you find Billy, bring him to the pub. We'll keep some food for you. Take the afternoon off. Spend some time together," Joan said.

"Thank you," Ellen said, looking at each of them, her throat tight. "For everything."

*

The first thing she did was to wash the drying blood from her hand before she changed out of her wedding suit. The flowers lay strewn in the kitchen sink. She was proud; she'd held herself together despite feeling hollow, worried, and humiliated.

What did it say about Billy? What would they be talking about back at the pub? They'd think he was a louse.

She took off the string of pearls and lay them on the table, then stared at her hat, vaguely aware of a noise coming from her like the whimper of a small dog. She crumpled onto the bed, crushing the hat in her hands. There had to be an explanation. He did love her. She knew he did. She pushed the hat back into shape, then carefully put it in the wardrobe for next week. It was almost eleven thirty – time to go out and wait for him.

The front gate of Phyllis's house had the best vantage point on the street. What would she say to him? Why didn't you call me at the pub, or send a note saying the boss couldn't give you the time off? Why didn't you try harder? You knew I would be waiting at the church. You knew I'd be humiliated.

The more she thought about it, the angrier she became.

The sun burned into her face and bare arms, yet she dared not move as she watched for the first of them. Some came on bicycles, some on foot, in groups of three, then five, then eight. She scanned each man from head to toe. More and more arrived until there were none.

He will come, she muttered to herself. Her whole body seemed to be burning from the hot sun, and still, she waited, not moving from the gate. In her head, an argument raged, telling her to move, to cross the road, to approach the men and ask, "Do you know where Billy Nolan is?"

19

Dana

A strange multi-coloured bird is performing acrobatics outside the kitchen window. It twists itself upside down to dip its beak deep into a white, bell-like flower. I run the kitchen tap, water spilling from the top of the glass over my hand. I tip the whole thing out before refilling it, hoping any imagined contamination has worked its way clear. Water touches my lips and slides across my tongue and down my throat, drowning my nagging doubts.

Jogging along the wet pavement, a fog-like drizzle sets in. I try to clear my mind, concentrating on my pace and ignoring the growing dampness across my shoulders. I dreamed of Daniel last night, of the way he'd looked at me as if I was the only one, and I woke in tears, my body tight and tense.

Soon, the asphalt footpath is replaced by a clipped lawn, and I finally stop. There's a low concrete wall running the length of the footpath, and I sling first one leg, then the other, over the wall and perch for a minute to catch my breath. The drizzle stops and pulling wet hair free from my ponytail, I slip the hair tie onto my wrist. A few metres away, something catches my eye. There, embedded into the lawn, is a black plaque with gold lettering: Cal MacKay, born 1920, died 1952. The name is unfamiliar, and I wonder why he died so young.

More plaques – some with faded, plastic flowers standing stiffly in shabby mouldy vases spiked into the ground – are laid out like a green and black chessboard surrounded by a low hedged border. A sign announces that I'm standing in the middle of the Garden of Remembrance.

Beyond is the lush green rainforest that casts a backdrop for the rows of headstones which appear to float in the fog. A lone figure in the distance limps among the taller tombstones. Leaving the garden, I stroll past a cracked headstone that pokes out from under the moss. Its date reads "1901." Beyond are corridors of crumbling old islander and European headstones in their segregated religious sections. There's a weathered grey seat, and I rest a minute to edge out a stone from inside one of my runners. A crow perches on a post and stares at me, its head cocked as if asking why I'm there. The quiet among the dead and long-forgotten somehow makes me feel calmer.

I settle back on the bench and tie up the shoelaces. My mouth is dry. There's a tap that splutters out water, and I let it run long enough for the imagined rust build-up to clear, then swallow a few gulps before remembering what Wally said. Spitting out the last mouthful, I wipe my hand over my mouth.

"That's probably wise."

Behind me is Herb in shorts, t-shirt and work boots.

"It tastes terrible," I say, coughing and spluttering.

"It's not really for drinking. Bore water for the plants." He points at a sign.

"How was I supposed to see that? It's nowhere near the tap."

There's a metallic taste in my mouth, and I wonder if the bore water will make me sick.

Herb shrugs. "It shouldn't kill you. An odd place for a run. Checking out past patients?" A tiny smile edges from the corner of his mouth.

Is he trying to joke? I smile anyway before realising what a frightful sight I am and gather my wet hair back into a ponytail.

"Just thought I'd take a look. It's a beautiful setting," I say, sweeping my hand around the cemetery as if showing him something he hasn't already seen.

"It's pretty old. Dates back to the late 1800's."

I notice he's holding a bunch of roses.

"I see you're actually here for a reason."

He lifts his hand as if just noticing the flowers. "Yeah. I like coming early when no-one else is around."

"Don't let me interrupt."

"Not at all. Would you like a tour?"

I look at my watch. It's still early. "Why not?"

The cemetery isn't big, and we wander around the old headstones.

"You're limping," I say.

"It's nothing. Old footy injury plays up now and then."

"We can do this another time if it's painful."

He stops and looks at me, narrowing his eyes. "Occupational hazard, I suppose."

"What do you mean?"

"Noticing people's health."

I grin. "I suppose so. Can't just turn it off." I look him up and down. "You've got a bit of bruise there. Someone kick you?"

He peers at the inside of his calf. "Dunno where that came from. Probably ran into something. Shall we?"

We resume walking, Herb explaining a bit of Kanaka history and me holding back on mentioning that the Kanakas were slaves. Probably not the place for a spirited debate.

"And this is where my grandparents are buried," he says.

We stop in front of a rather grand pair of black granite headstones: Bert Hipworth, born 1915, died 1971 (aged 56), and Carolyn Hipworth, born 1922, died 1975 (aged 53).

"And you were named after him?"

"My father, actually. He's over there."

Nearby is the large headstone of Herbert Hipworth II, born 1948, died 1978.

"I'm sorry," I say. "He was so young. Your grandparents were quite young, too."

Wally had said Herb's grandfather and father stood watching as the town was sprayed. Is it possible that Wally was right?

Herb's head drops. "Cancer, I believe."

"What sort of cancer? I mean, if you don't mind telling me."

He frowns. "I don't know. I was too young at the time, about eight or nine, and I never really thought to ask. I just know he got really sick and died a short time after. And I barely knew my grandparents." He looks at me. "You're right. They were too young. I'd never given it much thought."

"And your mum?"

"She's in Sydney. She can't bear to live here. Too many memories."

I nod. "You didn't grow up here, then?"

"Nope. Brisbane, then Cairns, and after uni in Townsville, moved back here to manage what's left of the family estate after Mum sold some of it off. Been here ever since. But now you've got me wondering what sort of cancer my father had."

He opens his mouth as if to say something, then doesn't.

"Remember when you asked me what surprises I was finding?" I say.

He looks at me with interest. "Yeah?"

"The surprises are the number of patients with cancer."

"Mmm," he says, rubbing his stubble. "I know we've had a few. That's why I thought it was important to have a permanent GP."

"For a town of this size, it seems particularly high. In fact, from what I can gather, Sugar Creek has the highest average number of cancer deaths in the state."

He raises his eyebrows. "Really?"

"I heard from Wally Gillespie that Agent Orange might have been sprayed in the area."

He rolls his eyes. "I wouldn't take too much notice of what he has to say."

"Even still, it's got me wondering."

"That's why you're here," he says with a smirk. "Anyway, it's probably because we had an older population for a while. Now there are more and more young people moving here, so I shouldn't think it would be much different from anywhere else."

He might be right, but his dismissiveness annoys me. "I think it's a problem, that's all. I should get back and let you …" I gesture towards the flowers hanging from his hand, forgotten.

"Yeah, thanks," he says, lifting them.

I take my time looking at headstones on my way towards the exit and glance back to see where he goes. He's walking away from his grandparents and father, but I'm too far away to see the grave those roses were meant for.

Reaching the gate, I remove the shoe that has been troubling me and take enough time adjusting my damp sock for Herb to drive past and toot the horn. My curiosity gets the better of me, and I double back, finding the roses at a fresh-looking headstone. With letters gilded in gold, it reads, "Amy Hipworth, born 1972, died 1998. Wife of Herbert Hipworth."

I've got goosebumps. Herb's wife. Not divorced – dead.

20

Ellen

It was almost twelve thirty when the first two men came out of the boarding house, showered and dressed. Ellen recognised them from the pub, and half lifted her hand to wave. The smell of Brylcreem and cigarette smoke drifted across to her. They didn't glance in her direction as they swaggered off, one whistling, the other carefully donning his pork pie hat. Others streamed out, their voices carried by the sodden breeze, their faces blended into featureless smudges.

A young, strong-looking man ran down the steps two at a time, laughing loudly. His name didn't come to her, but she was sure he was part of Billy's cane gang. She slipped the catch on the gate and hurried across the road.

"Hi," she said, trying to keep her voice casual.

The man turned and doffed his hat, sweat already glistening on his forehead. "Hello," he said, his voice deep. "Ellen, isn't it, from the pub?" He smiled, his teeth white against his tan.

She nodded. "Are you part of Billy Nolan's gang?"

"Nah. We work the same farms, but."

"I was just wondering if you've seen him."

He pushed the brim of his hat up, scratched his head, and squinted at her. "I don't reckon I have."

"So, you haven't seen him today?"

"Nope. But then I was loadin' this mornin,' so his gang woulda been cuttin'."

Her heart thumped. "I'm trying to find him. Could you do me a favour and see if he's still inside?" She fought to keep her voice even to hide her desperation.

He looked at the others heading down the street. "I was goin' to the pub."

"Please. I've been waiting for him all this while."

The man hesitated, shifting from one foot to the other.

"Please," she said, trying for a smile. "It won't take you long."

"All right. Wait here."

He sprinted up the steps and disappeared into the boarding house.

Before long, he emerged with a taller, older man. Frowning, they both looked in her direction and walked down the steps.

"Derek's in Billy's gang," the first man said. "Now I gotta go."

Ellen smiled her thanks and turned to Derek.

His hands, coarse and scarred, twirled a wide-brimmed hat. "You after Billy?"

She nodded, shading her eyes.

He coughed, loud and phlegmy. "Me too. Billy and Hector. Those blokes left us in the lurch without a word. Bloody annoying."

"What do you mean?" Her body trembled in response to words yet to come.

"They haven't been at work at all this week. Thought they mighta been sick or somethin', but they never showed up."

"You mean they didn't start work last Monday?"

Derek shrugged. "Nah. Never thought they were the sort to do a runner."

Her breath hitched inside her ribcage.

"Nice blokes, though. Musta been too tough for 'em. It's like that. Men come and go on the cane fields, especially ex-service." He put on his hat and turned to go. "But if you see either of 'em, tell 'em they don't have a job."

*

The next day, Ellen dragged herself to work.

"How are you, love?" Joan said, her hand resting on the bar.

Ellen lowered her eyes and tied on her apron. She turned away, pulled out a tray of glasses and began polishing them vigorously with a cloth.

"Sorry about yesterday," she said.

"Everything all right?"

Ellen nodded, not trusting herself to speak, and placed each glass in a perfect line in front of her.

Joan touched her arm. "Want to talk about it?"

Ellen shrugged off Joan's hand and forced a smile. "Better open up, hey?"

It wasn't long before the bar was filled with men laughing, yelling, thumping down their coins, wiping froth from their lips, and asking for another. It was easy to avoid Joan and not think.

Finally, it was closing time.

Paul saw the last of the men out, then locked the door. "Strewth, glad that's over. Rowdy bunch today."

Joan had disappeared, and Ellen wiped the counter just a little bit harder than necessary.

"I don't reckon that stain will come out," Paul said, grabbing the cloth from her. "I'll finish up here. I think Joan's after you, out the back."

She found Joan in the tiny office, standing in front of a filing cabinet.

"You need me?" Ellen said from the doorway.

Joan closed the drawer and turned, gesturing her to come in. "I'm wondering …"

Ellen realised it was a ruse to get her to talk, and she was in no mood for sympathy, or pity, or offers of help.

"Would it be okay if I knocked off now?" She just wanted to lie on her bed, to cry, to not think.

"I heard that Billy hasn't been at work all week."

Her eyes met Joan's. "How do you know that?"

"Hal Whittaker was in earlier." Joan untied her apron and threw it on the back of the chair.

"Who's he?"

"He runs the cane farm where your Billy works. He was asking around the other managers, and I overheard him. I thought you should know."

"Oh." Ellen sat heavily in the chair.

"It's okay."

What's okay? That my fiancé hasn't been at work, that he jilted me, that he's taken off?

She said nothing.

Joan took a step towards her. "I'm here for you. Paul and I both are."

Ellen stiffened, not wanting Joan to touch her.

Instead, Joan leaned against the desk, her eyes on Ellen.

The humidity seemed to saturate the room, and a crack of thunder startled them both. The rain came down, and Joan closed the window.

"Listen, love. You won't be the first girl who's been left, and you won't be the last."

"He didn't leave me," Ellen said, fidgeting with her engagement ring, wanting it off.

"But his things are gone from the boarding house."

Ellen looked up; how did Joan know that? "Of course, they're gone. He brought everything over to our room last Sunday. After I came to work and before he went off to the base."

Mind your own business!

It satisfied her to see the bewildered look on Joan's face. Why was it so important to her that Joan know what sort of man her Billy was?

"Oh, I didn't know."

The rain pelted against the window.

"He's not the sort of man to run out on me."

Joan looked at her carefully. "Because you're expecting?"

"Because he loves me." She stood up so abruptly the chair screeched across the bare floorboards. "Now, if you'll excuse me, Joan, I have to go."

"Of course, love, of course. And if I can help …"

Joan's voice faded as Ellen rushed out of the office, grabbed her bag, and fled into the street. Water gushed down gutters, and she dodged the drips tumbling off the shop awnings. All she could think about was that Joan knew. Her hand fluttered over her stomach. What was she to do? She looked up at the darkened sky. It was too late to do anything.

★

It was Monday, her day off. She hadn't slept and had hardly eaten any of Phyllis's chicken casserole. Even she seemed to know that Billy hadn't been at work all week. Word travelled fast.

Billy hadn't left her intentionally. She had to believe that. But what happened? She'd begin at Carolyn and Bert Hipworth's house.

She dressed and brushed her hair. Bloodshot eyes looked back at her in the mirror. Her appearance would have to do. Then she put on her shoes and closed the door. Although it was still early, the sun was burning the back of her head, and she wished she'd put on a hat. Their house wasn't far, and she hoped Bert hadn't already left.

Carolyn opened the door in her dressing gown, her face immediately twisting into sympathy. She grabbed Ellen in a bear hug.

"Oh, Ellen, you poor thing. I've heard the news. You poor, poor thing." She sniffed, dabbed her eyes, and blew her nose. "Come in, come in."

Ellen followed Carolyn, and they faced each other awkwardly in the lounge room.

"I'm so glad you've come. You know, Mavis and I, well … we wanted to give you some time. That's why we haven't come around. I just can't imagine what you must be going through." She touched Ellen's arm.

Ellen pulled away.

"I'm sorry for coming so early."

Carolyn tightened the dressing gown cord and put a hand up to her hair. "You're welcome anytime."

"I wanted to catch Bert before he goes to work."

"Bert?"

"I'd like a word with him."

Carolyn looked hurt. "Why do you want him?"

Ellen sighed. She couldn't worry about her feelings. "Is he here?"

Carolyn pushed her hair behind her ears, and her lips set in a firm line. "Well, yes. I'll get him for you. Though I can't imagine what you want with him." She disappeared down the hallway.

Ellen sat in an armchair, listening to their voices, Carolyn's imploring, and Bert's low. Maybe he was busy, or maybe he didn't want to face Ellen and her questions. Ellen drummed her fingers on the chair's arm, her foot jiggling, her body tight with nerves.

Carolyn stood in the doorway, her face composed back to sympathy. "He's coming. Can I get you something? A drink? Water, tea, gin and tonic?" Carolyn gave a slight smile. Her syrupy niceness was too much.

"No, I'm right, thanks."

"Okay, then. He won't be long." She slid into the armchair opposite. "How are you getting on? It's such a pity—"

"Ellen," said Bert, appearing in the doorway.

Ellen jumped up. Bert smelled of shaving foam, the same one Billy used. Her chest ached.

"Sorry for disturbing you. I know you must be busy. I need your help."

"Of course," said Carolyn. "Anything, Ellen. You can count on us." She brightened and looked at Bert. "Can't she?"

Bert moved to the couch and brought out his pipe. "Yes. What can we do for you?"

Ellen sat down again. This was going to be harder than she thought. She stopped fiddling with her engagement ring and took a deep breath.

"As you know, Billy went to the base last Sunday. He was there to test a topical cream." She licked her dry lips. "From what I can gather, he never left the base."

Bert dug out the bowl of the pipe with a matchstick, then stood up and got the crystal ashtray from the coffee table before sitting down again. He tapped the pipe's bowl on the edge of the ashtray, and she wondered if he was listening.

"I know he didn't," she continued, "because he never went to work with the others that afternoon. Hector, his friend, also went to the base and has not been seen since."

Bert pulled a tobacco pouch from his trouser pocket and pushed the pipe inside.

"Bert, I asked you if ex-servicemen were being called up. Because if they were, they might have had to stay, and I was worried about that."

He glanced at her before putting the pipe in his mouth and lighting it. He puffed and, when he seemed satisfied, leaned back on the couch.

She stared at him, wondering if she should wait before continuing. "You told me that wouldn't happen, but if he had enlisted, he would have at least contacted me. What I need to know is, did he and Hector leave the base, and if so, when?"

"Bert can find out," Carolyn said. "Can't you, honey? You're in charge."

He cleared his throat and shifted in his seat.

"It's not that easy."

"Why?" Ellen said.

Carolyn stared at Bert. "Yes, why?"

"Well, you're right," he stuttered. "We are experimenting with some topical creams and figured some ex-servicemen could do with a couple of bob. I don't look after that area, but from what I know, once the fellas have the cream on their arms, they wait around for an hour or so, and then they go. We pay them upfront but don't write down what time they leave. Look, I'll find out if they even turned up. We'll have a record of at least that."

It hadn't occurred to her that Billy might not have gone to the base. Her throat tightened.

"I'd really appreciate it." She stood up to go. "Thank you."

*

The next day, in the pub, Bert walked up to Ellen at the bar. "Do you have a moment?"

Ellen nodded.

"I'll meet you outside."

Ellen finished serving the next two customers before slipping out the front.

Bert was pacing, unlit pipe in his hand, and stopped when he saw her.

She could tell from his face that he didn't have good news and wanted to run rather than hear what he had to say. She took a deep breath.

"Did you find out anything?"

"Billy and Hector never showed up."

The air was sucked out of her as if she'd been punched.

"If there's anything else I can do, let me know," he said, his tone suggesting that he didn't mean it.

She nodded, then composed herself and returned to the bar. "Three beers?"

21

Dana

It's after seven when I head down to the pub for a meal after work. Crystal takes my order, and with my table number and a glass of chardonnay in hand, I weave around tables to find a spot. It's busy for a Monday night. Families just finishing up, couples, a few tourists taking photos of the stained-glass windows. Herb is with Jack and Steve in a grey-blue booth. They're in jeans and fresh t-shirts, except Herb's wearing his trademark Hawaiian shirt, the same one he wore the day I met him.

I don't feel much like being social. What was I thinking? I veer away, hoping Herb doesn't see me.

Too late. Herb waves, and so do the other two.

"Come and join us," he says.

I walk towards them.

"I don't want to disturb you."

"Come on." Steve pats the bench seat next to him. "You can't eat by yourself."

I'm perfectly capable of eating on my own and, in fact, would welcome it, but I bite back the comment.

All three of them are waiting, giving me encouraging looks. I'll eat, drink my wine, make small chat, and be home in no time.

I slide in next to Steve, Herb opposite. There's a whiff of rosemary and sage from someone. It's an aftershave I know well, and it takes me back to Daniel. I gulp my wine. It's hard not to remember the image of his bare chest, towel around his waist, kissing me, and the air filling with Paco Rabanne aftershave.

Jack leans back.

"How are you liking it here?"

"It's good, so far."

"Everyone being nice to you?" Steve asks.

My chicken parmigiana with salad arrives. "What are you trying to say? Isn't everyone nice here?" I smile my thanks to the waitress.

"Sure. It's a nice town with nice people. Special treatment for you, though, since you got your meal first. You don't mind, do you?" Steve says, reaching for one of my chips and popping it into his mouth. "Whoa, hot."

We all laugh as I offer the plate around. Steve grabs a couple more, and Jack helps himself, too. It's kind of nice to have the familiarity of belonging here and being one of them.

"His manners are appalling," Herb says, shaking his head to my offer of a chip.

"I think you're wanted," Jack says quietly to Herb.

There's a man in his forties standing a short distance away, looking at us.

"Excuse me a minute," Herb says, "and don't eat any of my chips, mate."

Steve gives him a fake look of hurt, and Jack shakes his head as Herb goes to talk to the man.

"There's always something," Jack says. "You'd think they'd leave a man to eat and drink in peace."

"I suppose he's always going to be in demand, being the mayor," I say, holding out the plate to Steve, who shakes his head.

"Go ahead, don't wait for us," he says. "It'll get cold." He turns to Jack. "Thought you'd get a bit of special treatment?"

I don't know what he means, but I do feel foolish waiting, so I pick up my knife and fork.

"So, are you both from around here?" I ask, biting into a chip.

"From Sydney," Steve says. "Arrived a week before you."

"Oh really? What brings you here?" The saltiness ignites my tastebuds for more.

"Travelling around. Thought I'd get out of the rat race, get some sun and surf. Jacko needed help, and here I am. For the moment, anyway."

I nod and look at Jack.

"Born and bred here, although I went to school in Townsville. I like it here better. Lot of work now that people are moving here and the tourists are coming in. That's Herb's doing."

"Since there's so much work, I might have to stick around for a while after all," Steve says.

"Hope so, mate," Jack says.

Crystal brings over their food – steak, salad and chips. A cheeky look passes between her and Jack; perhaps there's something between them. She leaves as Herb limps back to the table.

"My grandparents used to own this pub," Jack says, "until it ran into trouble, and the Hipworth empire bought them out in the late sixties."

That might explain the special treatment comment by Steve.

"I think I met your grandmother," I say. "Joan, isn't it?"

He looks up and smiles. "She's a character. Doesn't take any nonsense. I keep an eye on her now that my folks have retired to the coast." He suddenly looks worried. "Did she come into the surgery?"

"She can't tell you that, mate," Herb says, slicing his steak.

"Yeah, confidentiality and all that," Steve pipes in. "Another round?"

Herb shakes his head, and so does Jack. Steve looks at me and my almost empty glass. "Another chardy?"

"No, thanks," I say. "One's more than enough."

He looks at me as if I've just told him off for doing something wrong.

"I mean, you go ahead, by all means."

He raises his eyebrows. "Do you mind?"

"Oh, sorry."

Again, I've missed his body language. I stand to let him out, then swapping spots, I slide into his seat. The heat left behind is uncomfortably absorbed through my skirt.

He swaggers off to the bar.

"That bloke sure asks a lot of questions," Herb says.

"He's just inquisitive. Nice bloke, though, and a good worker, too," Jack says.

Steve is chatting with a woman at the bar, and I don't understand their comment.

"He's very friendly," I say.

"Yeah, he is," Herb says. "We might be able to convince him to stay. What do you reckon?"

"I hope so."

Steve comes back with his beer.

"Getting back to how I met Joan," I say, "she was here with Mavis in the lounge the other day. Seemed like a very nice lady."

Jack nods and wipes his mouth with the serviette. "She thinks she's looking after Mavis, but I reckon it's the other way around. She's a stubborn old stick. Still has a whisky every night before bed. That wouldn't hurt, would it?"

"I shouldn't think so," I say.

"Your granny, she'd know a lot then?" Steve asks.

Jack looks surprised by the question. "She's lived here since the thirties, so I reckon she knows a thing or two about the place. Why?"

"Nothin'. I just wondered, that's all," Steve says. "It's nice there are old people who know the area. I like learning the history of places."

"Mavis has been around for that long, too, I reckon," Herb says. "Between them, they'd know everything."

Steve places his empty glass on the table and gets up. "I reckon I'll call it a night. Evening, gents and doc."

He saunters off, and the woman he'd been chatting to earlier follows him out. Perhaps it's a coincidence or maybe he's just picked her up. But there's something about him that I can't put my finger on.

The waitress clears our table, and I hang onto the dregs of my wine.

"Want to know something?" Herb says, leaning towards us.

"But you got to keep it under your hat for the moment."

Jack and I nod.

He lowers his voice. "The tourist buses are going to include Sugar Creek on their itinerary. We'll have busloads coming in."

Jack's face breaks into a smile, and he slaps Herb on the shoulder. "That's bloody incredible. I dunno how you do it." He lifts his almost empty beer glass. "Here's to a prosperous town. We better get moving on that motel, mate."

Herb looks happy with himself.

"Congratulations," I say, wondering why I've been included but liking how it makes me feel a part of it all. Then I think about the extra demand that will generate for me. Now's not the time to voice my concerns, though.

"That'll mean a lot more business for the whole town. When's the announcement?" Jack asks.

"Probably next week at the council meeting. There's a lot to do before the first bus turns up, but I'm hoping we can get them rolling in sometime next month."

"April? That might be cutting it fine." Jack drains his glass and gets up. "I better get my beauty rest. That's great news, mate."

The crowd has thinned out, and the noise has died down enough to hear a jazz tune piped through the speakers.

I finish my wine. "I better get going, too."

"I'll come with you," Herb says.

"No need," I say. "Might be best to stay off that leg."

He puts his hands in his pockets. "My car is parked near your place, so I'm going that way."

Now I feel stupid. I don't know why that happens around him. "Okay," is all I say, and I walk out ahead of him.

He catches up to me on the footpath outside. "You're in a hurry," he says, grinning. "I'm the one with the gammy leg."

"Sorry," I say, waiting. "Are you in much pain?"

"It's a bit worse since this morning."

"You really shouldn't be on it."

"Is this a consultation?"

He's smirking.

"No, but I think you should come in tomorrow for a proper consult. It wouldn't hurt to check."

"I'll see," he says. "By the way, I rang Mum this morning to ask her about Dad's cancer."

"Oh, really? Did she know what cancer it was?"

"Leukaemia. She told me my grandfather had it as well."

"Mmm. That's weird."

"Why?"

"I've had a number of patients with leukaemia."

"Maybe it's just a coincidence."

"Something's not right. Cancer is generally caused by gene mutations."

"Is it hereditary?" He sounds worried.

"It could be, but it could also be environmental factors like exposure to chemicals, radiation, or even smoking."

His face is stern under the streetlight. "My dad never smoked, but my grandfather did."

We continue walking up the street, moths fluttering around the lamppost lights.

I take a punt. "If Agent Orange was sprayed around here in the sixties, that could also be a cause."

Herb scratches his head. "You're not still on about that? As the mayor, I'd know about it, and there's nothing."

"Would you really be across something that happened decades ago?"

He scoffs. "It's just Wally and his conspiracy theories stirring up trouble and putting the town under a cloud. There've always been scaremongering nutters."

"Wally claims it's in the water."

"Like I said, he's the biggest nutter going around. I wouldn't believe what he says." He points to his head. "Got hit in the head a few times. Who goes off to war three times without being a little bit mad?"

"Well, how do you explain the highest rate of cancer in the state, then, Mr Mayor? Perhaps *you* should dig a little more."

"I don't know, but as the health official, I'd appreciate it if you didn't spread this around. People will panic and –"

"And what, Herb? Listen, I know this could be difficult if it's true and gets out, and I know how hard you've worked to get Sugar Creek on the map. But this is a life and death situation, and I have a responsibility to make sure people don't get sick. Besides, they're already talking and wondering and coming up with their own theories."

We're standing outside the surgery.

"Alright, alright. I agree it's worth investigating. I promise I'll look into the council records and see what I can find out."

"Good. And while you're at it, can you find out where the rest of the medical files are? I don't have any from before 1995."

"Did you leave the surgery light on for any reason?"

I turn. There's light coming from the back. I fumble in my handbag for the keys. "Must have left it on accidentally. I'll just go and turn it off. See you later."

"I'll come with you."

I look at him with my keys in hand. "No need."

He hesitates. "I think—"

"Isn't this a country town where we leave the doors unlocked?"

He shrugs. "That still stands."

"See you later, then," I say. "And don't forget about that appointment."

"We'll see," he says.

"And the files?"

"Yes, yes. I'll get onto that."

I unlock the door. The light in the storeroom is on. I must have forgotten to turn it off. Nothing else appears to be out of place.

Although … I'm sure it was dark when I locked up.

I tug the handle of a filing cabinet, and it opens. I check the others, all unlocked. Linda would never leave them unlocked, but maybe I'm wrong. Now I regret not letting Herb come with me.

I go to the back door and try the handle. For a moment, I'm stunned – it's also unlocked; someone has been here. Why? Could it have something to do with my case? I dismiss that thought: no-one here knows about that. Is it the growing cluster of cancer patients? Has someone been searching for patient files? Or for drugs?

I breathe to calm myself, then open the door and peer into the darkness. There's nothing other than a clear, star-filled night. The light from inside settles on something at the bottom of the step near the rubbish bins. I quickly climb down the three steps and pick up a manilla folder. It looks old from the brown and yellowing edges and is empty. I twist it around and am shocked to read what it says on the side: "Deaths: Sugar Creek Base."

I snib the door and, as I turn, smell something – that same aftershave. My immediate thought is of Daniel, but I dismiss that idea and remember Jack and Steve. They both left before Herb and me. Could it be one of them? Surely not.

22

Ellen

"Listen, love, a lot of blokes take off."

"But we were getting married."

The middle-aged policeman lowered his head and peered over the top of his glasses, his hand resting on a blank piece of paper. A blunt pencil and letter opener lay beside an empty, stained teacup. He hadn't bothered to take down Billy's or Hector's name.

"I hate to say it, but that's probably more reason for him doing a runner." He sat back in his chair and picked at his teeth with the letter opener.

"No, that's not right. He loved me and bought me a ring and everything." She thrust out her left hand to show him the ring. "Why would he do all that? Spend all of his money on that?"

He put the letter opener down and leaned forward to look at her. "I can't answer that, love. But if I were you, I'd accept the fact that your fella has gone, and—"

"He left his clothes, all of his possessions. And what about Hector? His things are still at the boarding house." She sat back and folded her arms. "Don't you think that men who are running away would take at least a change of clothes?"

The policeman shrugged. "Ex-servicemen are not always of a right mind. He was in Malaysia and New Guinea?"

She nodded.

"Mmm. Probably saw and did things he's not proud of. It happens." His face softened. "Seeing the base might have brought it all back. It might not be you, love. It might well be something else."

She spun the engagement ring around her finger, thinking.

Billy hadn't talked much about the war, where he'd been, and what he'd done. He said it took a year out of his life, and he'd moved on. Forgotten about it, even. Maybe there was something to what the policeman said.

"But it's been more than a week. Don't you think he would have at least tried to contact me?"

"He might not be able to. He could be anywhere. If I were you, I'd go home and forget about him. If he's not right in the head, then you're better off. He's probably done you a favour."

"How do you explain Hector, then?"

"Mates stick together, love. Better now than when you're married. Take my advice and find a bloke who hasn't served overseas. There are a few in Townsville. Maybe go there."

The policeman looked at his watch and hoisted his bulk from the chair, signalling that the interview was over. He moved around the desk and turned to her at the doorway.

"It's for the best."

Ellen nodded, then headed off down the street in a daze. Had going to the base brought back horrific memories for him?

Oh, Billy, if only you were here. Where are you?

She didn't tell the policeman about the pregnancy because she knew what he'd have said: "Your fella might have felt trapped."

But he wasn't, was he?

With the sun hot on her head, she walked, relieved that the smoke from the burning cane had blown away with the morning breeze. People stared at her from across the street. There goes that girl, they thought. The one from the bar, the one who was jilted eleven days ago.

She kept going, head down, until she reached the outskirts of town. Here, the odour of burned cane was grassy and musty, and sweet and smoky all at once. Like Billy had been the first day she saw him in Sugar Creek. "We burn first, cut, and then load it all before we move on," he'd explained.

The cane fields were split into two by a dirt road, and smoke hung in the air. Beneath her feet, the ground was muddy and charred, but she trudged along, trying to avoid the puddles from the drenching rain the night before. She wiped perspiration from her forehead, pushing her hair off her face, and stared at a high, barbed wire fence.

A soldier, rifle slung on his shoulder, stood in front of a large wooden gate.

Should she tell him that she was looking for Billy and Hector? Or just Billy? Should she throw herself on his mercy and cry, hoping he'd feel sorry for her? She walked towards him.

"Um, can I go in?" she blurted.

The soldier glared at her. "Have ya' got permission?"

She stared right back. He was young enough not to have seen service, she guessed. She peered behind him at the "KEEP OUT" signs, the barbed wire, and then at his gleaming black boots.

"I'm here for the medical trial."

The soldier looked wary. "It's for ex-personnel."

"I was in the Australian Women's Army, in case you haven't heard of it." Her confidence grew. She folded her arms and cocked her head. "We girls did our bit, you know."

"Ya' got your letter?"

"Was I meant to bring it?"

"Yes. Anyway, you're too early. Come back at two next Sunday. They only do it on Sundays." The man smirked as he lay his hand on his rifle as if to remind her of his power. "If you'd read ya' letter, you woulda known that."

"Oh, yes. I forgot. Silly me. Thanks."

Now what? She looked at her watch. There was one more place she had to go before work – the railway station.

"Smoke's been bad, miss. Where ya off ta?"

"I don't need a ticket."

"Oh?" he said. "Ya after a timetable, then?" The station master pushed it towards her.

She took it and glanced at the piece of paper. "The train runs on a Sunday?"

"Yep, like clockwork. Every Sunday at four thirty."

"Do many people take the train on Sundays?"

The man scratched his chin and shrugged. "Dunno. We mostly get folks coming in from Brisbane, but some go off to Townsville. Never thought about how many go on a Sunday."

"Do you remember if two men might have got on the train? One was quite thick set, good looking with brown hair. The other quite tall with red hair. Do you know if they bought a ticket on Sunday the 26th of May? I know it's been more than two weeks, but might you remember? Do you have some paperwork that might tell you?"

The man frowned.

"You're that girl, aren't ya? The one from the pub that got jilted."

She was crestfallen. "Please, I have to know."

"Ya wanna know if he took off on the train?"

She nodded. "With his friend."

The man looked doubtful. "Not s'posed to say who's bought tickets."

"I just want to know if two men bought tickets that day. You don't have to tell me their names. I don't want to get you into any trouble."

He disappeared into another room, and Ellen fanned herself with the timetable. The deafening blast of a train's horn made her jump. It chugged past with open carriages laden with cut sugar cane.

"Okay," the man said, plonking a large ledger book onto the counter. "Five people bought tickets, but I can't say if they took the train the same day. You know people buy tickets in advance."

"Don't you write down their names?"

The man eyed her.

"Could you tell me if tickets were sold in the name of Billy Nolan or Hector …" She tried to remember his surname. "Burkin, that's it. Hector Burkin."

He looked at her squarely and shook his head. "Sorry, love."

Was that good news or bad?

"They coulda' hitched a ride instead, ya' know. To save money."

She nodded, murmured her thanks and went home.

The floorboards squeaked upstairs, and she heard Phyllis's slippers dragging along the floor.

All her worry, love, and grief blurred the page. Her pen was poised over the words, but then she snapped the diary shut on that day's entry. If only she'd been more insistent about not needing a ring, Billy might not have felt the need to earn extra money. The joy and love the ring once represented haunted her. Why was she still wearing it? Dragging it off her finger, she looked at it before putting it gently on the kitchen table. She opened the louvre windows and peered out into the darkness, hoping Billy might miraculously appear. Tears fell down her face, dripping onto the linoleum floor.

Had everything been a lie? Was it all a ruse? That's what the policeman had said.

Ellen wiped her eyes, moved back to the table, and picked up the ring. Perhaps she should sell it. She opened the wardrobe to look for the box and saw his wedding suit. It hung alongside his shirts, next to her dresses, his things neatly folded on shelves and in drawers. It prompted a smile: he'd always been neat and orderly.

She put the suit on the bed and lay next to it, bringing a sleeve to her face, breathing in the faintness of his smell, her stomach in knots. Where was he? Where was Billy Nolan? How could he torture her by leaving his things in the room they were to share as husband and wife? In a hot flash of anger, she swept the suit off the bed, hanger clattering to the floor, tweed crumpled in a heap. She buried her head in the pillow and cried like she'd done every night since.

A thunderclap woke her, and she peered at the clock. It was two in the morning, and she was hungry. She got up and forced down a sandwich Phyllis had left for her, then drank a glass of water and climbed back into bed.

The next morning, she woke to a magpie chortling on her windowsill. The day was bright, and the smell of frangipani drifted in through the open windows. She hauled herself up and went to the bathroom, splashing cold water on her puffy red face. She ran her hands over the swell of her belly and stared at her thin arms and legs.

How could a baby survive in a body like this?

Her stomach rumbled. She stepped over the mess on the floor and pulled on a fresh skirt and blouse. Then she ate a slice of stale white bread, smearing it with Phyllis's homemade pineapple jam before washing it down with hot black tea. When she was finished, she gazed at the floor. She had to move on, for the baby's sake. She needed money, and the sensible thing to do was to sell the ring and Billy's clothes. As she picked up his jacket, a blue leather hexagonal box fell out onto the floor and rolled under the bed.

Crawling on her hands and knees, she reached for the box and opened it. A thin, gold wedding band sat in cream velvet. He must have bought it and kept it ready in the pocket of his wedding suit. Ready for when he returned on their wedding day, ready for when he came back to this room to change, to walk to the church, to marry her.

Why would he run away if he'd bought a wedding ring?

She pulled herself up and tried it on – a perfect fit. The heaviness in her chest lifted. No. He didn't take off because he got jittery. Something happened; she was sure of it. Something happened at that military base. And she was damn well going to find out.

23

Dana

There's a message from Hannah waiting for me on my desk, and I ring her back during lunch.

"Sugar Creek Base is an old military base from World War Two."

"So, the deaths must have something to do with the war. Okay. I don't have to worry about that folder, then."

"Well, I dunno about that."

"Why? It's ancient history."

"After the war, it morphed into some sort of medical research facility."

I perk up at this. "That's interesting, but doesn't have anything to do with my cancer cluster."

"It's more than interesting. It's fucking mind-blowing. In fact, I'm kind of freaking out a bit and feel like I shouldn't even be discussing this over the phone."

"You were always the drama queen," I say, chuckling. "You want the cone of silence?"

"I'm serious. And I think you should know."

There's tension in her voice.

"Go on then."

"Back in the late forties, they tested topical creams on ex-servicemen. They also injected some of them with chemicals like diquat."

"What's that?"

"It's a type of herbicide. Although lord knows why it was injected."

"Into people?"

"Ex-soldiers. I found a paper on it by a Dr Cummins. Turns out it's not good for you." Hannah half-heartedly laughs.

"Human trials back then?"

"Seems so. They stopped it because patients were adversely affected, but I'm not sure what the effects were or how bad it was. What I do know is that some bloke died. Old Doc Cummins was scant on the detail. He'd never get away with writing that palaver these days."

"Really? It sounds like something out of the movies."

"And that's not all."

I tap my pen on the table. "Go on."

"Hold on a sec."

Hannah's voice is muffled as if she has her hand over the mouthpiece. Linda knocks and comes in with the next patient's file.

"You there?" Hannah asks.

"Yep."

"Sorry about that. Now where was I? Oh yeah. After that, they stopped for ten years or so. But get this. They reopened the joint, though no-one knows why."

"I think I might know." I tell her what Wally Gillespie had told me.

Hannah whistles. "I'll see if I can verify that. If what he says is true, it could explain your cancers. The TCDD he mentions can one hundred per cent cause cancer and birth defects. Preliminary studies also show that second and third generations can be affected."

The end of the pen suddenly tastes disgusting, and I drop it on the desk. "Jesus. Surely it can't be behind the cluster here?"

"Your old patient files should give you a clue. They'd be filled with various diseases if the town was exposed back in the sixties."

"There are no old files. I don't know where they've gone."

"Well, they've got to be somewhere. They should have been archived for at least seven years, and you've got patients who've lived there for decades, haven't you? There should be files for them, surely."

"Yeah, it's strange."

"You should find that empty plot of dirt old Wally told you about. Maybe there are dead bodies under it."

"Your imagination's really running away. You'd love this to become a murder mystery."

"I absolutely would."

"Listen, you've been a big help, but I'd better go."

"No worries," Hannah says. "Keep me posted. When this explodes, and you're splashed across the newspapers, I want some credit, too."

I laugh nervously. "I'm sure it'll all be nothing."

*

Two days later, Herb turns up at my surgery, pale and still limping. "Your leg worse?"

He nods. "A bit. Thought about what you said."

"Okay then, let's take a look."

The bruise is yellowing, but there are no others. I check his leg and foot, prodding the joints while asking him questions. He seems nervous, given his one-word answers.

"Are these the boots you wear all the time?" I ask, picking one of them up.

"Yeah," he says, pulling on his socks. He looks at me square in the eye. "Give it to me straight. No bullshitting. I've got it, haven't I?"

I narrow my eyes at him as I hand him his boot.

"What exactly do you think you have?"

He pulls on the boot roughly. "It's that cancer, isn't it? I saw the Harpers. They told me how it started with bruising and a sore leg."

I suppress a smile then see how anxious and upset he looks.

"Listen—"

"I lied about the bruise. I have no idea how I got it, and, believe me, I've wracked my brains trying to remember. I may as well get the blood tests and be done with it." He stands up and runs his hand through his hair. "Well? It's happening, isn't it? Cancer's in the family, and I guess I'm lucky I managed to get to thirty-two. And poor Amy."

"Amy?"

"My wife." He slumps into the chair opposite, his shoulders sagging, his eyes glassy. "She got skin cancer and died two years ago. This is just the final straw."

"I—"

"It's just … if we'd had a GP, then we might have caught it early." He talks rapidly, creating no space for me to interrupt. "That's why I got onto council and somehow became mayor. To fight for a GP. It's important, you know? We have to have good medical care. And I guess I haven't said thanks." He looks at me. "So, you may as well let me have it."

"You have bursitis."

"Jesus, that sounds even worse. Is it worse? Bloody hell, how long do I have, Dana?" He rubs his hands over his thighs.

"Herb, listen carefully. You are not going to die. It's not cancer."

"Thank god." He lets out a rush of air. "Sorry, you must think I'm a raving lunatic. I've got myself all worked up. Jesus, I feel a right idiot—"

"It's a very common condition in runners. Believe it or not, I've had it myself."

That shuts him up. He looks at me wide-eyed.

"It's very treatable with the right shoes," I say.

"Shoes?"

"Shoes. The bursa is a small, fluid-filled sac that cushions and lubricates your joints and bones. When it gets inflamed, it causes pain, swelling, and redness. Your foot is a little curved, probably from birth, but well-fitted shoes can mitigate this. You should replace your runners and those boots. They're worn on one side and forcing you to compensate, which puts pressure on the bursa. That's why you also have pain running up your leg. I'm surprised you haven't got pain in your lower back. I'm going to recommend a podiatrist in Townsville who'll fit you with an orthotic. Stay off your feet for a few days, elevate that foot, and no running for at least two weeks."

"That all?" he says.

"I also want you to do these simple exercises." I demonstrate.

"Now you try it."

He tries but struggles.

"You can hold my shoulder for balance."

His hand is hot; his face furrowed in concentration. He clings to my arm to keep from falling.

"Shit, sorry," he says.

"That's okay. Now do it again. Use your core ... that's it. Excellent. Now I need you to do that at least three times a day."

He looks pleased as if he's accomplished a tightrope walk, not a simple foot exercise.

I write down my instructions and hand them to him because I know he's only heard half of what I've said.

He reads the piece of paper and nods. "Sorry about before," he says softly.

"No need to apologise. I'm so sorry about Amy. It must have been very hard for you."

"It was. We met in Brisbane at uni. A dietician," he says proudly. "I was learning how to be a landscape architect."

This surprises me. I thought he just swanned around town doing mayoral things and was a farmer in his spare time.

"I've done the landscaping for most of the town."

"The palms down the median of Main Street?"

"Yeah, and your place – our old place. Amy designed the renovations and chose a lot of the plants. There's a tonne of herbs and indigenous plants with medicinal benefits."

"Amy sounds like a wonderful person."

"Oh, she was. By the time we found out, it was too late. It started from a melanoma then progressed. Nothing that could be done." His shoulders drop, and he breathes out as if it's the first time those words have found a place with someone else. "She was only twenty-eight."

I find myself softening to him and know now why he never looks happy.

The energy seems to have drained from his sad eyes as he lifts his head. "I've thought about what you said the other day, and you're right. There are a lot of people in this town with cancer. But I honestly don't know where to start. I've always dismissed Wally. Joan says he's crazy, and I guess I didn't take much notice. But if you've found out something, then, as mayor, I've got to get to the bottom of it."

I take a deep breath. "If I had the old medical files, I could see what sort of illnesses there have been and if they're linked back to that time. There may be old council files that could tell us something. I know you're busy, but either way, it might help to focus on what to do next."

"You're right. There might be something in the archives. I'll ask some of the council staff."

He looks at his watch. "Hell, I've been here so long. Sorry, I better go."

I'll ask him if he knows about the dirt patch another time.

"No problem. Glad I could ease your mind."

"Thanks. Even though I feel a right idiot."

"You were right to come and see me."

He smiles, dimples appearing that I've never seen before. The smile quickly fades, and the sternness is back.

I walk with him to the door, conscious now that the reception room is full.

"I'm glad you're here," he mumbles, face suddenly flushed, embarrassed. "I mean, I'm glad the town has you as a doctor. You're very good at what you do."

"Thank you."

"I'll let you know what I find out."

And then, he's gone.

24

Ellen

Ellen breathed in and tugged at the zip of her blue skirt. Giving up, she let the skirt slip to the floor. She'd managed so far by hiding the undone button under her apron, but not today. It wasn't as if she had a lot of clothes, but what she did have would be wholly inadequate in the coming weeks. She shut off the thought and rummaged through the wardrobe, settling on a light green dress that hugged the bulge of her middle too much for her liking. It would have to do.

The rings lay on the table, and she slid them on. For the baby's sake, she wouldn't sell them. They'd be a safety net of respectability. She'd be a widow, perhaps, not an outcast unmarried mother. All she had to do was save enough money, move away, have the baby, and take on a new life. Could she pull it off? She'd have to. She squared her shoulders and walked to work.

*

Ellen carried two shandies and a clean ashtray into the Ladies' Lounge, nudging the door open with her tray. At first glance, Mavis and Carolyn looked deep in conversation, but they stopped when they saw her. She was caught in a collision of their suffocating perfumes.

Ellen cleared her throat. "I hope you enjoyed your trip, Mavis."

Mavis nodded. "It was good."

"I still have your pearls. I'll bring them to your house after work tonight if that's all right?"

Mavis's cheeks flushed red, and she flicked ash into the full ashtray. "I'm, ah … I'm not home tonight."

Carolyn raised her eyebrows. "Not home? Where are you going?"

"Do you have to know everything?" Mavis snapped, frowning. She reached for her glass.

Carolyn pouted. "No need to get so touchy. I don't give a toss what you do."

"Good!" Mavis sipped her drink.

"When can I return them?" Ellen interrupted.

Mavis shrugged. "I'm in no rush for them."

"But—"

"Don't worry about them. When I'm ready, I'll pick them up from your place," Mavis said, a touch too firmly.

Ellen nodded, confused. Perhaps Mavis didn't want her at her home, didn't want to be tarnished with the embarrassment.

She reached for the empty glasses, and Carolyn touched her arm. "And how are you going?"

And there it was. Back to that.

"I'm okay," she said, quickly placing the glasses on the tray.

Carolyn shook her head and clicked her tongue. "Such a business. These blokes just seem to think they can get away with it. You have to move on. There are plenty of other fish in the sea." Carolyn grabbed her wrist. "What about Wally or Cal?"

Mavis frowned and flashed a look at Carolyn. "That's the stupidest suggestion I've ever heard."

Carolyn let Ellen go and looked at Mavis in dismay. "No, it's not. They're perfectly good, unattached men who would never do something so despicable."

Ellen picked up the full ashtray, stifling the impulse to pour the contents all over Carolyn.

"Billy is not despicable, and he didn't run away. He bought a wedding ring and packed all of his clothes neatly into our wardrobe. Those are not the signs of a man who was running. Something happened to him at the base, Carolyn. Despite what your husband said."

Carolyn folded her arms. "I'm not sure I like your insinuation, Ellen."

Mavis watched on with interest.

Ellen stared at the lipstick-stained butts in the ashtray. She needed to calm down.

"I know that Billy would have come if he could have."

Carolyn's face softened. "I know it's hard to believe. I … we understand. Don't we, Mavis?"

Mavis nodded.

"You're not ready to … I mean, you need time, that's all."

"I have to go. If you'll excuse me." Ellen turned away, fighting back tears and the urge to pitch the ashtray into the wall.

*

It was a busy Saturday afternoon, and the bar was filled with loud, noisy canecutters, many of whom knew nothing about her, not like the regulars who had shown curious sympathy.

Today she smiled, chatted, and acted as if nothing had happened. Today she kept up her vigil for the man in the brown suit. Mr

Taylor, she thought Billy had said. He hadn't returned since that day Billy signed up for the job. She was rewarded when she spied him in his usual corner spot. She'd find a way to speak to him, ask him about Billy and Hector, and get some answers. The man must know something. She kept watch on the line of men snaking their way around the tables to him.

Laughter, backslapping, the smell of cigarette smoke, beer, and sweat filled the bar. Ellen served the next man, filling another glass with cold beer, condensation and froth sliding down the side as she took his coins, and pushed the cash register shut. She'd wait and watch for her opportunity.

Two men sat on stools at the bar.

She smiled. "And what can I get you?"

"Two pots. And Rabbit will pay," the man said, winking and jerking his head at his friend.

"Come on, Lenny. Surely, it's your round, mate," Rabbit said.

She could see why he'd earned the nickname. His wild eyes were large and round, staring ahead like a rabbit caught in headlights.

"Keep ya' shirt on," Lenny said, his long, thin fingers carefully folding a piece of paper. "We'll be flush. It's the easiest way to make a buck."

"Yeah, so you keep sayin'," Rabbit said.

Ellen placed two beers on the counter. "There you go."

Lenny brought out a worn leather wallet from his back pocket. "I've done four of these now. There's nothing to it."

"What about that rash ya' got the first time?" Rabbit said.

Ellen took the pound note but made no move to put it into the register.

"What about it? It went after a few days. Nothing to worry about."

"What else is it doing to ya'? I dunno if I can trust these blokes. It was bad enough in bloody France."

"Listen, mate. It's harmless. There are no bullets here."

"I couldn't help overhearing you," Ellen said, leaning forward. "Have you been doing those experiments out at the base?"

Lenny turned and grinned. "Tomorrow will be my fifth go."

"Do you know Billy Nolan or Hector Burkin by any chance?"

"I know Hector," Lenny said. "Don't really know the other bloke."

"I haven't seen them for ages," she said quickly.

A couple of blokes down the other end of the bar tried to draw her attention. She nodded at them, still holding the pound note.

"Yeah, me neither," Lenny said. "Last time I saw Hector was at the base. I've been looking out for him 'cause he gave me a pack of his rollies while we were waiting, but I never saw him again. Scored myself a free pack of tobacco." He grinned, then raised his eyebrows. "The change?"

"Oh, sorry. Coming right up."

She returned with his coins.

"Thanks," he said, slipping them into his pocket.

"And Billy? He was there too, wasn't he?" she said.

It was hard to keep her voice casual. Interested but not desperate.

Lenny scratched his chin. "Hard to remember, but, yeah, I reckon Billy must have been there. Those two always stuck together." He narrowed his eyes. "Why?"

Ellen glanced again at the men at the other end of the bar, her heart thumping hard. "Oh, I haven't seen Hector or the other bloke in here awhile, and I just wondered. That's all."

She grabbed a cloth and wiped the counter, listening.

"Come to think of it ..." Lenny turned to Rabbit. "I haven't seen Jonno either since then. We all went in together, then split up and went into separate cubicles. Those blokes must have gone before I came out or waited somewhere else. Anyway, it's easy money."

He sipped his beer and wiped his mouth with his hand.

"What do ya have to wait for?" Rabbit said, brushing a lock of hair from his forehead.

"To see if you have any reaction, I think. Once they checked my arm, they told me to push off. Easy as that."

She left them, her mind a whirl, and attended to the men at the end of the bar. As the day wore on, she poured beer, smiled, and chatted as if she hadn't received news that had made her legs shake, and her stomach tighten into knots.

It was nearly closing time, and the pub was almost empty when she saw her chance. Mr Taylor stood up and gathered his jacket from the back of the chair.

Ellen glanced around – Joan was in the Ladies' Lounge; Paul was engrossed in a conversation with three stragglers at the bar – and headed over to him.

"Excuse me," she said.

The man slipped his arm into his sleeve, stopped briefly as if to appraise her, and then finished putting on his jacket.

"I'm wondering if you could help me?" she said.

He looked uncertain. "I don't know."

"My fiancé volunteered for the medical experiment at the base."

"So?"

"He and his friend did it four weeks ago."

"Listen, love. I can't help you. We're not taking women yet."

"I'm not looking to volunteer."

The man put his hat on his head. "Oh?"

From the corner of her eye, she saw Joan enter the bar holding a tray of empty glasses.

"I'm looking for Billy Nolan and Hector Burkin," she blurted, trying to keep her voice steady. "Do you know them?"

She was sure she saw a flicker of recognition. "Dunno who you're talking about. Never heard of them." He turned away. "I've got to go."

"Please," she grabbed his arm. "They signed on with you four weeks ago."

He looked at her hand and pulled his arm away, scowling. "Like I said, I don't know nothing about those men."

"Lock the door, will you, love?" Paul yelled out.

The man picked up the paperwork on the table and left.

She locked the door behind him, shutting her eyes tight to keep herself from crying.

25

Dana

The waiting room is empty, and Linda is massaging the side of her head when I come out of my office, jiggling my car keys.

"Headache?" I ask.

"Yep." She gives me a weak smile. "Mum is driving me crazy. She keeps losing things and blames me. Then I spend the whole evening trying to find what she's lost. She's even ringing me here."

"What sort of things is she losing?"

"Stupid things. Like, last night, she said her pearls were missing. She reckons Ellen, someone I've never heard of, borrowed and returned them, but now they're gone." Linda leans forward, forearms resting on the desk, and clasps her hands. "Except she's never had any pearls. Ever."

"I thought you were going to bring her in."

Linda rolls her eyes glumly. "She doesn't want to. 'There's nothing wrong with me.' The stubborn old bat. Anyway, I'll sort her out. You're off on house calls?"

I nod. "Do you want me to pop in and see your mum?"

"Christ, no. She'll go right off at me. I'll work on her." She hands me three patient files. "The Harpers first, poor things. Hope they're okay."

"Why don't you lock up early and go to the beach? Doctor's orders."

Linda laughs. "I might just take that prescription, Dr Janssen."

*

It's my first home visit to the Harpers. They've undergone chemo, and I want to check on them. My home visits so far have been confined to town, but today I roll the windows down and head out onto open road. It's not long before the turn-off onto Old Goanna Creek Road – a narrow bitumen road with cane fields on one side and grassland on the other, dotted with the occasional house. I look out for numbers on roadside mailboxes perched on rickety-looking poles. Another car is coming. This road isn't made for passing traffic, and I veer to the shoulder. A blue Holden Commodore, covered in a film of dust, slows on approach, and I recognise Steve. He raises his index finger, a thank you salute I've grown accustomed to, and I salute back. He beams in recognition, and I smile back, wondering what he's doing out here.

Soon I reach the Harper's driveway and drive over a cattle grate, down a gravel road lined with once-manicured shrubs, and pull up to a sprawling weatherboard house, much like my own. There's a thriving vegetable garden down one side; a yapping brown collie bounds over as I pull up.

Shirl is on the veranda. "Rover! Come here." The dog obediently leaves me while I take my brown bag out of the boot.

"Sorry, she loves visitors," Shirl calls out.

"She's a beautiful dog." Not that I'm much of a dog person.

Shirl holds Rover, letting me in the door before releasing him.

"Bob doesn't like her in the house anymore," Shirl says apologetically. She looks haggard, her eyes slightly bloodshot. "Come through."

She takes me into the loungeroom towards the back of the house. I immediately want to fling back the curtains and open the windows to let fresh air and daylight into this foul-smelling room. Lying on the couch is Bob, a bucket by his side. He's in old board shorts and a faded singlet too small for him, barely covering his stomach.

"It's the doctor, love," Shirl says, her voice at a pitch higher than necessary.

He grunts.

I move so he can see me without twisting around. There's a small amount of vomit in the bucket and a half-filled glass of water on the coffee table next to him.

"How are you doing?" I ask.

He lifts his head and licks his lips. "Been better."

"He can't keep much down." Shirl deftly removes the bucket and disappears.

"Are you drinking?"

Bob nods, but I check him for dehydration anyway and explain that vomiting is a common side effect of the chemo. He doesn't say much.

"Are you taking the anti-nausea tablets?"

"He doesn't want to," Shirl says.

"Bob, it'll make you feel better."

"The only thing that'll make me better," he says, "is to go to sleep and never wake up."

"The medication will help."

He closes his eyes and shrugs.

I turn to Shirl. "How are you feeling?"

She's fidgeting with her wedding ring. "Good."

"Sleeping?"

"Bob's not."

"And you?"

She shrugs. "We're both tired."

"Did they explain that your dosage of chemo is different from Bob's?"

"Yes," she says. Bob grunts.

I give them pointers on fluid replacement and diet and write another prescription for anti-nausea medication.

As I'm about to leave, Shirl pulls me aside, her eyes filled with tears. "He's just so cranky, Doctor Janssen. I don't know what to do."

"It's to be expected, Shirl. It's an understandable reaction to his illness."

"You heard what he said." She grabs my arm with sweaty hands. "He wants it to end."

"He only has another two cycles, and the nausea will subside with the tablets. Try to get him to take them."

Her nails dig into my skin. "He wants his life to end. And he wants me to do it."

There's desperation in her eyes.

I feel for them both. "It's probably the treatment making him say that. It's quite common."

She drops her hold on me and pulls a tissue from her apron pocket to wipe the tears away. "I'm at my wit's end."

"Do you mind if we sit?" I point at the cane chair on her verandah. She nods.

"Shirl!" Bob bellows from inside.

She jumps and turns her head like a scared mouse. "See? He thinks you've gone."

"He's not … hurting you, is he?"

She looks at me sharply. "Of course not. I can handle him. I just can't handle his mental state."

"Are you getting any help?"

"Friends and our son and daughter-in-law help out, but I don't know how much longer I can cope. My friend was telling me about anti-depressants."

"Has he had them before?"

"He took Ativan once, years ago."

"I see."

"But it's addictive."

"Maybe something a bit milder, I think."

"Yes, anything if it helps …" Shirl says, tears welling again.

I take out my prescription book. "I'm giving him a prescription for an anti-depressant and something milder for you. It'll help you both sleep, too."

"I need a cup of tea, woman." Bob's raging voice echoes down the corridor.

"Thank you," Shirl sniffs.

"I'll be back next week," I say, getting into the car while Shirl waves from the front door.

It's in the water, Wally said a couple of weeks ago.

I turn left instead of right and continue a couple hundred metres down Old Goanna Creek Road to a pair of weatherboard houses. They must have been the Jamieson's and the Thompson's. I pull over, leave the car idling, and stare at the three houses separated by a paddock or two. Behind the Jamieson's place, the pasture is being irrigated, and there are horses in the distance. Linda told me these were hobby farms and that horse agistment was popular. There must be a river nearby for irrigation. In the distance, beyond the flat cleared land, a thick line of trees undulates up the nearby mountain range.

I get back into the car and head towards the mountain, where the road is steep and windy and takes me down into a gully where the bitumen is replaced with gravel. The bush creeps suffocatingly close to the side of this potholed track. I should turn back, but I have half an hour before my next appointment.

A sign ahead reads, "Old Goanna Creek", and I stop on a rickety wooden bridge. Is this the contaminated water that feeds into the town? It's just a picturesque, gurgling creek with rocks, bush, and white water, not what I'd expect from an ancient poison spraying site. I'm beginning to discount everything Wally told me; perhaps Herb is right.

But I keep driving.

I guide the car around a steep U-turn, and it bumps and lurches, the seat belt tugging tight against my ribs. The road gets worse as I dodge water-logged potholes. I stop and peer over the passenger side; the steep drop makes me decide it's time to turn around. I drive on, looking for somewhere wide enough, hoping like hell that no cars come the other way. My hands are tight on the wheel, and there's no end to the climbing. Surely, I'm almost at the top.

The car isn't made for four-wheel driving, but I've got no choice other than to keep going. The terrain here is a thick, dark blanket of rainforest that I'm desperate to get out of. I curse my stupidity.

I remember a moment with my father, long ago, in a rainforest north of Brisbane. I'd run ahead of him as the path curled around enormous trees. Suddenly alone, I sat on a giant tree root, waited, and cried. But no-one came to find me, to save me. I had to save myself, and I did. I found my way out, back to my father lying on the picnic rug, a beer in his hand, and eating a chicken sandwich Mum had packed for us. He hadn't even noticed I'd gone.

Finally, I see a clearing to pull into, and I breathe a sigh of relief. I check my phone: no service. Leaving the car to idle, I step onto the gravel shoulder, shake out the tension from my hands and arms, and breathe in the fresh, cool air. I'm shocked by how sheer the drop is, but the view is spectacular. A coastline of white sandy beaches and blue ocean runs as far as I can see. Inland, an expansive forest spreads out like lava from nearby hills all the way to a small sprawling town, split in two by a railway line. Sugar Creek, I guess. In the distance, curls of smoke spiral up from burning cane fields. As I turn to go, my eye catches something else: a blemish in the middle of the rainforest, brown and bare.

26

Ellen

The minute Ellen walked outside, the heat hit her, so oppressive she wilted like the leaves hanging motionless on the surrounding mango trees. Sweat slicked her skin as she marched down the street towards Mavis's house. She wanted to be rid of the pearls and rid of Mavis. Just the thought of her humiliation was enough to avoid her and Carolyn. She wasn't sure if it was her imagination, but they hadn't been at the pub as much since that day.

But somehow, she felt that Bert Hipworth had lied to her. Mr Taylor had known something, too; he hadn't been able to get away from her fast enough. She'd returned to Bert's house, but no-one had been home.

She'd drop off the necklace, then go again and have it out with him.

The street was full of neat houses with tidy gardens and painted fences. A truck was parked out the front of number fifty-one, Mavis's house. She glanced at her watch – seven thirty in the morning. Perhaps it was too early to call in. She walked up the palm-lined concrete path and knocked on the door. She thought she heard footsteps, so she knocked again and again. Nothing.

She marched back up the street to Bert and Carolyn's home.

Bert opened the door and frowned. His unshaven face looked tired and pale.

"Ellen? What brings you here so early?"

"I'd like to talk to you about my fiancé."

Bert looked around and stepped forward. "We've gone over this," he said impatiently. "He didn't turn up at the base. Look, I know this is hard, but you must accept that he's run out on you. It's not your fault. The bloke's a louse."

Ellen's fists clenched tight. "You're wrong, Bert. Dead wrong. I found someone who saw Hector and Billy at the base. Saw them going in and never saw them again. And there's another bloke, someone called Jonno, who's also missing. What do you have to say about that?"

He glared. "Now you listen here. I don't know who this other joker is, but he's led you up the garden path. I'm telling you, again, for the last time, there is no record of either of those blokes being there."

Bert cocked his head towards the interior. There was movement in the back of the house. Muted footsteps. He turned back, and his expression softened. "You know me. My reputation is impeccable. Why on earth would I lie to you?"

"Maybe you're covering up something. Maybe the experiments went wrong."

"That's quite an accusation, Ellen." Bert reached for her arm, his fingers cutting into her. "I think it's time you left."

"Who are you talking to, Bert?" Carolyn said, coming down the corridor.

Bert quickly dropped her arm.

"Oh, hi, Ellen. Bert, why haven't you invited her in? It's too hot to stand out there."

"Ellen was just leaving," Bert said. "It seems she's accusing me of lying to her."

Carolyn looked incredulous. "Is that true, Ellen? You're still persisting with this?"

"I'm …"

Words deserted Ellen. Her heaving chest filled with a silent wail.

"Well?" Carolyn asked.

"I've made a mistake," Ellen said.

She stumbled as she hurried down the footpath and grabbed the gate to steady herself. The front door slammed shut behind her.

*

Joan stared at her when Ellen arrived for work later that day.

"G'day, love. You alright? You look a little pale."

Despite being tired, Ellen nodded. "I'm fine."

Nothing anyone could do would lift the heavy weight sitting within her. She set ashtrays on the tables and wiped down the bar, uncomfortable under Joan's stare, knowing she had more to say.

"Listen, love. You don't have to do this all on your own."

Ellen scrubbed the counter harder. "I'm not sure what you mean. I think I can get the stain out."

"I know what's going on, love." Joan's voice was gentle.

"Know what?"

"You're expecting."

Ellen looked up, scarcely believing what Joan was saying. "Expecting?" Her chest tightened.

"I had my suspicions from the moment I met you. No-one shows up like you did and then plans a wedding in a week or two."

Ellen went back to scrubbing the table.

"You've had such an awful time. I'm worried about you, and … well, it's only going to get harder. Have you given any thought to what you'll do?"

Ellen gave up on the stain and threw the rag into the sink. "I'm trying not to think about it."

"You poor thing."

Joan unexpectedly wrapped her arms around her. Ellen pulled away and sniffed, wiping her eyes with the back of her hand.

"You've got time," Joan said. "Four or five months along?"

She nodded.

"I know you don't want to think about it, but you have to."

She wiped the tears from her face with her apron. "I don't know what to do."

"You can't work right up to the birth."

Was she getting the sack? How could this be happening?

"But—"

"I mean you can work here as long as you can, but you'll be tired being on your feet all day. Then there's the birth. You need to think about what's best for the baby and you. People will talk. They're already talking."

Her heart pounded. "What are they saying?"

Joan pursed her lips. Her voice was slow, steady, and calm. "They reckon young Billy ran because you were expecting. You're beginning to show, love."

Ellen fidgeted with the edge of her apron. It was painful to hear his name. Desperate to sit down, she stared at the floorboards, deep grooves in the timber from years of footsteps like hers.

"And we're going to help you."

"We?"

Joan seemed taken aback. "Why, me and Paul. And Carolyn and Mavis, of course."

"They know?"

Joan nodded. "They do. And you can count on us."

These people she'd only known for five weeks were there to help her. A voice inside warned her to be careful. She'd seen Carolyn only that morning, yet she'd said nothing.

"Why?"

Joan sighed. "Because, silly, you're a good worker, we like and care about you, and, well, that's the sort of people we are."

Ellen blinked, uncertain, then stood taller, fragile relief lifting her slightly. "Even Carolyn?"

"Of course, even Carolyn. She's very fond of you; she'll do anything to help."

Had she now lost a friend, an ally, in Carolyn? Bert was right. Should she have believed some fellow from the pub over him? Bert was liked and trusted by everyone in town, and she'd accused him of lying. Perhaps whoever told him Billy wasn't there was covering something up.

But she kept thinking back when Bert had come home, the night of the dinner. He'd been so late, so short, so shocked when he heard Billy's name.

"Contrary to what you might believe, you are not an outcast," Joan said.

"I don't know what to say. No-one has shown such kindness towards me before. Thank you."

Joan smiled. "And I know of a place."

"A place?"

"For unwed mothers."

The words sent a shudder through her. Homes for unwed mothers weren't for a woman like her. She was engaged.

Except …

The pit at the bottom of her stomach and the ache in her chest told her otherwise.

"… and it'll cost you nothing," Joan continued. "You can wait until it's time and then give the baby up for adoption."

Ellen looked at Joan's hand resting on the counter, her leg, swollen with varicose veins, propped on the footrest of an old stool.

"Adoption? I can't give my baby away," Ellen retorted. "This is my baby, mine and Billy's. What will he say when he comes back? It's out of the question."

Joan's voice was gentle, her eyes sympathetic. "He's not coming back, love. You know that. Plenty of couples would give their eyeteeth for a baby, and they'd raise the child the way it should be. Surely you can see that's best for the baby and you?"

"I just can't." Tears slid down her face again, and she fiercely wiped them away. "Now, if it's all right with you, I'll open the doors. We're ten minutes late."

*

Ellen sniffed in the charity shop – the air thick and musty. She pulled a plain beige dress off the rack.

"Can I help you, dear?" A thickset woman with crooked, yellow teeth smiled.

"I'm just having a look," Ellen said.

The shop window shuddered from a gust of wind, and a crack of thunder made them both jump.

"Goodness." The woman tittered. "I reckon it's going to pour in a minute. Stay in here and take all the time you want, dear. I'm Wanda by the way. Sing out if you need any help. I'll be back there."

Wanda scurried to the rear of the shop behind the counter.

Another crack of thunder and the daylight faded as the sky grew black.

Ellen pulled out another dress while the tropical thunderstorm raged, pounding fat droplets on the verandah awning outside. She settled on three dresses, two sizes larger than her normal size. Surely they'd do; she didn't bother trying them on.

Then Ellen found herself in front of a rack of used baby clothes. She stared at a pale-yellow lace layette and stroked the satin ribbon. She looked at the price tag and pulled her hand away – too expensive. If she did as Joan suggested, she wouldn't need any baby clothes …

She felt as unstable as the weather.

"They're almost brand new," Wanda said.

Ellen flinched as if she'd been caught doing the wrong thing.

Wanda sidled up to her. "They grow out of them that fast. It's a shame to pay full price."

Ellen held the dresses firmly in front of her. "I am looking for a gift. For my sister and everything is so expensive brand new."

The lie slipped out easily. A beam of sunshine filtered across the rack of clothes.

Wanda nodded and smiled. "Well, we have some very pretty things. Boy or girl?"

"Maybe something in white." She picked up a pale-yellow bunny rug, singlet, and shorts.

"The shorts are a bit too big for a newborn, love. Perhaps something like this blue jumpsuit instead? And your sister might need some nappies. I have a little stack out the back." Wanda leaned in too close and whispered, her breath stagnant as a swampy pond, "She lost the baby, and, well, you can understand why she didn't want the nappies in the house afterwards. I can give them to you real cheap."

Ellen reeled back, shocked that someone had lost their baby, a possibility she'd never considered. "I'll leave the nappies for now and just take these, please."

Ellen paid and hurried out of the shop with her parcels, dodging the steamy puddles and dripping leaves. Arriving home, she threw everything onto the bed. She hadn't wanted to think about her future without Billy. Buying the clothes had made her realise something – she would be an unwed mother, a fallen woman. She wrung her hands and paced. What was she to do?

She sat down in front of her diary – Billy's inscription a comfort to her: "Write when you miss me to help you feel as if I'm nearby."

Adoption. The word made her shiver. What would her baby think of her? Would he ask why he'd been given away? Why his mother didn't want him? She hadn't thought of the baby's sex until now. He was a boy; she was sure of it. Billy had so wanted a boy.

"I do want you, little one. I do," she whispered.

How could she raise a child on her own? She had no money and no prospects. If only she had a sister or a mother instead of a useless, drunken father. She was on her own.

Her hand rested on her stomach, and she felt a flutter. The baby? There it was again.

She grabbed her fountain pen, and emotions formed into a word, a sentence, a paragraph. She wrote page after page until her hand ached, and she felt better.

27

Dana

It's almost dark by the time I finish my house calls and return to the surgery. Today's mail sits on my desk along with a note from Linda saying she's taken my advice.

As I finish off my notes, my thoughts wander back to the mountain and that bare patch of ground. I wonder if there's a road to it so I can get a closer look.

I flick through the post until I see a white envelope from the hospital board. I stare at it, then put it aside and open the others. Finally, I can't ignore it and holding my breath, I rip it open. It's just an acknowledgement of my statement and a line saying they'll be in touch, and I shove the letter into my handbag.

The phone rings, and I jump.

"Dana, mate." It's Hannah. "Thought you'd be still there."

"I could say the same about you."

"How are you holding up?"

"Do you mean in Sugar Creek?"

"Yeah, that too, but with the whole Daniel business."

It's nice that she checks on me. "I'm okay. I got an

acknowledgement of my statement but no date for the hearing. It kills me, to be honest. I just want it over and done with instead of hanging over my head."

"It'll come when it comes. At least you don't have to see that bastard again and are unlikely to run into him."

"A thousand kilometres away in a small country town does help."

"Speaking of which, how's your cancer patch?"

"Another case this week. So, growing. Plus, I may have found that barren patch of ground."

"Go on."

"Besides getting lost up a mountain on a dirt road today, I got quite a good view of the whole area. In the middle of the rainforest is a big patch of brown. There's no doubt that it's been deforested, but why, I don't know."

"Whoa, so it *is* there. And just to make this more interesting, you'll never guess what I found."

"What?"

"A newspaper article from the sixties. Your Wally Gillespie made a complaint about Agent Orange. The paper tackled the government and the military, who denied it, of course. There was an investigation of sorts, although I can't find any outcome or findings. And the newspaper just seemed to let it go."

"No evidence of Agent Orange spraying, then?"

"Couldn't find any. All we have is Wally's claims."

"Who everyone says is a bit of nutter."

"Well, yes."

"But if there *was* an investigation, wouldn't they have cleaned up any evidence?"

Hannah snorts. "Now that's pure wishful thinking, my friend. They may have said they investigated and said there's nothing to see here. So how would they then do any clean up. No, my bet is they've swept this all under the carpet. I mean let's talk asbestosis. That's taken umpteen years and still hasn't been rectified. And let's see, we've known smoking kills people for decades, but are cigarettes still on the market? Yes, they are. You've got a pissy little town that no-one cares about, so don't expect the authorities to do anything. Your Mr Mayor doesn't give a toss, either. Be real, Dana. You've got an unusually high cluster of cancer. There's something big going on right under your nose."

"All I have is an empty patch of dirt in the middle of a rainforest that could just be ploughed land. Look, I hear what you say, but I think it's just one of those things. And I don't think you're right about Herb."

She clicks her tongue. "He said Wally was a wacko. Maybe he doesn't want to stir up trouble. It's not in his interests, is it?"

"Probably not," I say, suddenly wondering about Herb. "I spoke to Jeffries, the haematologist and an oncologist in Townsville. They just dismissed me; didn't want to know."

"Bloody typical. Some of those guys are just plain arrogant."

"They just don't have time to get involved with my little issue. Let's face it, I don't have much to go on. My credibility is at stake, and I don't have a great record."

"You need a sample from that patch of dirt. And from any nearby creeks and, of course, the town's water. I can tell you one thing: if that dirt has been contaminated it'll fuck people up for generations. You know that stuff stays in the dirt for decades, and every time it rains, it runs off into underground bore water, streams, creeks, and the town's water supply. Look at Vietnam. Veterans are making claims in the US, too."

I'm suddenly exhausted. "I'll get samples so at least we can rule it out. I suppose I should alert the council's environmental health officer, whoever that is."

"I'd sit on that until you get the samples tested. See what you're dealing with first, then we'll work out where to go. You'll need to write a report. Get as much evidence as you can, then slam the authorities with it so they can't fob you off. That's what I'd do."

"Yeah, perhaps that's the way to go. I don't want to alarm anyone until I've got my facts."

"Absolutely. Good luck, mate," Hannah says.

I grab my handbag and turn off the lights. What if the samples show something? Surely Herb would want to do the right thing. He seems decent, and he did fight for the town to get a GP. If what Wally has said is true, Herb's family could have been directly affected. I hope, for everyone's sake, that I'm just chasing a dead end.

As I'm locking the front door, someone taps on my shoulder.

"Bloody hell!" I squeal.

"Sorry, doc. Wasn't sure if you'd still be here."

I swing around and confront Steve, his black hair wild in the dusky light.

"You shouldn't have snuck up on me like that. I'm closed."

"Yeah, I realise that. Sorry again."

I stare at him. "Why are you here scaring me half to death?"

He looks uncertain and contrite, and I feel a little bad snapping his head off.

"Um … I wondered if you'd like to have a bite. At the pub."

"A date?"

"Oh, no, nothing like that." Now he looks nervous. "I … I wanted to talk to you about something."

Is he backing out of a date, or does he want a free medical consultation?

"Look, I'm pretty bushed and just want to go home."

I walk away.

"Sure, sorry. Maybe some other time."

I leave him there and go home, wondering what that was all about.

28

Ellen

The policeman dunked shortbread into his tea, thick jowls wobbling like jelly as he chewed and licked crumbs from his thin lips. Dunk, dunk.

"You need to accept that your fiancé" – his mouth worked around the biscuit, crumbs dropping—"was a scoundrel. You gotta move on, love."

"How dare you say that?" Ellen stood and leaned over his desk, close enough to smell the tea on his breath. "Why don't you stop eating, do your job, and find my Billy? Don't just sit there and give me platitudes and excuses and tarnish the reputation of a good man."

The policeman stopped chewing and lifted his head, his face breaking into a scowl. "I've got better things to do than listen to some hysterical woman." He stood up, towering over her, intimidating her. "I've been patient every time you've come in here, and lord knows it's been a lot, but there's nothing that can be done. Now get out of here before I lock you up."

Somehow, she made her way out of the police station, her body trembling, heart racing. She was losing control.

She ran down the street and onto the main highway, stopping only to catch her breath, reminding herself she was almost six months pregnant. Tall stalks of cane swayed in the fields on either side of the road, ready to be burned and cut.

She walked on and on, the disastrous encounter with the policeman hurtling through her mind. She'd moved from rage to embarrassment to despair and hopelessness. No-one was listening to her.

The barbed wire fence of the military compound loomed nearby; invariably, that's where she always ended up. The rumble of a vehicle approached, and she locked eyes with its driver, who glared as he drove through the gate.

It was Bert. She lifted her hand to wave him down, but he disappeared down the narrow gravel track, leaving a billowing cloud of dust.

She stood there madly swatting flies from her face, her arms, her legs – for how long she wasn't sure – staring through the fence at the scrub, the guard, the gate, the track; watching for something, anything other than a wallaby.

As she turned to go, something caught her eye: movement on the other side of the fence. From the compound, down the track Bert had driven on, limped a stocky man in a dark, wrinkled suit. He said something to the soldier and waited for the gate to open. After walking through, he rested a moment while the gate swung shut. He glanced at her, then turned and headed slowly towards town.

"Hello," Ellen said to him, not sure why she felt the need. "Nice day for it?"

The fellow stopped, lifted his dusty hat off his large balding head, and stared. "You gotta be kidding. It's stinking hot." His eye twitched below a jagged scar. "What are you doing out here?"

She shrugged and scratched her arm. "Going for a walk. Mind some company? I'm going back into town now."

"Suit ya' self."

He pushed his hands into his pockets, and they began walking.

"Why were you at the base?" she asked.

"What's it to ya?" he said, his voice deep and gravelly.

"I'm just making conversation."

He turned his head to her, his face unshaven, circles around his eyes. "Not sure you'll get much conversation from me. I'm tired, and the leg's aching."

"Sorry."

"Nothing for you to be sorry about."

They walked awhile in silence, she matching his slow pace. A long ribbon of sunshine struck the road ahead of them. Beyond were the first houses.

"Those blokes back there are the ones who should be bloody well sorry," he said.

She glanced at him, but he stared straight ahead. "Why?'

"Have you heard about the experiments they're doing out there?"

He stopped walking, and so did she. They'd reached the outskirts of town and stood in front of a run-down weatherboard house.

"Yes," she said, her heart racing. "Ex-soldiers, aren't they?"

He nodded. "I'm one of them. They told me I was going to test topical creams. Instead, they stuck a needle into me and next thing I woke up in a bed, cold and hot at the same time, screaming."

Her mind raced "That's terrible."

"Yeah, it was."

"And your leg?"

He straightened up and glanced around. "That's the thing. They buggered up my leg. 'Scuse the French. It was perfectly okay, and now it hurts like hell." He winced as they resumed walking. "They gave me some aspirin and a few extra dollars and sent me on my way. And here I am talking to you."

"Were you the only one with that reaction?"

"Dunno. I was the only one in the infirmary."

"They should have at least driven you home and given you more money for your trouble."

"You're dead right, lady. I should have got a lot more. But I was bellyaching that much they threw me out. Sick of the sight of me, they said."

"How long did they keep you in there?"

"What day is it?"

"It's Monday."

"Shit," he said, stopping to rub his leg. "Sorry again. I'm a bit stunned. It's been over a week."

"A week of lost wages and a sore leg? If I were you, I'd talk to someone about getting more money. It's the least they could do."

The cicadas started up, and he looked at her wide-eyed. "Yeah, you're absolutely right. Those bastards should pay."

He grunted and began walking, his face contorted in pain.

Ellen thought of Billy, and the baby moved under the hand she rested on her stomach. She thought about her fear and if Billy had suffered. She thought about Hector and Jonno.

"This is my place," he said, his face covered in sweat.

They stood under the eucalypts, the shade pleasantly cool. She wondered if she should help him inside. The garden was overgrown and paint peeled of the weatherboard house.

"I'm Ellen," she said.

"Fred." He tipped his hat.

"Will you be all right?"

"Yep," he said with a pained grin. "Just need to get off this leg, and I'll be right as rain."

"Thanks for walking with me."

"Nice talking to you, love."

"Nice talking to you, too. Hope your leg gets better."

He saluted and limped off into his tumbled-down old house.

*

That night she tossed and turned in her bed, threading her way through the cane, the smell sweet and earthy. I'm here, a voice said, calling to her. I'm here. It was behind her, then in front. She walked in circles, unable to find her way to it. I'm coming, she yelled. I'm coming. Where are you? Only a warbling magpie answered. The stale smell of burned cane filled her nose and mouth. Her legs blackened from ash. She turned away; flames licked the horizon.

She gasped awake in the early morning light, bathed in sweat, breath squeezing out of her. Just a nightmare. She lay there, not wanting to relive it, yet compelled to.

That afternoon before work, Ellen walked to the church she'd avoided since the wedding. She settled into a pew at the back and squeezed her eyes shut, breathing in the dust, the wax, the burned-out candle smoke.

She wasn't religious, but prayer was the only thing she had left.

Ellen sought the Lord's forgiveness for her unborn baby and for herself. She hadn't prayed like that since she was a small child: begging her mother to live, to be there when she woke up, for her smile, for her face not to be bruised, for her arm to be in one piece. She'd prayed for her father to stay off the booze, for his anger to be gone, for his belt to stay on. She'd prayed hard for Billy where ever he was knowing deep down that nothing would bring back what she wanted.

198

A hand touched her shoulder, and she jumped.

Carolyn sat beside her and reached for her hand. Ellen waited for the admonishment, but there was none.

"Are you okay?" Carolyn whispered.

"I'm sorry for what I said," she replied.

"Do you want to talk?"

Ellen nodded. She deserved harsh words from Carolyn. What she'd said to Bert was unforgivable.

"I was worried about you," Carolyn said. "It's only natural that you'd not believe Bert, and I told him not to be so hard on you. I'd probably do the same."

She slumped back into the bench.

"But honey, you can't burn all your bridges. I heard what happened yesterday, and, well, you just can't yell at our policeman. He means well, and he protects our community and—"

"I know. I know. I'm just so tired and overwrought. I just snapped."

"It's understandable, but with the baby on the way, you have to think of him … or her," she said, her mouth twitching into a weak smile.

Carolyn's gaze rested on her bump, and Ellen instinctively placed her hand there as if protecting him.

"Thank you for being so understanding."

"You're welcome. Now, when you're up to it, or whenever Mavis gets back from Townsville, we'll get together with Joan and work out what's best."

Ellen nodded. "I better go before I'm late for work."

*

A few nights later, Ellen worked late to help Joan with the stocktake. It was easy money, but by the time she got ready to leave, she was more exhausted than she realised. Her back, legs, and feet ached as she trudged home down Main Street. It was only ten o'clock, but there was no-one around. She stopped in front of the thrift shop to rub the small of her back and wondered whether she could afford the nappies with the extra money.

She began walking again and turned into the next street. The sky was clear, the stars bright. She passed houses, focusing on their dim lights, the rumbling voices and faint sound of music from within, the smoky scent from wooden stoves. She thought about Carolyn and her words. What was best, she'd said. Not what was best for her and the baby. Why did it bother her?

Joan had told her she looked too thin, questioned her about what she was or wasn't eating, and lectured her about looking after herself for the baby's sake. She could look after herself, she'd said. She'd been doing it for long enough. That thought brought her back to Billy, making her eyes prickle.

As she blew her nose, she thought she heard footsteps behind her. She looked around but saw no-one. She turned into her street, and the footsteps came back. Her senses heightened, and she walked faster, clutching her handbag and glancing back over her shoulder. Only shadows. She crossed the street, the footsteps still behind her.

She wasn't far from home. Just a little further. She glanced back. The shape of a man, a big man, coming closer, catching up. She ran, her heart thumping, almost breathless, as she raced through the gate and up the stairs to pound on the front door.

When Phyllis greeted her, Ellen barrelled inside and slammed the door shut.

"Why, Ellen, what's going on?"

"Someone's, someone's ..." she puffed, gasping for air.

"Come and sit down. Get your breath."

Ellen followed Phyllis into the kitchen and leaned against the table, trying to calm down. Her heart raced as she gulped the water thrust into her hands.

Phyllis watched her. "What happened?"

"I don't know. Maybe it's my imagination, but I thought someone was following me."

"Did you see anyone?

"A man. I crossed the road, and he crossed and—"

Then the tears came, hard and thick in heaving sobs.

29

Dana

It's Sunday afternoon, and I duck into the library to reborrow the book I've been reading. In an old weatherboard house, it smells musty and the whole place needs refurbishing.

Hayley, the librarian, squints at me through black-rimmed glasses. "Doctor Janssen, I heard you were after some history of the area."

News travels fast in this town. "Yes, I'm very interested," I say.

"I'm setting up a historical display. It could be a bit of a tourist attraction. I thought you might want to see some of our old local newspapers. Steve said it was a great idea, too."

"Did he? It is a great idea."

Her low heels clacking along the worn wooden floor, she leads me to a small, dingy room where a pile of newspapers rests on a table. "Here they are," she says proudly. "And I'm going to laminate some pictures and put them on the wall."

I don't want to burst her bubble, but I doubt tourists are going to spend their time here leafing through newspapers. She seems to want my approval, though, so I nod encouragingly.

"I've got something else that might interest you," she says, leafing through the stack. "You might be interested in the history of our mayor." She pulls out a newspaper– dated 1972

The front of the paper is a full-page obituary of Herb's grandfather: an upstanding leader of the community and biochemist during the war who led the research at the Sugar Creek military base.

"Very interesting. Do you have anything about the base where he worked?"

"These papers go back to 1945 when the war ended. It's just so fascinating to read about it. Sometimes, I take them home and imagine what it must have been like." She rifles through. "They're in date order. Here you go. This one is from 1948." She scans the front page. "What about this?" She hands it over and continues looking.

"Anything from the sixties?"

"I haven't finished sorting the date order yet. But maybe you could come back another time when I have the sixties' papers in date order."

June 1948 An article on the front page that catches my eye.

Barmaid Ellen Lambert, who was jilted at the altar by Billy Nolan, claims the Sugar Creek military base is responsible for his disappearance after participating in medical experiments for topical creams. Police Sergeant Alcott dismissed her claims as the hysteria of a woman wronged. "These things happen," he said. "She has to accept it."

Hannah mentioned the medical experiments, and here it is. Where is the military base? Can I find that barren patch of dirt again? That's what I have to do today.

"Dr Janssen?"

"Sorry. Yes, I'll come back." I hand back the newspaper. "Got to fly, Hayley. It'll be wonderful when it's finished, and I'll pop back again next week."

Hayley beams. "Glad you like it. I'll try to have them ready then."

I head over to the grocery store and walk straight into Herb who's in the fruit and veg section.

"Groceries?" he says, stating the obvious.

"Yep," I say. "Have you found out anything yet?"

He holds a mango midair and looks at me. "About?"

"The old council and medical files I'm after, remember? We discussed it last Sunday. At the cemetery. You said you'd look into it."

"Oh, yeah. Haven't had much time. Sorry."

I squeeze my fingers gently around an avocado. It's good enough and goes into my basket.

"I'm not surprised," I mumble.

"What?"

"You heard me."

And I walk off. I can't believe it. Hannah was right. Why would he want to look into this? He wants it to go away.

He catches up to me. "What's going on? Do you want to talk?"

A couple of women with prams and wriggling toddlers pass us. We both say hello to them.

"Yes, I do."

"Out the front?"

"That's as good a place as any."

I move away from him and get the rest of my shopping. He comes out as I'm putting my groceries into the boot.

"What was that all about?" he asks.

I slam the boot shut and fold my arms. "I don't think you're taking this seriously."

I tell him about my trip up Old Goanna Creek Road and the bare patch in the middle of the forest.

"That's Bald Hill."

"Oh, so you know about it?"

"Yep. Been around forever. Algae killed off a few acres, and it's been like that ever since."

"Algae? Who told you that?"

"Can't remember. Sort of known that story since I was a kid. They didn't want anyone to go there."

"I don't understand. Algae? Isn't that found in the water? Don't you think that's strange? Have you even been there?"

He looks as if I've slapped him and put him in handcuffs.

"Honestly? No," he says, shaking his head. "We were just told as kids that the algae was dangerous. I never thought about seeing for myself."

"And you call yourself a landscaper? Wouldn't you question that childhood story?"

"I guess it's kind of stupid, now that I think about it. Algae could be in the creek, but it can't wipe out a forest."

I take pity on him. A little. "Well, you were a kid. Anyway, I'm going there."

"Now?"

"After I put my groceries away. Why? Do you want to come?"

"Can't."

"What? Are you scared of a little childhood story?"

He frowns, looking annoyed. "I'm not scared. I've got a job on. Not everyone has the afternoon off."

"On a Sunday? Could you draw me a map, then?"

He looks at his watch. "By the time I draw a map, and you ask me half-a-dozen questions, I could drive there and back. Come on. The ute's just over there. But no hanging around." He seems tired.

I need him on my side, and he should see Bald Hill for himself. "Sure," I say. "Let me drop off my groceries first."

*

The air-conditioning is on full blast when I slide into the ute. It's a pleasant relief from the relentless humidity. I look for a place to put my handbag on the floor, but a hand trowel covered in red dirt forces me to hold it on my lap.

Herb notices and reaches down past my leg. "Sorry, I'll get that out of the way," he says as he flings the trowel into the back. "Ready?"

I nod and brush the dirt from my arm and bag.

The clouds are building towards the hills, and I hope the rain holds off. I don't fancy walking through a sludge of possibly contaminated dirt.

"Hayley told me about her historical display," I say.

Herb keeps his eyes on the road. "Yeah, she mentioned it to me. I think it'll be good."

"She showed me some old newspapers, and I read your grandfather's obituary. I didn't know he was a biochemist."

We turn off the highway onto Old Goanna Creek Road.

"Quite well respected in his field, according to Mum. He worked out at the old base."

"How long was he there?"

"Years, I think. Since the war, at least. He started the research centre there."

"Where exactly is this mythical base?"

"Just ahead," Herb says, flicking on the indicator. "It's hard to spot."

He pulls over, engine idling, and points his thumb to the right. Squinting through his window, I make out a large iron gate almost hidden by scrub.

"In there?"

"Yep."

"I heard they did medical experiments after the war, and it was closed down for a bit."

"I think that's common knowledge. I don't know much else." He drives on. "I did make some enquiries, though. The council looks after the base now. Apparently, that's where the archives are stored. But I haven't had time to grab the keys and check."

He is trying. "Thank you. Sorry I was a bit testy before."

We pass the Jamieson's place, their car parked next to the house.

"I should have kept you informed," he says.

"How long have you been mayor?"

"Twelve months. Why?"

"Just wondered."

There's a lot he doesn't know, but is it his job to know every detail of the area's history? After all, he left when he was a kid. Perhaps I should talk to Joan or Mavis. They seem to know everything.

We pass the Harper's and Thompson's houses, and Herb turns left into a dirt road at a sign I'd missed the other day: "Bald Hill Road."

"I think I could have followed these instructions," I say.

Herb glances at me and smirks.

"I could have."

"We're not there yet."

The road is rough, hugged by tall trees. Soon he pulls over on a single lane small bridge and reaches across me to open the glove box. His arm brushes against my leg, and his touch jolts me. "Excuse me," he says. He grabs a map, studies it, then folds it up and throws it onto the ledge behind us.

We keep going and turn down another narrow dirt road. The faded sign says "Wombat Hole Track." The trees give way to weeds and the odd bedraggled patchy scrub. Nothing else seems to grow.

"Did the council clear all this?"

Herb pulls up, engine idling. "I don't think this is man-made, somehow."

"No-one ever wondered why?"

"I doubt anyone's come out here."

"But doesn't anyone check the roads? Like the council?"

"I don't know!" He drags his hand down his face and looks at me. "The thing is, the council was corrupt for years. Then some clueless administrators took it over five years ago. We've only just returned to elected officials, and it's been catch-up ever since."

He accelerates and turns into a narrower track where the trees are tall and lush.

"It seems to be okay along here," I say.

"Yeah," he says. "I'll have to push this up the priority list and get someone out here. The road is terrible."

And it is. We bump along, slowly dodging deep puddles of brown water. Bush scratches at the side of the car.

After about ten minutes, he finally stops and turns off the engine. "We walk from here."

I don't see a walking track, and the road is barely wide enough for more than two cars. Luckily, I have my runners and jeans on. I look at Herb's feet. "New shoes?"

He smiles. "My foot's heaps better. I should have told you."

"And perhaps as a caring doctor, I should have asked."

He laughs. He actually laughs. I'm surprised for a moment until his serious face comes back. He pushes through the undergrowth to a track that clearly hasn't seen a pedestrian for years, and I regret my burst of enthusiasm. Then he stops, and I almost run into him. There it is. Bald Hill. And it really is bald. A blank canvas of red-brown dirt. It's quiet, too, as if the birds and every other living creature knows not to be here.

"It's quite eerie," I say, folding my arms.

Herb picks up a damp clump of soil and rubs it through his fingers.

"I don't know if you should be touching it," I say.

"There's definitely no sign of algae," he says as if he can't fathom why he believed the lie for so long. "I don't know what's happened here, but it doesn't look right. We should grab some and get it analysed. You got a bag or a container?"

"Shit. That's what I forgot." The whole reason for being here, and I have nothing. I can't believe how stupid I am. I dig around in my oversized handbag and pull out a specimen jar. "What about this?"

"That's as good as anything. And sterile, too?"

"It certainly is. And before you ask, I don't usually carry a spare specimen jar in my handbag."

He gazes at me a moment with a hint of a smile before shrugging. "If you say so." He takes the jar and scoops soil into it, then rubs his hands together to brush off the dirt.

"It's not much," as he examines the contents.

I rummage in my handbag. "Oh, I do have a small plastic bag. Will this do?"

"It's better than the pee jar." He scoops up another handful. "Should have brought the trowel." He holds up the bag. "That should do it."

Unfortunately for us, the heavens open, and raindrops, big and fat, fall on my face.

"Shit," he says. "We better get back to the car."

I bolt back up the track. Herb yells, and I turn in time to see him trip. He tries desperately to correct his balance but falls headlong into the mud. The look on his face is priceless, somewhere between disbelief and embarrassment. He's quickly on his feet and unlocks the car.

I stifle the urge to laugh, but it doesn't work, and by the time I'm in the front seat, I'm positively belly laughing, holding my stomach.

"Never seen anyone sprawled in the mud?" he says, laughing, too. He has mud down the side of his face.

I shake my head as I just can't seem to stop, but I wrestle for control and composure. "Not like that." I find some tissues in my bag and wipe the side of his face. "Hold still … Sorry, but that glob of mud would have gone into your eye."

He looks in the rear vision mirror, and I hand him another tissue which he uses to wipe the rest of his face and his ear. "Better?"

I wipe my face, too, and pull out my wet ponytail so my hair can dry off. "Much better."

The rain has eased off, and he starts the car. We drive in silence for a while over the creek which has risen, white water rushing, leaves still dripping.

"Thank you," I say.

He glances at me. "What for?"

"For the laugh. Even though it was at your expense. I needed it."

"I suppose it's been full-on since you got here," he says.

"Something like that." The clouds clear, and the bitumen road looks dry. "But I'm settling in now, finding my feet."

His eyes are firmly on the road ahead, the laughter gone, serious face on. "I'll find some time to go out to the base. Now that I've seen that site for myself, I've got a lot more questions."

"The sooner the better. And I'd like to talk to Joan or Mavis. Surely, they'll know what's happened and can maybe back up Wally's claims."

"Joan's been here since before the war and will definitely be able to fill in the gaps."

"Why don't we see Joan next Sunday? Then, if you get the keys, I'd like to come with you to the base. If that's okay with you."

"Sure," he responds quickly. "I think we should. I'll tell Joan we'll drop in."

*

At ten o'clock the next day, Linda brings in a cup of tea and a couple of messages.

I return the first call – Hannah.

"I actually saw the brown patch up close," I say. "It's completely denuded. It's creepy, nothing but dirt and silence. Not even a bird."

"God," she says. "So, it's real?"

"Yep, and surrounded by tropical forest."

"Got some more interesting news for you."

"About the spraying?"

"No, not about that. It looks like someone else is investigating."

"Someone else?" I tap my pen on my notepad.

"I had a call from a journo from the *Sun Tribune* asking all sorts of questions."

"Why's he ringing you?"

"I deal with all the media enquiries."

"Do you?"

She laughed. "No! They patched him through 'cos no-one else would talk to him. But don't be surprised if he contacts you."

"What sort of questions?"

"Things like type of cancer cases, who's affected in the area."

"There's not much point in talking to me. I can't say anything, given patient confidentiality and all that. What's his name?" My pen is poised.

"God, I knew you'd ask me that. I didn't get his full name. Steven something. Anyone nosing around with that name?"

"Nope. The only Steven or Steve I know is a builder. Though he got here just before me."

"It must be him. How many Steves are there?"

" A heap. No, it won't be him. He's a bit of a tosser and besides he's a builder. He's off the list. Anyway, I'll wait and see if he contacts me. If the media gets hold of this first, it won't be good for the town. They're trying to build up tourism."

"Or maybe it'll speed up the whole process. Think about it. If it breaks in the papers, everyone will demand to know what's going on. Tourism will be the last thing to worry about," Hannah says.

"I know, but it's not fair to spring it on everyone before we have evidence. It'll just cause panic. Besides, it might be nothing."

"If it is something, your mayor won't want it known."

She's right. "I better go. I'll let you know if the journalist contacts me."

I hang up and remember Herb still has the soil sample.

30

Ellen

Walking into the Ladies' Lounge, Ellen saw Carolyn seated at a table for four and Joan on her feet, her face grim. What on earth had she done wrong?

"Why didn't you tell me about being followed the other day?" Joan asked, one hand perched on her hip and the other resting on a chair.

Carolyn stared at Ellen, an unlit cigarette teetering between her fingers.

"How did you know?" Ellen blurted.

"Phyllis bailed me up in the street and demanded to know why I'd allowed you to walk home alone after ten o'clock at night."

Ellen looked from Carolyn to Joan. "It's not a big deal. I'm not even sure."

"Not sure?" Carolyn said, frowning. "This is a serious matter for all women in this town, Ellen."

"I was tired, and well … I don't know. Look, it hasn't happened again."

Joan folded her arms. "That's because you won't be working back again. You'll leave at six on the dot. You've got a baby to think about."

"I need the overtime money, Joan, to look after this baby," Ellen snapped.

"Well, that's why we're here," Joan said, sitting down.

Ellen pulled out a chair and sat too. "Are we waiting for Mavis?"

"She's not back yet," Carolyn said, lighting her cigarette.

"Is she *still* in Townsville?" Joan asked.

Carolyn dragged on her cigarette. "As far as I know."

"Is she ever coming back?" Ellen said, wondering if Mavis had forgotten about her pearls.

Carolyn shrugged and blew smoke across the table. "No idea. It's not my business."

"You had a falling out?" Joan said.

"No!" Carolyn retorted. "She's got her own life, and she's a big girl."

"She got a fella?" Joan said, a knowing look on her face.

"How do I know?" Carolyn snapped back. "We're not here to talk about her. We're here to help Ellen."

Joan cleared her throat. "Yes, yes, you're right. I took the liberty of picking this up the other day." She spread a leaflet across the table. "You don't have to look at it now. Maybe just read it at home."

Ellen shifted uncomfortably as she read the title: "St Andrew's Maternity Home."

"It looks so lovely, Ellen," Carolyn gushed. "It has nice gardens, and the rooms are spacious and clean, although you do have to share. That's okay. It's not for long."

Ellen glanced at the black-and-white photos of smiling faces, a manicured lawn, white bedspreads, and fresh-cut flowers in vases.

She turned the brochure over and glimpsed the words "For unwed mothers."

She'd have to give it some thought; she knew that. There was no hospital in town, but this place had midwives and doctors, according to the brochure.

"I took the liberty of enquiring about spots, and they said they were filling up fast," Joan said.

"Must be baby season," Carolyn chuckled.

Joan shot a disapproving look towards Carolyn, then turned her attention back to Ellen. "I hope you don't mind, but I put your name down."

Ellen jerked her head up. "What?"

"They said you could change your mind," Joan continued. "It's only to get a booking. At least now you have options."

"That's very thoughtful of you, Joan. Don't you think that's thoughtful, Ellen? At least you have options," Carolyn said, stubbing out her half-smoked cigarette.

Words stuck in her throat. She didn't know whether to be angry or grateful. How dare they interfere? All she could say through gritted teeth was, "Thank you."

Carolyn clasped her hands and tilted her head. "And what do you think you might do afterwards?"

Ellen folded her arms. "I'm not sure what you mean."

"Do you think you might like to come back here or move on and make a new life?"

Carolyn's singsong voice irritated her, and she caught her sideways glance at Joan. She felt this whole thing had been rehearsed. Perhaps they were trying to get rid of her because she was an embarrassment to the town.

"I'd have you back working here in a heartbeat," Joan said. "But all Carolyn is … all we're wondering is … have you any plans once you've given up the baby?"

Ellen's head began pounding, and the baby shifted. "I don't know yet. I want to keep the baby."

Carolyn sat back in the chair, crossing her arms about her waist. "Of course you do, but how will you raise, feed, and clothe him? Who will look after the baby while you work?"

Ellen felt her cheeks flush. Why were they so pushy? She chewed the inside of her mouth and jiggled her knee under the table. "I'm not sure yet."

The two women seemed to talk over each other.

"You've got to think about the baby."

"It's best for the baby."

"If you love your baby, you must do what's best for him."

Ellen had never felt claustrophobic before, but right now, she was trapped. She clenched her jaw and looked around the room: the floral pattern of the pressed iron walls, a cobweb hanging from the corner window, and a beam of sunshine burning into the worn, green carpet. A panicky longing to get out sat in her limbs.

"Well?" Joan said gently.

She could no longer ignore her situation. She wanted to argue, to fight, to say they were wrong. She'd be fine on her own, and she'd have the baby and then …

Then what?

She had to face the fact; she had no idea. No idea about what she'd do or how she'd cope. Unmarried with a child, dependent on her for everything.

"These people will find your baby a good home, with a mother and father who will love him like you would," Joan said. "I don't think you've got much choice, love."

Ellen picked up the brochure and shoved it into her apron pocket. "I'll think about it."

She pushed the chair back, mumbled her thanks, and went back to work.

*

That night she pulled the brochure out. "A haven," it said. "A place to have your baby safely in comfort and for little cost."

She put it down and rubbed the bump that was her baby. *I don't want to give you up, but how can I look after you?* Perhaps they were right. Perhaps the best thing to do is to hand him over to a couple who could give him everything she couldn't.

*

A month later, she was at the greengrocer. A woman in a blue hat stared at her and tutted.

Ellen turned and frowned. "Excuse me?"

"You should be ashamed of yourself."

Ellen blinked, aghast. "What are you talking about?"

Another woman clutching a toddler on her hip sidled up alongside. "We don't need your kind in our respectable town."

"Look at her. Brazen hussy. I suppose you think working in the pub you might trick another poor hapless chap into marrying you?"

"I … I don't know what you …" The words dried up in Ellen's throat as the shock hit her like a slap across her face.

The woman behind the counter joined in. "I ain't goin' to serve someone like you. Put ya stuff down, and get outta my shop."

Ellen dropped the fruit and fled. "Slut!" She heard someone say as she left.

Shaken, she made her way home, certain that everyone was staring at her, the insult ringing over and over in her ears. She fumbled with her keys and turned the handle, only to find that the door wouldn't open. She'd taken to locking her door since being followed.

"What on earth?"

She turned the key again, and the door opened.

"Idiot!" Her mind was in a fog, trying to remember if she had even locked it in the first place. "Must remember to lock the door."

She glanced around as she threw her handbag on the bed. "Neat as a pin," Billy would have said. She kicked off her shoes and lay down, rubbing her swollen feet, her stomach protruding more than she'd expected. How could she walk down the street now? Slut – such a horrible word. Is that what everyone was saying behind her back? Perhaps Carolyn and Mavis were thinking that, too. She hadn't seen Carolyn since their meeting weeks ago, and she knew Mavis had returned yet hadn't come by to collect her pearls. Only Joan and Paul were on her side, but how long before the women of the town stopped their husbands from coming to the pub?

Her legs and back ached. She heaved herself off the bed and pulled her dress over her head. She'd run a bath and soak. As she made her way into the bathroom, she froze as she passed the kitchen table.

There sat an envelope, her name scrawled across the front.

The breath heaved out of her. Someone had been in her room. Phyllis perhaps? But she always left mail on the front doormat. She looked under the bed and crept up to the bathroom door, half expecting someone to be there. But there was no-one, and nothing appeared touched or moved.

She stared at the envelope – an ordinary, white envelope, although bulky – and picked it up with trembling hands. Sliding her finger under the seal, she loosened the flap, her heart racing, tipped the contents onto the table, and then sat heavily on the chair.

She counted out one hundred pounds, hardly believing her eyes.

There was a note, the writing unfamiliar: "Take the money and leave. Build a new life."

She turned it over and over, expecting something else to materialise, but there was nothing. Who could have given her more than six months of wages? Joan? Carolyn? She shook her head and counted the money again, trying to make sense of it, but the effort was too much.

Maybe Phyllis knew something. She threw on her dress and raced up the stairs.

"Hello, dear," Phyllis said. "You look like you've seen a ghost. That man hasn't followed you again, has he?"

"No, no, nothing like that. I'm just puffed from climbing the stairs."

"Come in, and I'll make us a cup of tea."

"I wondered if you collected any mail for me today by any chance?"

Phyllis shook her head. "Sit down and rest yourself. You'll have a cup of tea?"

"A cuppa would be nice." She settled on the kitchen chair and decided to say nothing about the money.

While Phyllis made the tea. "Stay right there and rest."

Phyllis looked at her over her teacup. "Have you decided what you're going to do?"

Ellen put her cup down. "Do?"

"About the baby?"

"I'm thinking about going to St Andrew's Maternity Home. What do you think?"

"I've heard of it. I'll hold your room for you rent-free, even if you decide to keep the baby," Phyllis said carefully. "But the easiest thing would be to let him go to a good family and for you to start again."

"I've lost everything, Phyllis. Everything. I don't know if I can face losing my baby, too."

Phyllis leaned across and touched Ellen's arm. "I said it's the easiest option. But regardless of what you decide, I'm here if you need me."

"Thanks for the cuppa and for your support. It means a lot to me. After all, I've still got time."

She could start a new life. Someone meant for her to have that money, but how long would it last? Now she had more options, and the possibilities churned through her mind.

The baby kicked.

31

Dana

Herb and I are standing on Joan's neat and tidy front porch. No sign of dust or leaves despite the wind from last night's storm.

"Joan's lived here in this town since before the war," Herb says as he presses the doorbell, its singsong chime echoing inside the weatherboard house.

"She'll know what happened at Bald Hill," I say.

"She might not know anything."

"You did. We should start with that, don't you think?"

He shrugs. "Don't know."

Don't know? I open my mouth to say something when the door opens.

Joan beams, her eyes shining with delight. "Herb, how are you love?" she says before turning to me, her eyebrows raised. "And Doctor Janssen? You didn't tell me you were bringing the doctor, Herb. I hope it's not a house call intervention."

I'm not sure what that's supposed to mean, but I'm annoyed that Herb hadn't told her. I regret leaving the arrangements to him.

Herb laughs and glances at me. "No, Joan. Dana wanted to tag along."

Tag along? I glare at him.

He looks startled for an instant. "Hope that's okay," he says as he ushers me through the door.

"'Course it is. Come in. Nice to see you, Dr Janssen."

"Thank you," I say, stepping in front of Herb. "I hope you don't mind me dropping in on you like this."

"It's lovely to have visitors," she says. It's hard to tell if she is pleased or not.

The home smells of mothballs and last night's fatty roast lamb. We follow as she slowly hobbles down the cool,¬ dark corridor of her Queenslander. She really should see me about those swollen ankles, but I don't say anything, given her alarm at my presence.

"You have a lovely old home," I say, looking around at the timber, tongue-in-groove wall panelling.

She turns slowly to look at me with milky-blue eyes and smiles. "Lived here since before the war. I tried living in the pub but just couldn't relax. Anyway, I have all the mod cons, courtesy of my wonderful grandson. He fixed my kitchen, does repairs, and looks out for me when I need him."

"He does wonderful work," I say.

"Yes, he does. Best in town." Joan puffs out her chest in pride.

Mavis sits in a sunroom just off the kitchen and smiles as we enter.

"Now, you know Mavis." Joan raises her voice to her. "You know Dr Janssen. Remember we met her at the pub?"

"'Course I do. My daughter works for her. She says lovely things about you, dear."

"So nice to see you again too."

"G'day, Mavis," Herb says. "You're looking well."

"I am well," Mavis says. "Any fitter, and you'd be in trouble."

She laughs, and Herb turns crimson as he plonks himself into an armchair.

"Do you need any help?" I ask as Joan puts on the kettle and gets cups and saucers from the cupboard.

"Take these, love." She hands me exquisitely patterned bone china cups.

"These are beautiful," I say.

"Wedding present from the thirties. It's nice to bring them out every so often."

"Have you lived here since then?"

"Yes. Married here, bought a pub with my husband, Paul, and I love it. I hope you like it here too."

"It's wonderful, and I can see why you never left. I saw the display in the library. I'm surprised there's no historical society in town."

Joan grunts and hands me a plate of biscuits. "It's terrible. That woman doesn't know anything."

"Really?" I say innocently, even though I agree with her.

"I know everything there is to know about this town, and I told her she should have come to me in the first place. But there's no telling these youngsters."

"And that's why I'm here," I say, pleased that she seems willing to open up. "I'd love to hear your recollections. Especially about Bald Hill."

By the alarm on her face, I've mentioned something touchy, but she quickly composes herself. "My memory isn't very good now. Can you take those and put them on the coffee table?"

I do as I'm told, hoping I haven't jeopardised everything. Herb is splayed on the armchair, picking at what I presume is a splinter from his thumb.

"You must be important," Mavis says. "She only gives me a cracked mug." A coarse chuckle builds, turning into a phlegmy cough.

"Are you all right?" I ask, ready to assist her.

Mavis nods. "Went down the wrong way. At least I'd be in good hands if I was choking." She chuckles again.

I really like her.

While she pours the tea, Joan chats about Jack and how he should find a good girl and settle down, but not with that strange-looking girl, Crystal. I nod politely, looking for an opening to get back to what she might know. Herb stares vacantly at the ceiling as if he's heard this before.

"And so should you, Herb. It's time," Mavis says. She turns cheekily to me, her eyes boring in. "He's a very eligible bachelor, you know."

"I'm not ready for another relationship," I blurt.

Joan stops pouring, holding the teapot in midair. Herb shifts about, staring at his big feet. It suddenly occurs to me that he might think it's a possibility. God, I really need to steer the conversation to the spraying. And Herb is not helping in the slightest. Only the whir of the ceiling fan breaks the awkward silence.

Mavis's eyebrows shoot up. "What happened to the last one?" she says.

I feel my face reddening now that I'm reluctantly in the spotlight. Even Herb shoots me a look. "It … um, it didn't work out. These things happen. And now I'm too busy working."

"Good for you, love," Joan says.

"Watch that one. She's into matchmaking," Mavis says.

"Don't be ridiculous. It was one time. You're the one trying to matchmake," Joan retorts.

Herb takes a homemade chocolate chip biscuit from Joan's plate and stays out of it by throwing the whole thing into his mouth.

"She learned her lesson," Mavis says, turning back to me.

"Anyone we know?" I ask, hoping to deflect any further probing.

Joan hands a cup to Herb, who doesn't drink tea. I wonder how he'll get out of this.

"Mavis and Wally," Joan says, passing around the milk. "They were apparently seeing each other for months before I found out. Kept disappearing to the coast. Then they split up, and Mavis took off. I merely got them back together when she came back. Late fifties, wasn't it?"

Mavis looks over her teacup. "You're telling the story."

"Even arranged their wedding. Herb's grandmother was bridesmaid, and his dad the ring bearer. Ah, it was a lovely wedding."

Mavis rolls her eyes. "It was okay."

Herb puts his cup down, untouched, and gets straight to the point. "We wondered what you knew about Bald Hill and the spraying done by the military in the early sixties. I know it was a long time ago, but do either of you remember anything?"

Mavis holds her cup midair. "Nasty business, that place. Your grandfather did the wrong thing."

"My grandfather?" Herb looks puzzled.

Joan interrupts. "Don't mind her. Your grandfather did nothing wrong. She wasn't even here in the sixties. You mean the crop dusting? It was done all the time. They were testing new fertilisers and pesticides."

I get the impression Joan's been asked this before. It all sounds quite rehearsed, and I glance at Mavis. Her lips are pursed in disapproval, but I can't tell if it's about the spraying or Joan's dismissal.

"Do you know what exactly they were spraying?" I ask Mavis. "Did they spray around Bald Hill?"

"There was an algae outbreak there," Joan says. "We were told never to go there for fear of spreading it,"

Mavis puts her cup down with a bang. "That military base was doing experiments on men. If it wasn't for Wally, that place would still be open. And that's what I said to that young friend of Jack's when he was here last week for lunch."

Joan looks indignant. "He was very nosy. Insinuated that the town has been poisoned, which is ridiculous. I mean, if it was, we'd all be dead or dying. He was asking all these questions and got quite rude about it. Fancy dredging up a thing like that."

"Who was asking?" Herb says.

"Steve someone. He works with Jack. I didn't like him one bit," Joan says.

Could this be the journalist, Hannah mentioned? Can't be.

"Steve Messina? He's a nice bloke. New in town," Herb says.

"Well, he's not that nice," Joan says, pursing her lips. "Enough of the past. I've heard that you're bringing in tourist buses, Herb. That's so good for the town. Tell me all about it."

It's clear that Joan doesn't want to discuss the military base and knows exactly what Herb likes to talk about. While she's engaged with him, Mavis and I take the empty cups, and Herb's full one, into the kitchen.

"You mentioned the military base was doing experiments, Mavis."

"Horrible business, especially when young Billy went missing. Then Ellen ... I was truly scared for my life. If Bert found out what I did ... I hate to think what would have happened to me."

Is she talking about the woman in the article I'd read last week? I wish I'd taken more notice. "Who are Billy and Ellen? And what were you scared of?"

Mavis looks like she's somewhere else, in a time I'm not part of.

"Mavis?"

She looks at me, eyes suddenly sharp. "Be careful of that Steve man. He's not nice. Now, I better trot off home. Linda needs lunch, and she has to find something for me."

She walks abruptly back into the sunroom. "Herb, be a dear and give me a lift home."

"Of course," he says.

In the car, I twist around in my seat. "Do you know what they were spraying back then?"

Mavis narrows her eyes, her voice dropping into a coarse whisper. "I'm not allowed to talk about it. It was bad enough when Wally made such a kerfuffle. There was all sorts of trouble." She brings her hand to her lips as if zipping them shut.

"Oh?" I say. "Who says you're not allowed to talk?"

Mavis jerks her head in the direction of Joan's house. I glance at Herb, who says nothing.

We continue the short distance to Mavis's house in silence. I'm not convinced she has dementia, either. She seems smart as a whip, and I'm not buying her forgetfulness act. She knows a lot more than she lets on, but I'm not going to get much more out of her right now.

I help Mavis to the front door. Not that I'm much help; she shrugs off my arm, and I hover behind her.

Back in the car, I turn to Herb. "Off to the base now?"

He looks confused.

"You did say we'd go after we saw Joan."

"I forgot all about it. Sorry," he says, not looking too contrite. "I've been really busy."

Frustration bubbles inside of me. "We've just wasted our time. We got no information at all. And what's the deal with saying I was tagging along? This was my idea in the first place. I'd have been better off without you."

Herb starts the car and sighs. "Yeah, well, those two can be like that. They only want to talk about what they want. I thought it'd be better to have you lob in with me rather than pre-warn them. They don't like people prying, especially people they don't know. See how they bagged poor old Steve?"

I yank on the seatbelt and slam the tongue into the buckle. "Oh, really! You know, we doctors, especially women doctors, are privy to a hell of a lot more secrets than the average male mayor. We happen to be entrusted with a lot of information. And now we've wasted more time. Leave it with me, and I'll tackle them again. On my own."

He looks surprised. "I didn't think …" he says, backing the car and turning. "You're probably right."

Apology accepted I want to say as I look out the window, mulling over what the two women had said. "I'll get the keys and sort out the files. Don't worry about that."

"No," he says firmly, stopping at an intersection. "I'm sorry that I let you down, but I'm the one who should go out to the base. You can come if you want. There actually has been a lot on. I'm really sorry. Am I forgiven?"

I soften under his gaze, anger dissipating. I know he works hard, and his heart is in the right place, even if he's stretched.

"Okay," I say. "I'm worried, that's all. I want to get to the bottom of this before anyone else does. Steve is already asking strange questions, don't you think?"

"He's an inquisitive guy," Herb says.

"There actually is a journalist called Steven making enquiries about all this. I've been warned that he wants to talk to me."

Herb's hands tense on the steering wheel. "And you think our Steve is him? Is that what you're driving at?"

"I don't know, but he was asking about the town being poisoned. Isn't that a strange thing to ask?"

Herb scoffs. "If he's a journalist, then I'm a brain surgeon."

"All I'm saying is there's someone else investigating, and I've got patients falling sick and dying. Something needs to be done."

He pulls up outside my house. "We're on the same page about that."

I wonder if he really is levelling with me. "Do you? It's not really in your interests, is it? Let's face it, you're a politician. If this gets out, tourism here will be dead. You've been great at pretending that you're concerned, but I think you're just humouring me."

He drags his hand through his hair and turns to me, his face pained. "That's absurd. If I didn't care about my community, I wouldn't have become mayor or bloody well employed a doctor, let alone you."

"Then what have you done about the soil sample? You said you'd drop it off."

He looks at me blankly. "I … I … It's still in my shorts. They're being washed while I'm out." He blinks and groans. "Sorry."

I shake my head and slam the car door. I can't rely on Herb.

After he's gone, I head back out to Bald Hill, hoping like hell I can find the place again.

32

Ellen

Lugging her suitcase, Ellen stopped to rest at the top of the stairs just before the ornate front door of the triple-storey timber house. She looked around at the wide-set verandah, set off with white fretwork and surrounded by gardens. The house was high enough to glimpse the sea beyond rolling hills. The nearest town was half an hour away, and Sugar Creek another hour beyond that. According to the pamphlet, it dated back to 1872 when the Hendersons, a prominent family who made their money from sugar cane, lived there, raising their ten children. Thirty years later, the St Andrew's Anglican Church bought it, converted it into a school, and then a "home for unwed mothers."

She waited until Paul drove off in his truck, trailing a soft mist of dust down the gravel driveway, before taking a deep breath and opening the front door.

The smartness of the exterior wasn't the same as soon as she crossed the threshold into a corridor of worn floorboards and peeling wallpaper.

Inside, she was met by two paper-skinned nuns, their faces lined in permanent scowls of disapproval and judgement. There was no point explaining her situation; no-one believed her. The house was filled with subdued young women like her.

The centre of her life for the next two months was the kitchen – endless chopping, dicing, and frying, and the peeling, dry skin of hands too long in hot soapy water. Nights were spent crammed into hot, stifling rooms, listening to girls crying, sniffing, and wailing. No talking to or getting to know the story of each girl who worked, and disappeared within weeks. Every morning she woke to the shrill sound of the whistle and decided to pack up and leave before remembering within minutes, there was nowhere else to go. Each day, the baby kicked and pressed on her organs, protesting the lack of room in her ever-growing abdomen.

*

The pain was unbearable. Then came relief, just long enough to catch her breath, before her body contorted again with pain, she hadn't known possible. The midwife's words didn't register. Her body screamed from within, commanding her to shrug off hands as she crawled towards the corner of the room. A howl from deep inside her rose to a crescendo of sound followed by a minute of relief.

"Ellen, you need to listen to me. You need to be in the bed, not on the floor. It's not done to have a baby like this."

The invisible knife twisted again, taking her breath away.

"Please don't let me die," she screamed.

"You're not dying. You're having a baby, and it's coming now! Get up!" the midwife yelled.

Ellen allowed the woman to pull her up. "Oh, god. Make it stop," she sobbed. "Please make it stop."

She fell on the bed, and the invisible knife stabbed again and again.

She tried to kick, but the midwife's hands were too strong, roughly pulling her legs wide and pushing her feet into stirrups.

"You're nearly there."

"I can't," Ellen cried. A demon had possessed her body, tossing it around, contorting it, stabbing at it with blinding savagery.

"You can," the midwife said calmly. "Now, I want you to listen. Just focus on what I say. Okay?"

Ellen nodded and let the voice in until her body convulsed and writhed as she began pushing the thing out of her.

"Stop! Don't push yet. Hold it in."

She tried, but her body, like a runaway train, had its own mission.

"Now, push with everything you've got, dear. NOW!"

And she let her body take over, pushing the agony out of her.

"The head's crowning."

Is that good? she wondered. What's a crown? But there was no time to think; the knife twisted.

"One last push as hard as you can."

With a final, mighty thrust, something slippery slid through her legs, and, just like that, the pain vanished. She fell back onto plump pillows, puffing like she'd run a hundred miles, her body dripping in sweat, weak and shaking.

A cry opened her eyes. Wrapped in a towel in the midwife's arms, the red-faced baby screamed.

"A boy!"

"A boy?" Ellen said, smiling. "Billy, we've got a boy."

"Now rest. You've earned it, love."

"Can I hold him?" Ellen said.

The midwife hesitated. "We're not meant to."

"Why?"

The midwife looked around the room as if she expected someone else to be there, then handed him to Ellen. "Just quickly."

Sandy hair like Billy's, pointed ears like hers.

"He's beautiful," Ellen said, her eyes filling with tears. "I'd like to call him William."

The midwife leaned over and took the baby. "Time to rest."

Ellen murmured and closed her eyes, holding the image of her son's little face in her mind as she drifted off.

A hand nudged her shoulder, waking her. "Time to go, love."

Ellen opened her eyes. "Huh …"

"Time to go back to your own bed."

Back to the room she shared with three other pregnant, unmarried women. Back to the life she'd grown used to over the last two months.

Ellen nodded and allowed herself to be helped out of bed. No wheelchair for her this time. She stood up, surprised to feel no damage or aches, just an emptiness.

"Now, back to your room for a bit."

A bit? What did that mean? What happens now?

"Can I see William?"

"We've talked about this, Ellen."

Talked about what? Not seeing her son? So tired. Had they given her something? Why couldn't she think straight? Why couldn't she move from where she stood?

"Come on, there's nothing wrong with you. You've just had a baby. It's not an illness."

Not an illness? *Then why do I feel as if a truck has run into me?* She straightened her shoulders and shook her head. "I'd like to get my baby."

The nurse frowned. "We need this room, and you have to leave."

A tall, tight-faced woman came in. "What's going on here? Why isn't Ellen back in her room?"

"She wants her baby, Matron."

"I want William. I can't leave without my son."

"Everything's done. Now let's go." Matron's fingers wrapped around Ellen's thin arm, and she was propelled out of the room and into her own.

"You're allowed to rest for the remainder of the day, and tomorrow we'll chat about the next stage for you."

Ellen nodded and sank into her bed, wondering who had changed the sheets. Her waters had broken on it, yet the sheets were crisp and fresh. Perhaps Susan or Pauline had done it. She wondered where they were.

"What time is it?" Ellen asked.

"It's two in the afternoon," the nurse said.

The others would be in their work areas. "Pauline?"

"She's in the delivery suite."

"Ah," Ellen said, sinking her head into the pillow. "When can I hold William again?"

But the two women were already gone. Her head sank into the fresh pillowcase, her eyes closed, and she drifted off.

33

Dana

There's a blue Holden Commodore and I nudge in behind, blocking it in on the narrow road. No-one comes here, Herb said. How does he know? And he calls himself mayor.

The car probably belongs to a hiker. I hope I'm back before them. I sneak a look inside. It's a mess of men's clothing, a dirt-stained shovel, food wrappers, and empty beer cans. I shake off the image of a serial killer hiding a body and head into the bush.

It's dim and dark under the canopy, and red cookie-dough mud cakes my runners, making it slow going. I check that I'm headed in the right direction; getting lost is not my plan for this Sunday afternoon. There are broken branches ahead, probably by Herb last week. The silence is unnerving. My imagination slides back to the Commodore. Who else is out here? Folding my arms around me, I stop, suddenly uncertain, my bravado slipping rapidly away. I shake my head to clear the anxiety and will myself to take another step. I listen for sounds of assurance, rustling breeze or even birdsong, anything to make me feel as if everything is normal.

The hair on my arms standing on end warns me first. Something is not right. Twigs crack ahead of me. Throat clearing. A man. That's enough for me to turn around and race back to the car. I fumble for my keys, my hands sweating, not waiting for what or who it is until I'm safe. At last, the door opens, and as I get in, I hear a voice.

It's Steve, smiling and waving, a camera hanging from his neck. I calm down, annoyed at my cowardice. Of course, he has a shovel in his car. Still, he's not one of my favourite people, and I'm not interested in chatting.

I start the car; the radio plays an ad for the latest computer.

"Hey, wait," he yells and comes over to me. "I wanted to speak with you, doc. Have you got a minute?"

I turn down the radio and roll open the window a smidge. "You can make an appointment."

His eyes widen. "Oh shit, it's not a medical thing. I just want to ask you something."

I stare at him. Not this again. "Look, I told you before that I'm not interested. Okay? I'm sure you're very nice, but my job takes up all my time and—"

He grimaces. "That is definitely not the question I had in mind. We've really gotten off on the wrong foot."

"Then what?"

Stepping back from my window, he straightens up and drags his hand through his hair. "I should come clean with you."

I roll down the window a little more. "About what?"

"My real name is Stephen Romano, and I'm an undercover journalist for the *Sun Tribune*."

Hannah was right. I turn off the engine but don't get out.

"Journalist?"

"Yep, sorry. In another life, I was a carpenter before deciding it wasn't for me. It comes in handy, though, if I'm undercover. That's what I wanted to talk to you about the other night. No-one else knows, but I figured, as the town's new doctor, you'd have some views about what's going on and could possibly help me."

I get out of the car, lean against the doorframe, and cross my arms. "What are you investigating?"

"The disappearance of three young ex-servicemen in 1948. I believe they were murdered by the military here in this town."

"That's pretty shocking, but it's well before my time. I hardly think I can help you."

"They were part of a top-secret medical trial. A fourth one died from the trials, but I believe the other three might have, too. I'm trying to find medical records from that time and wondered if you had them in your office."

"Medical records aren't ever kept that long."

"I know, but in regional areas, you'd be surprised about the number of files and documents found in basements or back rooms. People don't know what to do with the stuff."

"I don't think they'll be out here in the bush. See anything interesting?" I point at the camera around his neck.

He touches it. "Can you keep this quiet?"

I shrug. "Depends what it is."

We stare at each other, and I wonder if he's telling me the truth.

He takes a deep breath. "I believe this was also where the military tested deadly insecticides and herbicides. Namely, Agent Orange." He cocks his head to one side, and his eyes slowly widen with realisation. "That's why you're here. Because of the cancer cases. How many are there now? You want to see for yourself if it's true. Am I right?"

"I can't discuss my patients." Who knows what he'll put into his article? I jerk my head in the direction of the path. "I need to get a soil sample."

"Right then. Let's go."

I put my hand up still not sure if I can trust him. "I don't need any help."

"I'm sure you don't, but I'd like to come anyway."

"Suit yourself."

I can't stop him, but I'll have to trust him. We get to the dirt patch, and as I scoop the soil sample into a plastic bag, I hear the click of his camera.

"Hey, what do you think you're doing?" I say, straightening up.

He's grinning. "Just taking a picture."

"Of me? How dare you? If I see that picture in the paper, I will sue you. Do you understand?"

He looks surprised. "It was of the paddock. The sun wasn't out before, and I think this is a much better shot. I'm sorry if you thought it was a picture of you."

"Well, it better not be," I say. Another misunderstanding with this guy. I walk off to hide my embarrassment, leaving him to catch up.

"You probably know how lethal that stuff is," he says. "There are more than two million people in Vietnam, even today, suffering the consequences from the defoliation in the sixties."

I'm not sure what to make of this Steve. We walk on in silence, with just the noise of the undergrowth crackling under our feet, until we get back to the cars.

Curious, I turn to him. "What do you think happened to those men?"

"My theory is that the experiments went wrong, and they died. They probably just buried them somewhere, maybe even here. Have you met Wally Gillespie?"

"Yes, I have."

"He's a wealth of information. Told me a heap of stuff about those experiments. He was mates with Herb's grandfather who ran the base."

"And what happened?" I scrap the mud off my shoes with a stick.

"A man called Fred was injected with something, and when he woke up a week later, he could barely walk. They let him go home, but he died a few weeks after. There was an investigation, the experiments stopped, and the base was closed. There's no record of the three missing men, and the military claimed the blokes weren't ever involved in the experiments. I have reason to believe they were there, and if I find any files or paperwork on them, I can prove it."

I throw the stick away and look at him, listening carefully. I'd read something about this in the library's historic newspaper exhibition. He might be telling the truth.

"The base reopened in the late fifties and early sixties. And from what Wally tells me, they started testing chemicals, herbicides, and Agent Orange, getting ready to use them in Vietnam."

"Did you get that from Wally only? Because he told me that, too."

"A journalist at the time wrote an article, quoting some unknown military sources who corroborated it. And there was an investigation, but it went nowhere."

"That's interesting." We might be able to help each other, even work together on this.

"Don't you think it's odd that no-one is asking why this town has the highest rate of cancer in the state, let alone the country?" Steve says.

I look at him. "Hannah told you?"

"No, she wasn't that helpful. I found out from the Department of

Health. It's on the public record. This story is getting bigger, and that military base is at the centre."

"Have you been there yet?"

"Nope, but I fully intend to. So, what about it? Do you want to help me find those files?"

"I'm not sure you'll find anything from 1948. I don't even have files from before 1995, so I've got no way of knowing what's happened before then."

A breeze springs up, and there's that familiar distinctive smell. Why didn't I realise it before?

Steve's aftershave.

"You broke into my surgery, didn't you?" I say.

He looks like a mouse caught in a trap. "I was just trying to find those old files."

My mouth falls open. "My patient files are confidential!"

"I'm sorry, but this is important. We could save lives."

"Did you take any files?"

"Only one. It has something about deaths in Sugar Base. But the folder was empty so I just tossed it. I swear that's the only one."

"That's why you were there the other night. I surprised you. That whole story was made-up, wasn't it?"

The guilt on his face gives it away.

"Bloody hell. You're just full of it, aren't you?" I get into the car and slam the door.

"It's not like that," he yells.

I start the engine and wind down the window. "What's it like then?"

"I have to be careful. There are bigger forces here who don't want this to get out."

"Like who?"

"Like some people in this town, for a start. Be careful about who you trust."

Is he talking about Herb?

"I thought journalists did things the right way. You know, contact people for a comment and stuff like that. You can bugger off. And I better not see anything quoted by me. Today is strictly off the record."

He looks at me in dismay.

I raise my voice. "You got that?"

He nods.

I back the car away and turn it around before glancing behind me. He's there, arms limp by his sides, his mouth still open.

*

The following week, the head lab technician rings me.

There are traces of diquat, Tordon, and dimethyl sulphoxide, plus concentrates of dioxin TCDD and 2,4-D in both samples. There's a report to follow in a week, he says, but I'm hardly listening. I already know what this means.

"Will you report this, or do you want me to?" the tech says. "One of us has to."

So, we have to spill the secrets the town has kept for so long? A place that has taken me in, accepted me, and given me an opportunity. This is how I'll repay them? Repay Herb?

It feels unreal. The enormity of what I've done comes down on me in a wave of nausea. Why did I dig and probe and question? I could have left it all alone and just treated my patients.

I should take the easy way out and park this thing with the guy on the other end of the phone. Then I think of the people who have already died and the ones who still will. Bob Harper is back in hospital, now in palliative care.

"Dr Janssen?"

I could just provide the lab report and let the health department do the rest. But what if that's not enough for them to act?

"I have a full report to write," I say. "I'll do it."

I need those old medical files.

34

Ellen

The truck jerked on the potholed road, riddled with puddles from the last downpour. Ellen's hair was blown across her face by the wind from the open window, and she pushed it back, her elbow resting on the window rim.

"We tried out one of the canecutters who said he had experience, but he didn't work out. You want to know why?" Paul didn't wait for her to respond. "We caught him drinking. He'd pour one for himself and one for a patron." Paul laughed. "Can you believe the cheek?"

Ellen pulled her gaze from the cane fields and stared at the sign ahead – two more miles to Sugar Creek.

"We gave him the flick. You'd think we'd have learned not to take on another cane cutter, but Joan was desperate. So, we tried another bloke, and he spent all his time chatting and smoking."

Ellen felt his glance drift from the road to her. She hadn't the energy to respond. She'd wanted to get out of town, but the money she'd found on the table had gone in the first month on so-called expenses. Now it seemed she had a debt to Joan and Paul, who'd paid the rest, and the only way to pay it off was to work in the pub for next to nothing–indentured to a pub in the town that had left her with no baby and no husband.

"And that's why we're so happy to have you back."

I'll bet, she thought, but she nodded.

Paul pulled up in front of Phyllis's house. "Do you want me to wait while you collect your things?"

She was expected to stay in the pub – Joan's kindness had a twist. She got out and stood, resting her hand on the open door, remembering Billy's clothes still hanging in the cupboard, her mind momentarily paralysed.

"Ellen?" Paul held her bag.

"I've got a lot to pack up, so I'd like to take a little time. But thanks." She took the bag from him.

"When you're ready," Paul said. "I'll see you later?"

Ellen turned towards the house. She was meant to start work in three hours. No time to pack or to think. She opened the gate, went down the side path, and unlocked the back door. Inside, she gazed around her room – the same as when she'd left it three months earlier. She threw the bag on the floor and then took the back steps to see Phyllis on the verandah.

"Why hello, dear." Phyllis looked up from her book and smiled. For some reason, that smile always calmed Ellen. She put her book down on the cane side table. "A cup of tea? I've just made a pot."

Ellen smiled. "You stay there. I'll get it."

Phyllis nodded. "I've missed you."

Ellen settled on the other chair with her cup of tea and explained that she would have to move back to the pub.

"Bloody Joan. She's" —Phyllis frowned then shook her head—" Never mind. Listen, just stay here."

"I can't pay you, Phyllis. Besides, Joan wants me to live there, and I'll be working long hours. It's probably best."

"It's only best for Joan. Look, I like having you here, and I'm not interested in the money. Stay here and just pay expenses. No rent."

"Really?" Ellen said. "You're so kind."

"You've had a tough time. I know what it's like to be on the wrong side of people in this town."

"Oh? What do you mean?"

"Let's just say Joan and I don't see eye to eye. She says one thing but does another. So be careful around her. Everything is all about Joan and what's good for her. And, if I'm being honest, I like the fact that you'll live here and not with her. She hates not being in control, and it gives me a little thrill to disrupt her plans. So, you'll stay?"

"I'll pay you back. Really, I will."

"No! And I mean that," Phyllis said. "You're keeping me company. But I'm glad that you'll be here."

Ellen nodded and sipped her tea. She didn't know what else to say, but she was relieved. She hadn't wanted to live at the pub.

"There's been a bit happening since you've been gone," Phyllis said.

Ellen's interest was piqued. "Like what?"

"They've shut down the experiments."

Ellen put down her cup, hands shaking. "Why?"

"Someone died."

"Who?"

"One of the canecutters."

"Oh my god. What happened?"

"One of the men got quite sick. They kept him for a week or so then let him out, but he could barely walk. The fellow started spouting off at the pub that they were poisoning ex-soldiers. Anyway, he died, so now there's a real kerfuffle over it."

Ellen blinked, dumbfounded. "What was his name?"

"Frank, or Fred, I think."

Fred, the man she met outside the base months ago.

"And what happened? I mean, how did he die?"

"Gangrene, I think. And it wasn't picked up, poor man. He'd fought in France and then in Malaysia. Imagine going through something like that only to die here from the hands of our own. It's terribly sad. Anyway, the experiments ended, and I wondered about your Billy."

Phyllis seemed to wait for her reaction; Ellen wasn't sure. Her mind whirled back to Billy and Hector. What if they'd died at the base?

Ellen stood up abruptly. "I have to go. Thanks for the tea."

"You're welcome anytime, dear. Do what you need to do."

Ellen gave Phyllis a tight hug.

"Oh, goodness. What was that for?"

"For being such a nice person. For knowing what to say and when to say it."

Ellen was grateful that there'd been no other questions. The woman had given her hope and resolve. She was ready to fight to get her life back.

*

Her thongs slapped against the bottom of her feet, echoing along the street towards Bert and Carolyn's house. She was going to get some answers. Ellen rounded the corner and stopped, squinting at a woman coming out of a white gate pulling a large pram. It looked awfully like Carolyn. She walked quickly until she was close enough to hear her voice, the high lilt of cooing over the child.

"Carolyn?"

The woman spun around, her mouth open, the look of shock suddenly smothered with an awkward smile. She moved to stand protectively between Ellen and the pram.

"Why, Ellen, you're back?"

"Yes. Got back an hour ago," Ellen said. Her gaze moved to the side of the pram. "Babysitting?"

Carolyn's hand fluttered to her mouth, and her eyes flitted nervously. "Oh, the pram? Yes, well … We're on our way out, so now's not a good time. Maybe later?" Carolyn's looked at the ground. "I didn't think you'd be coming back."

"I have to work, and Joan offered me my job back, so here I am. May I?"

"I… I… We really have to go."

"I won't take a minute."

Ellen dashed past Carolyn, pushing her aside, and peered into the pram. The baby was sleeping, his hair sandy like Billy's, his little ears peaked like hers. William. This can't be real, she thought. Her hands bunched into fists as she fought against a rising scream. With determined self-control, she stared at Carolyn instead. "Why is my baby with you?" She knew she was acting crazy, but she didn't care. She reached past Carolyn to wrest control of the pram. "That's my William!"

Carolyn pushed her with such force that Ellen fell against the fence. "Listen to me. Just calm down and listen. It's not your baby. He's mine."

Ellen beat back a sob. "He looks exactly like my little William."

Carolyn pulled her face into calm composure. "Most babies look alike."

"Why do you have mine?" Ellen's crossed her arms.

"I don't know what happened to your baby, and I'm sorry about that, really I am," Carolyn said gently. "Bert and I adopted Herbert Junior, or little Herbie, as we call him, five weeks ago. We've been on a waiting list for a year."

Ellen stared at the child. "Five weeks ago?"

Carolyn nodded. "I expected better from you, Ellen, after all I've done to help."

Little William was born three weeks ago.

Ellen watched Carolyn walk brusquely away and squeezed her eyes closed, wondering if she was losing her mind.

*

Ellen arrived at work, unable to erase the image of Carolyn's baby.

"Where's your stuff?" Joan said, her face stern.

"Thank you for the offer, but I've decided to stay with Phyllis."

"I see." Joan folded her arms. "You still need to pay back the debt as soon as you can. I don't pay enough for you to afford rent, and I need my money back."

Ellen tied on her apron. "It's okay. I've come to an arrangement with Phyllis. And don't worry. I'll pay your money back within the agreed timeframe. I'm very grateful for all you and Paul have done. Now, is it time to open?" she said, smiling. She enjoyed seeing the surprise on Joan's flushed face.

Soon the pub was filled with noise and smoke; being busy stopped her from thinking.

Lenny and Rabbit walked up to the bar and smiled. "Good to see ya," Lenny said.

"What'll it be, fellas?" She liked these two.

"Two pots, thanks," Lenny said.

"Where you been?" Rabbit said, ignoring the warning frown from Lenny.

"I had a little break. What about you? Did you end up doing the experiments at the base?"

"Yeah. Didn't like it one bit. It was nothing like they said," Lenny said. "I chickened out the last minute when I heard about that bloke who up and died. That was enough for me. I done enough for that mob."

Lenny picked up a glass. "Anyway, it's closed down now, so we gotta stick to sugar cane, don't we, mate?"

"Yeah," Rabbit said. "Pay's not as good, but you know what you're in for."

She tried to keep her voice even. "I suppose you never ran into Hector again?"

"Nah. He probably found something better."

"Maybe we could too," Rabbit said.

Lenny held up his glass. "Nice seeing ya' again, love."

"You too," she said.

After last drinks had been called, the pub emptied, and Ellen cleaned the tables. The crowd had seemed as boisterous as always, but something had changed. There was an air of discomfort around her. People smiled and asked how she was, but no-one asked about the birth. It was as if the last three months hadn't happened.

35

Dana

I'm at the post office to pick up two shipments of Lily's paintings. The smaller of the two sits perfectly flat in the back of the station wagon. It's the second package, as wide as it is tall, that stumps me. It's not heavy, just awkward as I try to angle it along the back seat. The wrapping rips as I nudge it, and as one painting begins to fall, another pair of hands comes from behind me to catch it before it reaches the road.

"There you go," Herb says. "What's this?"

It's obvious what they are. "More paintings."

"Where will you put them?" he says, helping me slide the last one in.

"Yeah, I know. There's no more space in the surgery or the house …" I say, slamming the door shut.

"Or the pub."

"I'll store them at home until I work it out."

"Maybe you should put a price tag on and sell them."

"The art gallery is interested, but they haven't gotten back to me.

My mistake was telling Lily that I'll try to sell them. Now I've got all this."

"They're really good. Has the council's arts officer been in touch? I think he wants the two in the pub."

"I'll have to check the price with Lily first. Haven't seen you around," I say, slipping my thumb inside the key ring and flipping the keys over and over.

He shrugs. "Just took off for a few days and headed to Sydney to see Mum."

"Oh, is everything all right?" It's none of my business, but he looks even more tense than usual.

"Yeah," he says. "All good."

A tourist bus pulls up outside the pub, and a crowd emerges. They're noisy and excited for nine thirty in the morning. Men in baseball caps point at the buildings, middle-aged women with leathery, tanned skin fan themselves.

Herb leans against the car, hands in his pockets, and stares at the bus. "There's probably a market for your sister's art right there."

"Maybe. Anyway, thanks for your help," I say, deciding it's time to go.

He touches my arm and looks at me, his blue eyes intense. "I'm sorry about stuffing up the soil sample. I'm going up to Bald Hill tomorrow to get you another one."

The keys flip around and around my thumb. "Don't worry about it. I went up there already and got what I needed. The samples have been sent off."

He looks surprised. "Oh?"

"I did manage to find my way there all on my own."

"Right. Of course, you did. If you need –"

"Yes, I do need something."

"Sure, anything."

"The keys to the base so I can get those patient files. I know you're busy, so just point me to the right person at the council offices, and I'll do the rest."

The laughter from the pub suddenly dies down. There's some sort of commotion, but it's obscured by tourists taking photos of the pub's facade.

Herb is distracted by the tourists. "Yeah, okay. I'll see you later."

Was he even listening to a word I said? I get into the car, and as I reverse out, I see Jack and Wally in a heated discussion with Herb, who's trying to shepherd them away from the tourists.

At home, I manage to lug the paintings downstairs. It's a spacious area with a kitchenette and small bathroom. Jack told me the owner before Herb used it to house his mother in the seventies. Since then, it's been vacant, and Herb has left it as it is. I lean the paintings against the wall and resolve to follow up with the gallery.

*

Back in the surgery, I put the receiver down, my stomach tight with nerves. The hospital board is sitting to hear my case on Friday – two more days and I'll know my fate. What if I'm struck off and can no longer practise? No, that wouldn't happen, would it? I'm being irrational. I should have warned Herb about this upfront, but instead, I cowardly hoped the whole thing would resolve quietly.

I phone Herb to ask if he can come to the surgery after work. He agrees, and now I'm even more nervous. Why did I get myself into this situation? I never should have taken this job. Three months in, and I've grown to like it here. The people are nice, and I'm better at the job than I thought I would be. There's still so much to do, and maybe now I'll never get that chance.

My head hurts. I try to shrug off the growing anxiety.

"Your next patient, doctor," Linda says.

And just like that, I'm in doctor mode. Everything else must wait.

After the last patient has left, I make myself a cup of tea and wait for Herb. I rehearse what I'm going to say: just the facts and potential outcomes.

There's a knock, and the door nudges open. "G'day," Herb says, taking off his hat. His shorts and boots are marked with mud.

"Come in."

He looks worried and tired. "Look, if it's about this morning, I was listening. It's just that Jack was getting hot under the collar with Wally because he was mouthing off about Agent Orange to the tourists. He's getting worse now, telling anyone who'll listen."

I wait for him to stop talking, but he goes on. I've learned that he does this when he's nervous.

"I'll get the keys, and we'll go on Sunday. I know you said you wanted to go on your own, but I can't let you have the council keys if you know what I mean. And—"

"It's not about the files. You better sit down."

His eyes widen, and he slumps into the chair, fidgeting with his hat. "The report's back, isn't it?"

I shake my head and take a deep breath. "I'm sorry. I should have told you this right at the outset. I don't know why, but …"

The words I rehearsed flounder in the back of my mind. I'm adding to his burden and making such a mess of this.

"What's happened?" he says.

I tell him everything except for Daniels's affair. Just the facts. He sits very still while it all tumbles out of me, and when I stop, he doesn't move or say anything, just stares at the floor. I wait, bracing myself, not knowing what to expect. Maybe he's not understood?

"I'm really sorry, but if this goes the wrong way, I might have to leave."

Dropping his hat to the floor, he lifts his arms above his head to stretch, then exhales. "What about your patients?"

"I'll organise another doctor to take over."

He gets up abruptly and paces around the room. "You should have told me."

"I know, but if I'd told you, would you have employed me?"

"Probably. We were desperate."

"Oh."

His face softens. "It wasn't like that. Your credentials seemed too good to be true, and I wanted the best ... You are the best."

"And the only candidate by the sounds of it."

"There's that, too. I suppose we'll deal with it when we know. Friday, you reckon?"

My voice cracks. "I don't want to leave."

And just like that, the tears start. He's suddenly around my side of the desk, patting my back and murmuring that it'll be okay while I sob like a baby. I pull away reluctantly, thrown off balance by the feeling of his strength and security. Maybe it's been too long since a man cared about me. I bite back the rising lump of self-pity.

"I don't normally cry like that," I say, dashing tears away from my face to regain a scrap of composure and dignity.

He hands me a tissue from the box on my desk. "I wish you felt that you could've told me."

I dab my eyes and blow my nose. "Thanks for understanding. I wasn't sure what to expect. Thought you might send me packing."

"Then you don't know me too well. As I said, I ... we need you. The town loves you." He attempts a smile. "If I let you go, I'll never hear the end of it. Can I ring the board?"

I shake my head. "No, goodness, you can't do that. It's a medical thing. They don't care about the town needing a doctor. It's best to let them do what they've got to do."

"Okay. But if you want me to, I will."

"Thanks," I say, waiting for him to go, suddenly self-conscious, knowing how frightful I must look.

"You alright?"

I take a deep breath. "I just needed a good cry, and you're very kind to lend me your shoulder."

"Anytime."

I walk towards the door, and he follows.

"I'll see you on Sunday?" he asks.

"Yes."

"Pick you up at eleven?"

"Okay."

"Do you have any idea when the results will come in?"

"The written report is likely next week" – it's not a lie—"and then I'll have to complete my report. If I have to leave, I'll get it done before I go."

"Let's wait and see what happens first." His hand brushes my shoulder. "Now, are you sure you're okay?"

I nod.

36

Ellen

Ellen peered at the soldier's gleaming black boots, marvelling that there was not a speck of dust from the gravel road. He stared straight ahead, ignoring her. She moved to the familiar shade of a large eucalyptus tree and looked down at her own shoes, dusty and scuffed.

Waving a fly from her face, she glanced at her watch – almost eleven thirty. Could she throw herself at his mercy, tell him the whole story, and appeal for help? It was probably pointless, yet she couldn't keep going like this. One last time, she told herself, then she'd stop. She'd pay out her debt and make another life a long way from Sugar Creek.

Taking a deep breath, she stepped out of the shade and walked confidently up to the soldier. "I'm here to see Bert. Bert Hipworth."

The soldier eyed her with disdain.

She faltered for a second and blurted, "I've got an appointment."

"What time?"

She relaxed a little. This man didn't know about her. He hadn't been warned by the others.

"Eleven thirty."

"You'll have to wait until he comes out to get you."

Bert was at the base. Her confidence grew. "He told me that you'd let me in."

A moment of uncertainty, and then his mouth set in a firm line. "My orders are to not let anyone in. You'll have to wait until he comes out." He stared ahead, dismissing her.

It was hopeless, just like the other times. She should go back. Instead, a determination to get into the base overwhelmed her. Today would be her last attempt, she'd decided; she needed to try harder. She wandered back to the eucalypt and waited. For what, she didn't know. Shading her eyes, she looked back at the stretch of road she'd come down. In the opposite direction, a soaring barbed wire fence ran alongside the gravel road as far as she could see.

She began walking, wondering if there was another way into the base. A blowfly buzzed around her head, then left to land on the lifeless flesh of a cane toad. Small flies orbited its head, and the smell of rotting flesh forced her into the centre of the road. She hurried on, open cane fields on one side, the impenetrable fence on the other.

A train rattled in the distance beyond the fence, and she squinted at the shimmering heat haze. A cicada started up. Something troubled her foot, and she stopped, taking off her shoe to let a small stone roll out. Give up, a voice inside her said. But she kept going, wiping the sweat from her face with her handkerchief, thankful for the growing cloud cover.

A rumbling jeep headed towards her. She moved to the side to let it by. Instead, it slowed and pulled over, swirling dust up after a week without rain. She coughed as a broad-shouldered man in the familiar khaki got out.

"You're to come with me, ma'am," he said.

He strode to the passenger side and opened the door for her.

"Where am I going?"

He looked at her in surprise. "To your appointment."

"Oh," she said, hesitating at the open door, suddenly nervous.

This is what she wanted, wasn't it? To see the place that took her Billy. She got in the jeep. The soldier closed the door behind her and drove back to the base, saluting the guard at the open gates. They drove over a cattle grid and along a gravel road lined with low-lying scrub. The driver slowed past several parked vehicles and a large water tank with rust stains snaking down its side. There were two colourless, fibro buildings with narrow windows, one marked with "Infirmary." Had Billy been there? Then past a concrete building cut into a granite hill, no windows or doors, only a mass of grey with tangles of barbed wire on top.

She expected to stop, but the soldier drove on. The road wound around thick scrub, past rusted machinery lying to the side.

"Where are we going?" she asked, nervously pushing strands of hair from her eyes.

The driver stared ahead, ignoring her.

The road became potholed, flinging her about, and she clung onto the side bar of the door to steady herself, pushing down a rising panic as the road narrowed.

"I'd like to go back now," she said, licking her dry lips and looking at her watch. "I … I have to go to work, but thanks all the same. When you come into the pub, I'll shout you a drink for your trouble."

He kept driving. Her fingers danced over the door handle, and she calculated how she could open it and jump. She'd roll into scrub, but she could do it. Then the jeep slowed and pulled into a clearing by a cane field. A single car was parked next to scrub.

The soldier moved quickly to her side to open the door.

"We're here?" she said, getting out.

He nodded.

"But what—"

He returned to the jeep and drove off in the direction they'd come.

She stood, clasping her sweaty hands, unsure what to do. The driver's side door of the parked car opened, and Bert climbed out, his face red, his eyes bulbous, his suit several sizes too big. Like her, he'd changed, too.

"What do you think you're doing?" he said. "Lying about an appointment to see me."

A coldness crept through her veins. "I'm just looking for answers," she said flatly.

"Answers?" he said as if he didn't know what she was talking about.

"You've given me nothing but lies." Her nails dug into her clenched hands. "I think I deserve a truthful explanation, and you know it."

"I've got nothing to say to you," he said, his jaw clenched. "I don't know why you bothered coming back."

"You know why. I want to know what happened to Billy. Is that why you came here?" – she waved her hand—"Why not meet back in one of those buildings? In your office?"

He slammed the car door and came towards her. "I've told you about Billy. You're an embarrassment, the laughing stock of the base. 'The crazy sheila's out the front again.' Stop coming here and stop hanging around my house."

Her anger flared. "All you've done is lie. You've taken Billy from me and now my baby. Why?"

He sneered. "What makes you think it's your child?"

"I know my own child, Bert. I'm not a complete idiot." She trembled. "Carolyn doesn't know, does she?"

"You better be careful about what you say."

She pointed her finger at him, her anger erupting. "Or what, Bert? You can't hurt me any more than you have already; I've lost everything. I know something went wrong with those medical experiments. I saw you that night, remember? I was at your house, and you were in a right state. Something went horribly wrong that day, didn't it? Those men died, didn't they?"

"You don't know what you're talking about."

"And instead of coming clean, you disposed of Billy and Hector and that other chap, Jonno."

"That's bullshit."

"I think the authorities will be very interested when I tell them."

"No-one will believe you. A slut trying to get a man to marry her into respectability? I don't think so."

"Maybe, but how do you explain the disappearance of Hector and Jonny? And now that Fred has died, I think there'll be a lot more interest in my story. Where did you dispose of them? In those cane fields, perhaps? Is that why this base owns them? Maybe you set it alight? What a handy way to get rid of bodies. But the police have ways of finding evidence, Bert. They'll come after you, and I'll make sure of it."

He stepped closer, his face growing darker, angrier. She wasn't fast enough to dodge the slap, and she lost her footing, falling into the culvert, her face stinging.

His eyes narrowed. "You shouldn't have come back here."

She quickly got to her feet, but he grabbed her arm, causing her to scream in pain.

"Help!" she yelled.

"No-one can hear you out here."

Surrounded by cane fields and bush, she realised the mistake of coming here on his terms. Her body was overcome with a rage she'd never known – for her Billy, William, and her lost life.

"You should have stayed away; you had the money." His nails cut into her arm, hurting her.

She sliced his face with her fingernails. "Your money?" she spat. "Let me go!"

"This is your own fault. I never wanted to do this, but you've left me with no choice."

Years of abuse from a drunken father had prepared her, and she twisted out of his grip. In an instant, he grabbed her again and punched her in the stomach. She fell to the ground, writhing.

"It's not too late to do the right thing," she gasped.

"You should have thought about that before you came here."

Then he was on top of her, pinning her down with his knees. She kicked and scratched, twisting her head from side to side, but he shifted his weight so she couldn't move. He was too strong. His breath, hard and fast, smelled of stale alcohol. Like her father's.

"Get off me!"

He sneered. "I do want to thank you for the baby."

That hurt more than the punch and the slap. "Give him back!"

"Joan did me an enormous favour. She organised it all for her best friend, Carolyn. Now they're both off my back."

"No," she cried. "Joan wouldn't have done that to me."

"You're more gullible and stupid than I thought. But rest assured, little Herbie will grow up with a good family. A family who will give him everything that you or Billy never could."

Her anger found new strength, but the more she struggled, the tighter he gripped.

"Quite a fighter for someone so skinny." His eyes were wild.

"You're right," she said, fighting a rising panic. "No-one will believe me, and the baby is better off without me. Please let me go. I'll leave town."

"It's too late, believe me. This is best for everyone."

"Don't make things worse." His hands lifted from her arms to her neck, squeezing the air from her.

Her hands now free, she felt around on the ground, praying for a rock.

He smiled. "Don't struggle. It won't take long."

Something sharp pierced her hand, and she wrapped her fingers around it. It would do. She sliced the barbed wire across his eye and cheek, blood gushing over her. He let her go, bringing his hands to his face.

"You fucking bitch!"

She kicked him off and ran into the cane fields, scaring the crows into flight.

He shouted again. "You slut."

She weaved in and out of the young cane stalks as fast as she could, thankful they were tall enough to hide her. Her chest lurching, she stopped to gasp for air, sweat running into her eyes. She looked behind but couldn't tell if he was near. A breeze picked up the smell of petrol and smoke. The cane field was on fire. She began running again.

She heard the cane train before she saw it and headed towards its shrill whistle and the clunk of metal on railway sleepers. A high wire fence loomed at the edge of the cane field. She hadn't expected it and fleetingly wondered why it was between her and the train line. The smell of smoke grew stronger, and when she turned, flames leaped high into the afternoon sky. Running along the fence, she prayed for an opening. "Please, God, let there be something. Anything."

She lurched at the wire and scrambled for a foothold but slid down.

She tried to lift it to get under, but it was so taut a rabbit couldn't get in. There was no way out except back to the road where he'd be waiting. Waiting to kill her. There was no bargaining.

Surely there'd be an opening. The train was getting closer. She shook the fence again, hoping for any slackness. The wire came away just a little. Was it enough? She lay on the ground, lifted the fence, and tried to roll under it. The jagged edge caught on her dress, gouging her leg. But she was through.

Hiding in the undergrowth on the other side of the track, she waited until the train came into view. It seemed to be slow enough, but not having jumped on a moving train before, she wasn't sure. The train chugged past, its trays empty. The driver turned to watch the flames, and she jogged alongside, trying to keep up. There was a short ladder on the side of a tray, and she grabbed it with one hand, reaching with the other for a firmer grip. Her legs were suspended, her feet scrambling to find leverage on a rung. She almost let go; her arms were so weak. But with the last of her strength, she leveraged herself up the next rung and crawled onto the empty tray. Lying on her back in dirt and straw, she stared at plumes of smoke drifting across the sky, trying to catch her breath and calm her racing heart.

*

After the train left the cane field behind, she pulled herself up on one elbow to get her bearings. She knew the cane trains went through the thick rainforest behind Phyllis's house. She could hide out there until it got dark enough to go home. As the train got closer to town, she jumped, stifling a scream from the pain as she thumped onto hard ground, her swollen face slamming into damp moss.

She lay among bushes and gravel, surrounded by vines, ferns, and trees so tall their canopy almost shut out the sunlight. Groaning, she pulled herself up and limped into the undergrowth. Her ankle throbbed, but she ignored the pain, pushing on until she reached a gurgling stream. She sank into the damp ground, scooping handfuls of water into her mouth. When she'd had enough, she removed her shoes. Her toes were covered in blisters. Plunging her feet into the cool water eased the pain. She glanced at her watch – a few hours until darkness.

A hollowed-out tree with giant roots snaking out was large enough to hide her. Everything ached, her throat especially. Her arms and legs were scratched and bloody, the bottom of her dress torn and caked with dirt. She raked out leaves and twigs and straw from her hair.

Her little William had been stolen from her. Joan had betrayed her. And Bert would kill her to stop her from talking. But for the time being, she felt safe.

37

Dana

Dread rolls in a wave through my body as I force myself to dial the number of a man, I've never met yet holds my future in his hands. A woman answers, friendly and efficient as she puts me through. Dr Kumar, the board chair, tells me about the case, his voice measured and revealing no emotion, rehashing what I already know while I doodle a circle over and over and harder and harder until the paper is torn.

"Dr Janssen," Dr Kumar says with such gravity that an ache squirrels into the pit of my stomach. I look at the wastepaper bin, ready to throw up. "The board has found that you have no case to answer."

My breath catches. "No case?"

"Yes," he says, and I can hear the smile in his voice.

"But ..." is all I can mutter. Like a popped balloon, the air rushes out of me.

"The error didn't cause harm or injury beyond the underlying condition the patient was being treated for. She'd not ticked the allergy box because she'd never had penicillin before. And it was an extremely rare reaction; no-one could have foreseen it. Indeed, your quick action in recognising the anaphylactic symptoms was commendable. The patient fully recovered."

"But what about her family?"

"They have now withdrawn the complaint."

"Thank you so much," I stutter, not quite believing what I've heard. "I'm okay to continue practising?"

"Why, of course. And from what I hear, you're doing a sterling job up there in Sugar Creek. I've received glowing reports."

"From whom?"

"Several people, the specialists in Townsville but mainly the town's mayor. He speaks very highly of you. Keep up the good work."

"Thank you."

I sit there stunned. Herb must have called, even though I'd asked him not to. I'm so relieved I don't know whether I should be happy. Or upset that he ignored me. Perhaps I should be grateful. For a moment, I allow myself to feel the joy and punch the air. I ring Mum and tell her the news. Then I call Herb, disappointed when he doesn't answer. I leave what I hope is a bright, breezy message for him instead. Then I ring Hannah.

"Did they mention what happened to Daniel?" she asks.

"I didn't think to ask."

"I heard that he lost his position in the specialist training program and has to be supervised for another twelve months."

"Oh really?"

"Apparently, he was caught on the security cameras going into the stairwell with Petra that night."

"You're joking." He had been furious with me, and I was so distraught I hadn't wondered where he'd been.

"That's why you couldn't find the bastard when you needed help."

"You haven't said anything to anyone, have you?"

"About you and Daniel? No, definitely not. But he's a snivelling, two-faced rat and deserves to have the book thrown at him. He should have lost his job."

Afterwards, I sit alone in the silence of the surgery, thinking about Daniel, about how I'm truly over him, his lies, and his deceit. I can't help but feel happy. My confidence soars until I remember the work I must do.

*

Herb gets out of the car and bounds up my front steps. I've been watching out for him from my bedroom and open the front door before he gets a chance to knock.

"Good news. I knew you'd get through," he says, smiling.

I guess he's happy that I'm staying. One less thing for him to worry about, perhaps.

"And thanks for your intervention, even though it was totally unnecessary," I reply.

"I know you asked me not to, but I had to do something. Sorry."

He looks ruefully at me, and I relent. "It's okay."

He looks relieved.

I slide into the passenger seat of the ute, which looks like it's had a spit and polish.

"Before we go, there's something I need to tell you." He turns to me, wary. "Steve, the builder, is a journalist." I tell him about my encounter at Bald Hill.

His happiness fades behind a tight frown, and he runs his hand through his hair. "Bloody hell. I can't believe that. What a snake."

It's time to break the rest of the news. "It gets worse. The test results prove there are remnants of Agent Orange in the soil and water."

He groans, and his shoulders slump. "Jesus."

"After I send my report, the whole thing will be in the hands of the Department of Health and the Environmental Protection Authority."

He starts the engine and then looks at me, stern and businesslike. "Then what?"

"There should be a clean-up operation. But given that nothing happened last time this was raised, it might be better to have Steve on our side."

"How the hell is that any better?"

"The goal now is to have a healthy, rather than a prosperous town, right?" I suggest.

He looks at me with quiet resignation. "Everything I dreamed about for Sugar Creek will go. Even if it's cleaned up, there'll be no more tourists. Who on earth would want to live here or even risk visiting?" He shakes his head. "Dana, once this is out, it'll be over for this town."

We head out of my street. "I can't believe that it's up to this generation to clean up the mess left by those bastards in the sixties," he says. "I don't suppose I can bring a class action on behalf of all those in the community who died, including my own family?"

"Why not?" I say. "They should pay."

"But who'll really pay? The military? The government? The Shire Council? It'll take years before we see a cent. Let's face it. It's a disaster whichever way you look at it."

"Except we're saving current and future generations. People have a right to live in a safe environment; you must keep that in perspective. Money and growth aren't worth much if the population is dying. Not to mention what it's done to the environment."

He breathes out slowly. "I know." He indicates at the intersection to turn right.

"Ah … Can we make a detour first?" I ask.

"Where to?"

"I kind of promised Steve that he could come."

His mouth sets in a straight line. "You're joking."

"It's better that we have him on our side. If the authorities try to drop this like they did in the sixties, then the media may be our only hope," I argue. "He's waiting at the pub for us."

Herb sighs and turns left instead.

*

"G'day, mate," Steve says as he leans in through Herb's open window. "Thanks for letting me tag along."

Herb just grunts in response.

"Dr Janssen," Steve says as he slides in, forcing me across to the middle of the bench seat, my leg touching Herb's as I clip on my seat belt.

"I gather that you know why I'm coming?" Steve says to Herb.

"Yep," Herb says.

We drive on in silence until we reach the base.

"You do exactly what I tell you, and don't go wandering off," Herb says to Steve.

"Yeah, sure, mate."

Herb unlocks the padlock and swings the gate wide, driving up an overgrown and disused road and round a bend to a large grey building. The concrete monolith is just what I thought a base might look like. Beyond is a group of outbuildings, which look more like temporary school portables with rust stains, old graffiti, and broken windows.

We park and get out, the day dim under a sky of dark cloud.

The large metal door is rusty, and after searching for the right key, Herb unlocks and pulls it wide, resting a rock against it to keep it open. It reveals a long, dark corridor. He fumbles for the light switch. "The council maintains it for storage," he says by way of explanation.

"I reckon the council needs to get in here and do a bit of maintenance, mate," Steve says, touching the water-stained walls.

Herb ignores us and strides ahead to another door at the end of the corridor. I cough the dank mustiness from my lungs. Herb tries the last of the three keys he's been given and pushes open the solid door. He flicks on the light switch, and before us is a cavernous room filled with hundreds of filing cabinets and boxes piled high.

Steve breaks the silence with a long, low whistle. "What is this place?"

Even Herb looks surprised. "Just a dumping ground for old records. I had no idea." He looks at me. "I don't know how we'll find what you're after."

"Patient files on the label here," Steve says, moving towards some black cabinets. "Even has the dates on the front."

The patient files date back to 1960. I was only after files between 1980 and 1995.

Steve tugs on a couple of drawers – all locked.

I look at Herb. "Any keys for these?"

Herb looks in dismay at the keys in his hands. Only three, and each one already used. "Sorry. I should have thought to ask. I'll get the keys in the morning, and maybe we can come back tomorrow night."

Steve produces a set of keys. "Move aside." He chooses one and unlocks the drawer. "There you go."

"How have you got a key?" I ask.

"There's always a master key for these types of cabinets. It gets me into a lot of them."

"You mean it helps when you break and enter," I retort. "Can you open these others?"

Herb shakes his head at Steve. "You're … I don't know what you are."

Steve grins. "Just a helpful bloke. Now let's get to work."

Herb turns to me. "Do you know exactly what you're looking for?"

"The files of cancer patients, particularly those who died in the eighties or nineties or earlier if they're here. See if you can find any of these names."

I hand him a list and look around for Steve, who seems to have disappeared.

We're absorbed in hunting down files, and I'm ecstatic when I find one, yellowed and brittle in my hands. Herb finds another, and we keep searching. I figure I need about ten as a sample.

"Look at this."

Steve is standing on the far side of the room, holding a folder, his usual smugness gone.

"What's wrong," I ask.

He just shakes his head and hands me a folder: Hector Bradbury, aged 23, single, no next of kin declared.

I open the folder and read the document aloud, releasing its musty secrets.

"Three drops of pure sarin on a piece of flannel wound around his left forearm. Results: within half an hour, Bradbury was drenched in sweat. He lost his hearing first and then fell into unconsciousness. He was injected with atropine but stopped breathing twenty minutes later and was pronounced dead." I shiver.

Steve takes a deep breath. "That's one of the missing men."

I find a box to sit on, resting the folder on my lap. "Sarin is a highly toxic nerve agent."

"Isn't that what they used in the concentration camps?" Herb says. "What the hell were they doing using that on our own blokes?"

Steve looks up and sighs. "They were conducting human experiments, mate."

"Atropine is usually used to treat poisoning, but I'm not sure whether it would have helped a sarin exposure," I say, imagining I can smell the gassy chemical. "Where did you find this?"

Steve jerks his head towards the open door of a small room with banks of grey cabinets. "It was unlocked. I'm shocked this information wasn't destroyed. They just handed it over to a council. It's damning evidence, that's for sure."

"I'm not surprised stuff like this has been left lying around," Herb says. "I think it just became a dumping ground for anything they didn't know what to do with. I've just found a bunch of immunisation records from the twenties."

I close the folder and hand it back to Steve. "Are you okay?"

He rests his forearms on his knees. "I didn't expect to find anything, to be honest. Just thought this would be a dead end." He gets to his feet. "I've got to find the files of the other blokes, then we can go. This place gives me the creeps."

"I've only got a couple more on my list. Herb, why don't you help Steve?"

Herb and Steve disappear into the room, and I look at my watch. We've been in this airless, concrete bunker for four hours, and I'm battling the feeling of claustrophobia, yearning for fresh air. I force myself to keep going through the list of names.

I flick through the cabinet and find Herb's grandparent's files – died from the same cancer – as he'd said. The signature of the medical practitioner is from Dr Cummins.

I suddenly get an idea and drop what I'm doing. "Steve, what was the doctor's name who signed off on Hector Bradbury?"

Steve comes out of the room, looking at a folder, and squints. "Um, looks like Dr Common."

"May I?" I say, taking the paperwork from him. "It's Dr Cummins."

Steve gives a half smile. "I suppose you doctors can all read each other's crappy writing."

"It's part of our training."

"Really?"

"I'm joking," I say, making a face. "Are you nearly finished?"

"Give me another half hour, okay?"

Herb comes out and picks up his father's file. He looks sad. "My name is in here."

"Yes, it is."

"But what are these other names?"

I look at him quizzically and then at the paper he hands me. "Siblings: a brother and a sister," I read aloud.

He shakes his head, his hands trembling as he puts the file down. "I never had any siblings."

I'm in dangerous territory. Patient confidentiality applies even for the long-dead.

"I'm so sorry," I say.

"They're dead?"

I read from the file. "Yes. Died at birth."

"I don't understand why my mother never told me."

"It was probably too painful."

"Could Agent Orange have done this?"

"It's possible."

"Jesus." He shakes his head, his face pale. "I need some air. I'll wait outside for you."

"Okay," I say, calling after him. "We won't be long."

I'm worried about him. I shouldn't have let Herb look at his father's file. What else is in these files? My energy is drained from the ghosts we've found, and I bundle up the paperwork. I wonder about Dr Cummins. I'm almost certain Hannah mentioned his name, too. I flick through the pages of my notebook. There it is.

"Are you ready to go?" Steve calls out.

"Yep," I say, picking up the files and packing my notebook back into my handbag.

"Better lock up." Steve pulls out his keys and locks the cabinets.

I feel uneasy with the silence and just want to get out. It's almost as if someone else is in here with us. It's the year two thousand, a long time in the future for these poor souls whose lives were cut short in this ghastly place.

"What did you find?" I ask, looking at the folders tucked under Steve's arm.

"A killing field," he says grimly. "That's what I've found."

38

Ellen

High-pitched squealing jolted her awake, so loud it almost drowned out the nearby gurgling water. It came from above her. Hundreds of flying foxes or fruit bats hung from the branches like black icicles. She'd never been able to tell which was which. One swooped so close its wings almost touched her, and she cowered into the tree's hollow. It was nearly dusk and the hot, sticky air stank of urine.

She lifted herself up against the safety of the tree, keeping an eye on them. Then, carefully, she tested her ankle by stepping around the tree roots. Her limbs stiff, pain shot through her ankle as if caught in an animal trap. She bent over and examined the swelling bulge that spilled out of her shoe.

She searched for anything recognisable. There was no path to follow; she'd run blindly, taking little notice of where she was going. Another stupid mistake. A new doubt entered her head: what if she walked in the wrong direction? She thought about Joan, who'd told her a story about two people lost in this rainforest during the war. They'd never been found. Joan, the liar, probably invented the story to scare Ellen. Joan, whose concern for her was nothing but an opportunity to get her hands on little William for Carolyn. How stupid she'd been to believe those women had genuinely cared about her.

No-one cared enough to look for her. They'd think she'd taken off. Joan might be angry, assuming she'd left to escape her obligation. And Bert? Hopefully he believed she'd died on that burning cane field.

She put her hands over her ears, trying to block out the screech. Mosquitoes bit her arms and legs, and she fought against a mounting scream and paralysis of indecision. Which way?

She looked up. Was the sun setting in that direction? The longer she waited, the darker it became. *Do something!* She followed the stream, trying to reassure herself that crocodiles couldn't be this far inland. Limping, the going was slow, and she stumbled over a tree root and fell into a shrub. More jagged scratches on her legs and two black leeches sucking on the fleshy part of her calf.

"Oh god, oh god, oh god," she screamed, slapping her legs. "Get off me."

The one good piece of advice her father had given suddenly came to her. "Calm down. Don't pull them off – they'll just bury into your skin." It was a rare day when her father was sober. He'd understood her hysteria.

"Wait for them to suck your blood, and they'll drop off," one of her brothers had said, laughing.

"Calm down and remember. Find the head." She shuddered. "With your fingernail, slide it under the head to break the suction." It worked, and she grabbed the black, slimy thing and flung it as far as she could. Then she tackled the next one.

Large droplets battered her and the leaves as she pushed on. The noise of the flying foxes faded into the background as the rain got heavier. Hardly able to see, she started crying, calling out quietly for Billy. There was no answer. The roar of the sudden thunderstorm drowned out her sobs, and she sank into the ground to give herself up to the elements, the leeches, the mosquitoes, and everything else in the rainforest. This was what hell was like: deafening, hot, and wet.

Then, just as suddenly, the rain slowed until only fat drops tapped like Morse code on the large leaves. She almost welcomed hearing the flying foxes again. She got to her feet; if she were to die in this place, she would die trying.

Pushing her soaked hair back from her face, she listened. Hope coursed through her wet aching body. There it was again – a familiar rattle. She heaved herself through the undergrowth, ignoring the pain.

It was closer than she realised, and at the edge of the rainforest, she stepped out and inhaled the fresh evening air, listening to the comforting clang of the train in the distance. She clambered up a small rise to the track. Saved.

The rising full moon lit the way as she followed the track until the outskirts of the town came into view. She slid down the slight embankment and limped to the road. There were no cars. The train station was ahead, and she turned towards her home sticking to the footpath. The smell of roasting meat wafted from a house, and her stomach rumbled. She'd not eaten since that morning's slice of white bread with jam. She licked her lips as she thought about where to go. Most people would be home, eating and listening to the wireless. Should she risk going home for a change of clothes, her purse, and her rings before leaving? To get something to eat? She had twelve pounds left – enough to get away. But how and to where? She couldn't go to Phyllis. It could be too dangerous. It was better for her not to know in case Bert came looking. He might have asked about her already.

A truck roared in the distance, coming towards her. She ducked into someone's garden and squeezed behind a shrub. A dim light shone at the rear of the house; someone was home. Voices nearby. Men. Two of them walked in her direction from the house opposite, stopping a few feet away. One handed a cigarette to the other, the flash of the match landing next to her. She kept still, despite the incessant itching on her arm. A strong waft of smoke from the cigarettes blew past, and she stifled a cough. When they walked to a parked car down the street, she shifted her position, suppressing a groan from the throbbing pain in her ankle. The men laughed. Finally, one got into the car and drove away, while the other went back into the house opposite. Her limbs stiff, her damp dress stuck to her legs, she struggled out from behind the bush and headed off to her street.

She froze. A vehicle was parked in front of Phyllis's house. Was it Bert's? It was hard to tell in the dark. A glow from a match being lit came from inside the car. Perhaps they were waiting for her. Or maybe for someone from the boarding house across the road? She couldn't risk it.

She could think of only one other place, and she hobbled into the next street. She tugged at the church door. Locked. The alcove was large enough to hide her, and she collapsed against the church wall, not daring to remove her damp shoes for fear of not being able to get them back on. Shadowy wings moved over the moonlit front yard – dozens of flying foxes moving quietly like bombers across the cloudless sky.

She shivered. Here she was, back at the church where she should

have been married. She slumped against the timber wall, tried to
ignore the pain, and waited.

39

Steve enters the corridor to head outside. I glance around the room for one last time, my hand hovering over the light switch.

"Who closed the door?" Steve asks.

I look down the corridor at the exit, sealed. "Maybe it swung shut?" I offer.

He tries the door. "Fuck," he mutters. "It's locked."

A rising terror pitches in my stomach. "How could it be?"

The look on Steve's face is knowing and questioning at the same time. "Well, who is already out there, but your Mr Mayor.

"No!" I say.

"He's got a lot to lose."

"He'd never do that. The wind's come up and blown the door closed, that's all," I say, desperate for it to be true. "Remember, he used a flimsy rock to hold it open. Try it again."

Steve tries the handle, but the door doesn't open.

"Let me." I push past him and try for myself, but there's no budging the door. I fumble in my handbag for my phone. No reception.

Steve pulls out his phone. "Flat."

"We'll just yell," I say, taking a deep breath.

He holds up his hand. "Shh. Listen."

There are voices outside.

"Who else is out there?" I slump against the cold wall for support, suddenly afraid.

Steve plants his ear on the door. "It sounds a bit like Jack."

"What?"

"He gave me the sack yesterday. Told me to pack up and get out of town."

"Why would he do that?"

"After I started asking about the spraying, he asked what I was doing. Told me to keep my nose out of things if I knew what was good for me. My guess is he's got wind of what's going on."

I try to keep my breathing steady. "Then what is he doing here?"

"Dunno. Maybe he heard Herb was coming out here." He rattles the handle. "Hell, I don't know."

"You're fuckin' ruining everything," comes his voice from outside, loud and angry.

"Yep, it's definitely him," Steve says.

A car starts up and rumbles away. We look at each other.

"Herb," I yell, my voice cracking.

Steve yells too, and we listen for something, anything. There's nothing but the wind whipping under the door.

"Maybe Herb's taken off with Jack?"

"Leaving us here? He wouldn't do that."

"Then where is he? You'd be surprised what some people will do. He was probably humouring you, or maybe Jack made him see what's really at stake." Steve turns to me. "Money and power."

I wince. I can't believe Herb would do that. He's a good man, isn't he? I remember how gentle he was when I'd cried my eyes out. He cares. He wants what's best for his community.

"You'll see," Steve says. "He and Jack are probably knee-deep in developing this town. We come along and shake things up; they collude and lock us in. They've probably concocted a story about us leaving town. No-one will ever know where we are."

"That's ridiculous. My mother will ask questions; so will your newspaper and your family."

But when will they ask? I only speak to my mother once a week. My patients will wonder. Why didn't I confide in Linda? Maybe Steve is right. Maybe it wouldn't be hard to concoct a reason for me leaving.

"Herb," I yell again, putting my ear to the door. "Herb." Silence.

"Hold these. Let me see if these work," Steve says, handing over his files.

I concentrate on regulating my breathing as he pulls out his keys. He tries them all but none fit. I fight the mounting panic and hug the folders close to my chest, my hands clenched, my body covered in sweat.

"One last thing to try," he says, pulling a thin wire from the key ring.

He jiggles and prods for what seems like hours but it's only a minute in truth.

"There!" Steve says, pushing open the door.

I've never been so glad for fresh air. But my relief is suddenly quashed. Herb's car is still there.

I drop the files in the dirt and run. "Oh my god," I scream. Herb is lying on the ground. I check his pulse, steady. He's breathing well. There's a gash on his forehead and blood oozing down his face. Probably concussed. "Call an ambulance," I say, throwing Steve my phone.

"There's no reception out here, remember?"

"Shit."

I feel around Herb's pockets for his keys and toss them to Steve. We work together, me holding his legs while Steve heaves him into the back of the ute.

"He's a heavy bastard," Steve says, sweat dripping down his face. "The surgery?"

I nod as I climb into the back, cradling Herb's bleeding head in my lap, hoping like hell that he'll be all right.

He grins like a drunk and looks up at me. "What the hell?" he says before closing his eyes and groaning.

"Just lie still," I say, relieved. "We're taking you back to the surgery. You're going to be fine."

Back at the surgery, Herb manages to get out of the ute with our assistance and responds well to my questions. I'm relieved – concussion seems unlikely. While I clean him up, Steve fires questions at him.

Jack found out what was going on. He was angry and told Herb to stop. No, Jack had no idea that we were there, too. The door had slammed shut just before Jack pulled up.

"Now what?" I ask, washing my hands.

"We keep going," Herb says.

"Will you go to the police about him?" I ask. "I think you should."

"There's no point. It'll just rile him up more. No, you both do what you need to do, and I'll take care of Jack."

*

The next morning, I begin compiling my report, methodically reading each file and typing up the names, birth details, and diagnoses.

When I get to Herb's dad, I leaf through his details – born at the St

Andrew's Maternity Home in 1948, adopted two days later by Bert and Carolyn Hipworth. Interesting, but not unusual.

The treating doctor was the same for everyone – Dr Cummins. I call Hannah to find out what she knows about this guy.

"Dr Cummins was the regional GP, delivering babies and providing patient care," Hannah says.

"As well as signing off on medical experiments." I check myself gnawing the end of my biro and throw it on the desk.

"Looks like it. From what I can gather, he must have worked from at least 1948 until the early 70s."

"Hold on, I've got a file from 1994 here. Jesus, his signature is there."

"He must have practised for almost fifty years. How is that possible?" Hannah says.

"No idea," I say. "Thanks again for your help. Better keep moving."

Before the next patient, I ask Linda, "Did you know the previous GP, Dr Cummins?"

"Yeah, sure. He'd been our local GP for as long as I can remember. Lovely man very highly regarded. Enjoyed a drink at the pub and was a World War II veteran. He retired to Mission Beach. Not sure when. Mum and Dad will know more. Why?"

"I've seen his name on a lot of files dating back a long time."

"Well, he was the only doctor in the region. I think he might have even delivered me." Linda chuckles. "Hey, Mum wanted me to ask you over for dinner tomorrow night. Are you free? Her long-term memory is very good, and you can ask her about Dr Cummins."

"Thanks, I'd like that."

That night I finish the report. I have to be careful to include all the facts – the details of the soil and water samples, the patient deaths that I've sampled from each decade since the sixties, and the current cancer cases. It's time-consuming, and it's late when I finally finish. I fax it off and head to the pub for dinner with Herb and Steve.

Waiting in the dinner order queue, I notice Herb, a purple bruise over his right eye, with Steve at a table, deep in conversation. I order a salad and head over.

"Just in time. Maybe you can talk some sense into him," Steve says.

"Or vice versa," Herb says, rolling his eyes.

I slide into the chair next to Herb and opposite Steve.

"We're debating the merits of when the article I'm working on should come out," Steve says.

"Have you finished your investigation?" I ask.

"Just about." Steve sips his beer.

"Surely there's more to do," I say. "Shouldn't you talk to the Department of Health first?"

Steve smirks. "You trying to tell me my job?"

"Why don't you wait a bit, mate?" Herb says. "There's no need to go off half-cocked, creating a scandal and scaring the whole town. I've got a council meeting tomorrow night where I'll tell them what's going on, and then I have to talk to the Department of Health and work out an action plan. A story now will only cause panic. A planned communication strategy is critical."

"Would you like me to come to the council meeting too?" I ask.

"No need. You might have to be involved later," Herb says.

"I know how the wheels of bureaucracy work," Steve says. "It'll be months before the officials even read Dana's report, let alone get something done. Believe me, getting the media well and truly involved is the best tactic. Sorry, mate, but it's going to get a little rough. You may as well give me a statement. I'd like one from you too, Dana."

"Me? I think you should talk to the department. They're coming on Wednesday."

"You've sent your report?" Herb says, turning to me.

"I faxed it half an hour ago and rang them this morning. So, talk to them, Steve."

He nods. "Okay, I will. Maybe I'll do my article on the missing men first to give you some time."

Herb looks relieved. "Thanks, mate."

"Anything else about Jack?" I ask.

"He's gone to Brisbane," Herb says, rolling peas from one side of his plate to the other with his fork. "To see his lawyer, I believe."

"He's gonna need one," Steve says. "The land he's bought is across the road from the base. He bought the Harper's and Thompson's places last month and a whole lot more. Apparently, he's buying up for development. Herb, your planners have already given the green light, but once this is out, that's all going to stop."

I give Herb a sidelong glance. He's abandoned his fork and is shredding layers of a cardboard beer coaster into tiny little bits.

Steve drains his glass and pushes his chair back. "Thanks for the tip, Dana, but think about giving me a statement. You too, Herb. I'm heading back to Sydney at the end of the week, so before then, perhaps?"

Steve waves to Crystal as he leaves.

Herb looks positively glum, his elbows on the table, his head in his hands.

"Are you all right?" I ask

"What will happen on Wednesday?"

"They're sending out a team to check the water first because that's probably making everyone sick and has to be dealt with right now."

"Yeah."

"You'll go down in history for doing something about it, cleaning up the town, and saving your community."

He shrugs, tiredness ringing his eyes. "I don't care about going down in history. The whole thing is just a disaster."

"I know."

"I'm just …" He looks at me. "It's just that I know what's going to come, and I'm dreading it."

"I know." I put my hand on his arm, thinking about how much responsibility he has as the mayor.

"This affects the health of many generations. First my grandparents, then my father, then probably me. There'll be so many others." He looks around the almost empty pub and sighs.

Mavis walks in and waves as she heads to the bar. I wave back.

"Possibly, but now that you know, your health and everyone else's will be monitored closely. If you do have any issues, they'll be caught early. There might be more resources allocated, like more doctors and nurses. A proper health clinic like you always wanted."

"What about other genetic mutations? Who knows what else my grandfather was exposed to? There'll be hereditary issues from him, too."

"Your grandfather?"

"He was in World War II and as a biochemist he was probably exposed to a heap of stuff."

"I doubt it. Since your father was adopted, you wouldn't be affected by your grandfather."

"What the hell are you talking about?"

I realise what I've just done. "Um, I thought you knew. Your father was adopted. It was in his file."

He throws the scraps of beer coaster onto the plate. "Jesus, something else my mother hasn't told me."

I fall silent. Someone over at the bar laughs.

"Thanks for everything yesterday," he says, getting up.

Mavis comes over with her glass of wine. "Well, you two look nice and cosy." She winks at me. "Going already, Herb?"

Herb composes himself instantly. "Hi, Mavis. How are you?"

"Doctor Janssen is coming over tomorrow night for dinner. How about you? Got a lamb roast on."

"I have a council meeting at eight, but I'd love to come." He attempts a smile. "What time?"

"Around six. You can trot off to your meeting after dessert." Mavis gives Herb a knowing look. "Pineapple meringue?"

"Will definitely not miss that," Herb says.

"I better go. Joan's waiting for me. We're off to bingo."

"Me too," Herb says.

Mavis looks startled. "To bingo?"

Herb blinks. "Ah, no," he stumbles. "I'm going to ring my mother."

And I stare at the salad in front of me, not noticing it had arrived, my appetite completely gone.

40

"There's another delivery at the post office," Linda says, poking her head around my door. "Do you want me to pick it up on my way home?"

I groan and look at my watch. "I told her I couldn't take any more." Lily's paintings are multiplying rapidly. "I'll go. There are no more patients, are there?"

"No. All done."

There are more paintings at the post office than I'd expected, and the packaging has come away from one of the larger pieces. A nail juts through it, catching the edge of my skirt and ripping a hole the size of a matchbox. Damn.

When I finally get home, I duck into the surgery to see if Linda is still there and ask her for help.

"I'm just locking up, and then I'll be there in a jiffy," she says.

We unload them all except for one. It's large, so we have to inch it carefully out of the car. "Watch out for that side," I say. "There's a nail jutting out. It's already torn a hole in my skirt."

She glances down and frowns. "That's such a pity. There's a dressmaker in town who might be able to fix it for you."

"It was old anyway."

The skirt is the least of my worries. I'll ring Lily and tell her that I've got enough. Perhaps she can go through the art gallery from now on. Let them work for their commission.

We carry it into the room under my house, both of us puffing.

"It's like the dungeon of an actual art museum," Linda says. "They're wonderful. I really love this one of the daisies. She's certainly got a delicate touch with the paintbrush. They'll all sell at the exhibition."

I sigh, wondering why I'd taken this project on. "I hope so. Let's just push this one across the floor." We move it, and the nail rips through the fragile lino, exposing the old wooden floor. "Bloody hell." We give one last heave and rest it along the wall with the others. Then we examine the damage.

"Perhaps you can just … pat it into place?" Linda squats down and tries to roll back the strip of lino, but it won't sit flat.

"Bugger. I'll have to tell Herb. Hope he's not too upset," I say.

Linda hoists herself up with a grunt. "Maybe he can glue it back down somehow. This floor looks like it hasn't been touched for a thousand years. Anyway, the lino is pretty much worn out. I'm sure he won't care."

I peer at the floor. "He's got enough to do already without this. It can't stay like that. It's right in the doorway and is a hazard."

"Easily fixed." Linda quickly grabs the flap of lino and gives it a tug, ripping it even more until she's holding a tear-drop shape of lino as tall as she is.

"Oops," she says, grimacing. "I'll just put this down here, will I?"

I'm speechless and dismayed that she's made it a lot worse. I wonder what Herb will say. We've ruined the floor completely.

"I'll get someone in to fix it. Okay?" Linda says.

"My fault. I'll sort it out. We should have just lifted the painting in the first place," I say. "You've been a big help. Thanks."

"Sorry about the floor, but really, Herb won't care." She looks at her watch. "Hell, I better go and help Mum with dinner. I'll see you in an hour?"

"Yes," I say. "I've got a nice bottle of chardy chilling."

Then she's gone, leaving me with the guilt and the damage.

*

The lamb is tender, and the wine delicious. Herb smears a generous dob of butter on fresh bread.

"Mum, we were wondering about Dr Cummins," Linda says, pouring more gravy. "He delivered me, didn't he?"

Herb places his butter knife on the floral side plate and looks at me. He's been preoccupied all dinner and hardly said a word.

"No. I had you in Townsville, love."

Linda frowns. "How did I not know that?"

"Guess you never asked."

"He was here for a long time, though, wasn't he?" I ask.

Mavis wipes her mouth. "Our Dr Cummins arrived just after the war. I didn't much like him. He was a bit strange, but it's understandable since he'd been a POW. In Malaysia, you know."

"You knew him?" Herb asks.

"Not that well. He came to Sugar Creek to work at the base. Somewhere along the way, he became a GP and was here until ninety-five."

"Then he died, didn't he? Cancer?" Linda asks.

"I think so." Mavis lowers her voice. "Between you and me, he was well and truly past it. It was clear he wasn't well, but he refused to budge. Everyone ended up going all the way to Townsville or Cairns to see a doctor."

He must have been complicit, knowing what had happened but doing nothing about it. I wonder if he got Wally's investigation shut down.

"And now, thanks to Herb, we have a lovely doctor instead, who incidentally knows about a nice wine too." Mavis beams at me and holds up her glass.

I wipe my mouth with the white linen napkin, horrified at my lipstick smeared all over the beautiful fabric. "That was delicious," I say.

Linda holds up her hands and smiles. "I had nothing to do with it. Mum's always been a great cook."

Mavis looks at Herb and me. "I hope you two have still got room for dessert?"

After prawn cocktails and a roast lamb with all the trimmings, I don't know how I can fit another thing in, yet I nod.

"You bet," Herb says. "I've always got room for your desserts. Pineapple meringue pie?" He looks hopeful.

Mavis laughs. "Naturally."

Linda turns to me. "She's been making that pie for I don't know how long and is known everywhere across Far North Queensland for it."

"I'll vouch for that," Herb says enthusiastically.

"How can I say no?" I say as Mavis disappears into the kitchen. "Just a tiny bit for me."

"We'll have dessert out on the verandah. It's going to be a stunning sunset, I think," Linda says.

Mosquito coils smoulder in the corner of the verandah, and Herb leans on the railing staring off into the distance.

"You okay?" I ask.

He nods. "It's a lot to process. Cummins working on those

experiments. My father … Mum had no idea that Dad was adopted. I don't think his parents ever told him." He turns to look at me. "One day, I'd like to find out who his real parents were and where I came from. But my immediate worry is tonight's meeting. It won't be good, and well …"

"I know," I say, standing next to him. "You've got a lot going on now. Remember, it's the right thing to do, and I'm here to help. You know that, don't you? I can still come with you."

"Yeah, I know." He attempts a smile and then sighs. "I'm not sure how everyone will take the news. I can handle it tonight. But you'll probably have to come to the town meetings."

"I will."

"Dessert is served."

Linda holds two floral, bone china plates and hands one to each of us. "I know the slices are generous, but she doesn't know how to do small. Just leave what you can't eat."

"Thanks," I say, eyeing the large slice of pie, a cross-section of crust, and plump yellow filling topped with large curls of meringue.

Mavis brings out two more plates, and we seat ourselves on cane chairs.

A breeze has come up, rustling the nearby palm trees. The first mouthful is pineapple heaven, soft on my palate. I must have moaned because when I look up, Linda is giggling, and Herb is smiling.

"Glad that you like it, love," Mavis says, looking pleased.

"It's like nothing I've ever had before," I say, licking my lips.

"I've been making it for years. Well before the war. It's just lemon meringue but with pineapple instead. Caught many a man with that pie."

"Mum!" Linda says, chuckling.

I want to lick the plate but scrape the last bits off instead. Herb has already finished.

"Another slice?" Mavis asks.

"Couldn't fit another thing in," Herb says, patting his flat stomach.

"No more for me either," I say, handing my empty plate to Linda.

"Linda tells me you're exhibiting your sister's paintings?" Mavis says.

"Yes. There'll be a showing at the gallery in three months. Of course, you'll be invited to the opening."

"They're beautiful," Linda says. "We had a bit of difficulty with the ones that came in today. Even ripped the lino."

"Downstairs," I quickly add.

"Are you still storing them under the house?" he asks, his eyes trained on me.

"Um, yes. I hope that's okay."

"Sure," he says.

"I'm afraid it's right in the doorway, Herb. It was my fault, really," Linda says.

"No, it wasn't," I say.

"I'll pop in when I can and see if I can fix it. I've never actually got around to that part of the house."

"Quite a history, that house," Mavis says.

Herb looks at his watch. "I hate to eat and run, but I have to get to this meeting." He gives Mavis a peck on the cheek. "Thank you for a wonderful meal, Mavis and Linda." He nods to me. "I better go."

"You'll stay for a cup of tea, Dana?" Linda asks.

"Of course. Love to," I say, waving to Herb. "And I'd love to hear more about my house."

41

Strips of orange and gold across the sky seem to melt behind the hills, and a breath of cool air floats across the verandah. Mavis puts down her dessert plate, leaving most of her pie. She places her hands, freckled with age spots, on her lap and stares into the distance. Then she turns and looks at me with eyes as sharp and bright as a bird's. "Phyllis Laurel originally owned your house until she died in the seventies. Cancer, I think."

I'm not surprised; another one lost.

"She took in boarders after the war. They lived downstairs. But she never took another one in after the incident."

Linda looks at Mavis. "Incident?"

Mavis pauses before sitting back in her chair and clasping her hands. "It was around 1948. Phyllis rented the room to a young woman, Ellen. She was new in town and was getting married. So, of course, we wanted to help. We had a grand old time getting ready. I even lent her my pearls. And, because she was alone" – Mavis looks directly at me, I guess because I'm alone, too—"we were sort of unofficial bridesmaids. Me, Joan, and Carolyn. But when we got to the church, the groom hadn't shown up."

"That's terrible," Linda says. "Poor thing."

"It was very upsetting, but Ellen never cried. Just kept it together." Mavis shakes her head. "I don't think I could have done that, especially since she was also pregnant. We didn't know it at the time. It was scandalous in those days. No wonder she tried to get married in a hurry." Mavis paused. "The thing was, she was insistent that her fiancé was at the base, and that was why he was a no-show. Wouldn't let it go. We didn't believe her, to be honest. I thought she'd made the bloke up, but Joan had seen him in the pub."

"Her fiancé was at the military base?" I ask, my mouth dry.

"Yes. There were a whole lot of fellas who volunteered to do medical experiments for extra money."

"And that was common knowledge then?"

Mavis shrugs. "Everyone knew about it."

"Is that the incident?" Linda says.

Mavis shivers. "It's nearly dark, and I need a cup of tea. Pop the kettle on, darl."

We collect the dessert dishes and follow Mavis inside to make the tea. We settle into the lounge room – the good room, Linda whispers – and make ourselves comfortable.

Mavis sips her tea. "That's better," she says, smiling at me. "Nothing like a cup of homegrown tea to finish off a meal."

"Mum, did the fiancé ever turn up?" Linda asks. "What happened to the woman, and why have I never heard this story?"

Mavis puts her cup down. "One thing at a time, Linda. I have to get my memories in order. No, the fiancé never turned up. It was months and months later when I finally went to pick up my pearls, the ones I'd loaned Ellen."

"Are these the same pearls you keep raving on about?" Linda asks.

"Stop interrupting," Mavis shoots back. "And no, if you must know. I should have collected them sooner, but I'd forgotten. I was too much in love with your father, and we'd been away in Townsville. You know how gossip spreads in a small country town." She winks. "Still does."

When she smiles, her cheekbones stand out like apples, and her eyes twinkle. I can see the beauty she'd once been.

"I really didn't think she'd come back to Sugar Creek," Mavis says, "but she did. I guess she had nowhere else to go after the baby was born. Anyway, she wasn't home. So, I decided to wait out the front of her place. Your place, Dana. I'd borrowed Wally's truck, and it was almost dark. I waited for, I don't know, maybe half an hour? At least four cigarettes."

Linda looked at her mother in shock. "You smoked?"

"In those days, we all smoked. We didn't know any better. It was what you did. I quit just after you were born."

Linda shakes her head in disbelief.

"What happened then?" I say quickly.

"Well, I went to the pub and thought Ellen might still be there because that's where she worked, you see. In fact, I don't know why I didn't go there first." Mavis shrugs. "Anyway, Joan was mad as hell because she hadn't shown up. Watch out if you get onto Joan's wrong side. She was bellyaching about how ungrateful Ellen was."

"Where was her baby?" Linda asks, her face screwed up in confusion.

"Oh, yes. She had to go to the unwed mother's home to have her baby. Keep up, Linda. She was alone and pregnant, and with nowhere to go, that's where she went. She gave the baby up for adoption and came back to Sugar Creek."

Linda rolled her eyes. "Okay."

"Was that the St Andrew's Maternity Home?" I ask, remembering the name from Herb's grandmother's medical file.

"Yes. That's it. Anyway, the hotel was closing up. It was a Monday, and I only ever went there on the weekend with Carolyn, you know. We'd have a shandy or a gin and tonic and sit in the Ladies' Lounge, flirting with the GIs. There were some handsome ones during the war."

"Mum, back to Ellen."

"Anyway, after that, I left."

"Oh." I expected her to say more. "What about your pearls?"

"I had to get Wally's truck back, so I went to his house, he lived on the outskirts of town, because he didn't like the shack on the farm. Anyway, he was in a right flap, saying someone had set his cane field alight and that he was going to lose his entire crop. He grabbed the keys and ran right back out, leaving me to walk home on my own. And it was dark! He sold the farm a few years after that. The government offered him too good a price, and he was sick of farming. Not a lot of money in it, and too much responsibility looking after the canecutters. Especially when some of them came back sick from the experiments."

"Mum, that's what we want to know. What about the experiments?"

"I'm getting to that. Hold your horses."

Linda clucks her tongue in exasperation.

"If you stop interrupting and be patient, I'll be able to keep my train of thought."

We both nod.

"Well, I decided to check one more time. Ellen's was on my way, and it wasn't far from where I was living at the time. The town was tiny in those days. I ran into old Mrs Falconer, who asked me to help with something. We chatted for a while before I realised how late it was. It was a full moon, which normally spooks me. I don't know why. Plus, Ellen told us that someone had followed her home one night, which frightened every woman in town. But anyway, I must have forgotten about that because I could have gone there in the morning, but I didn't. It was just as well in the end."

Mavis sips her tea. "There were no lights on when I got there. I should have just turned around and gone home, but I couldn't imagine where she might have gone. It was at least eight, I reckon. There were no lights on upstairs, either. Then I remembered Phyllis had gone to Townsville to see her sister. I knew that because Mrs Falconer was about to go to the Henderson's to fill in for her at bridge. I decided to go around the back, just in case, and saw a light through the window. A torch moving about. I got such a shock because I thought maybe someone had broken in. But your old mother was brave back then, or maybe stupid, so I snuck closer to get a good look. It was Ellen. I knocked on the window, trying not to scare her, and whispered, 'Ellen, it's me, Mavis.'"

Mavis looks at Linda and puts her hand to her chest. "I gave her such a fright. I got a fright, too. You should have seen the state of her. Her hair was sticking up in all directions, her face was streaked with blood and dirt, and even her dress was torn. 'God,' I said, 'what happened to you?' She burst into tears, raving about her baby and Bert and Billy. I held her and tried to calm her down."

"Bert?" Linda says.

"Yes, yes, yes. Bert Hipworth. And you talk about me losing my memory. Really, Linda."

"Go on," I say, goosebumps spreading down my arms.

"Anyway, she was hysterical. Told me that Carolyn and Bert had stolen her son, Bert tried to kill her, and she had to get out of town before he came back." Mavis sat back in her chair. "I don't mind telling you, it was an unbelievable story. You could make a movie out of it. But something seemed to gel. We all wondered how Carolyn got that baby. They'd been on a waiting list, so she said, but I'd never heard of a waiting list. They were desperate for people to adopt babies, not like today. Back then, with no contraception, girls had no choice but to give them up. It was quick and easy."

Mavis looks sheepishly at Linda. "At least your father married me."

"Mum! You mean I wasn't a honeymoon baby?" Linda counts on her fingers.

"I thought you might have worked it out."

"Eight months. Well, I'm glad you stuck together for a while at least. I know Dad was a difficult man."

"But a loving one, especially when it came to you." Mavis turns to me. "She's the light of our life. And so are our grandchildren."

"Wait, so Herb is their son?" Linda says, scratching her head. "But he's only thirty-something."

"No, she means Herb's father," I say, not moving.

Mavis continues. "Bert Hipworth died in the early seventies. Cancer. And Herbie, as he was known, died from cancer, too. He married a young lass from Townsville and died when Herb Junior, the mayor, was a little tacker."

Linda nods. "Does Herb know that his dad was adopted?"

Mavis shrugs. "Don't know. Probably."

If only Herb had stayed to hear this.

"And Ellen?" I ask.

"Oh, yes. Back to that night. Even though she was in such a state, she was absolutely clear on what happened. Her fella, Billy, and a couple of others had died from the experiments, and Bert tried to cover it up and strangle her. If I hadn't seen the red marks around her neck, I wouldn't have believed it. Whether he set fire to the cane field to smoke her out or kill her, I'm not sure. I know that was where Wally had gone because his farm ran alongside the base."

Linda shakes her head and slumps into her chair. "That's incredible."

Mavis purses her lips. "It's very sad. That poor woman's life was ruined by that base and that man. I never liked him. I wondered why Carolyn even married him. Sometimes she hid bruises on her arm by wearing cardigans. In this stinking heat. I wasn't fooled, but in those days, no-one talked about it. So, I knew what Bert was capable of. Ex-soldiers can't always turn off. They're trained to kill, and you can't undo that straight away. Your father was different, love. He seemed to compartmentalise it. He went to Korea because of my rejection, to be honest. I've never told anyone, but I had to get away. After hearing what happened to Ellen, I was scared. I helped her throw a few things together and let her keep the pearls. Sell them and use the money to set herself up. Then I led her to the community hall. I had the keys and told her to stay there until I came back."

"Then what?" Linda says.

"I went home and tried to sleep. The next morning, just before dawn, I walked around to Wally's place. While he was sleeping, I snuck in, left a note, took the truck, picked up Ellen, and drove to Townsville. I put her on a train to Brisbane, and from there, I don't know where she went."

"Wow. That's quite a story, Mum."

"There's more. I went home scared to death. I don't mind telling you. I couldn't tell Wally. Then I saw Bert a couple of days later. He had a jagged cut across his eye and down his face. I plucked up the courage to ask him what happened, and he said he'd run into a barbed wired fence. Ellen did a good job on him. He could have lost his eye."

Mavis's eyes narrow. "But there was something about him, like a lion looking for prey. He asked if I'd seen Ellen, and I told him I hadn't. After that, I just wanted to get away. So, a month later, I broke it off with Wally and got on the train to make a new life in Brisbane."

Linda leaned over and rubbed her mother's arm. "And that's where you did your teacher training?"

Mavis nodded. "They were desperate for teachers. And I loved it."

"It all sounds horrible, Mum, and you were too scared to tell anyone?"

"Yeah, I was. This is the first time I've spoken of it. Your father eventually sold the farm and went off to Korea a year or two later." She sighs. "I thought he'd forget me, but we couldn't keep away from each other. He found me when he came back, and that's when, well, you know the rest." Mavis looks tired. "But I'll tell you one thing. I never wanted to come back here until that man died."

"Is that why we moved so much? I thought it was because of Dad's work." Linda stares at her mother, and I think about poor Herb, who knows none of this.

Mavis nods. "Your father found a job here just after we separated in the early sixties. I stayed in Townsville. I couldn't bear to come back. I should have gone to the police, but they wouldn't have believed me. Just like the bruises on Carolyn's arms. They didn't even believe Ellen about Billy."

"But what about the pearls, Mum? You had me looking for them the other day." Linda is frowning. "I'm confused."

Mavis raises her eyebrows. "Your father gave me another set, Linda. I hope you don't think ..." Mavis starts chuckling. "Oh, dear ..."

I get to my feet. "I better go and let you rest. Thank you for sharing that. You were incredibly brave."

"Nice of you to say. Yes, it is probably time for bed. Dr Janssen, we really love having you here in our town."

I blush. "Thank you, Mavis. I really like being here, too."

"And almost everyone is lovely." Mavis puts her hand on my arm. "But a word of advice. Keep away from Joan and her grandson, Jack."

"Mum, I thought you were friends."

"Only for company, love. I never really liked the woman. An opportunist. She had a part to play in taking that baby off Ellen, pretending it was for her own good. But it wasn't. And to be honest, I've had about enough of her. Yesterday I found out she was spreading stories about me having dementia. Ooh, I'd like to give her a piece of my mind."

"Now, Mum, don't get yourself worked up over her. She isn't worth it. And we know you don't have dementia." Linda looks at me.

"You are as sharp as a tack, Mavis," I say. "Those tests showed no sign of dementia, remember?"

"Just forget about her. Don't see her for a while," Linda says.

"You're probably right. Now, give me your hand" – Linda helps Mavis to her feet—" Drop in again, Dr Janssen. Any time."

"I will, Mavis. I will," I say.

42

I walk the last patient of the day out of my office and catch the look of exhaustion on Linda's face. I know how she feels. Now that the news is out, my voice is almost hoarse from talking to patients, scared and worried that they might already have cancer, reassuring them as best as I can and organising tests, just in case.

"Well, that's a day we could have done without," Linda says after she locks the door.

"You're not wrong. What do you think?"

Linda raises her eyebrows. "I reckon everyone is panicking. Some are going to just pack up and get out."

"What about you? How are you feeling?"

She shrugs. "Just a bit numb. I mean, I know Dad's been sounding the warning bell for years, and I should have taken more notice, but … I ignored it and moved away. I suppose I haven't really spent more than a few years here, anyway, but I feel for those who have. It's just not fair."

"At least the authorities are taking it seriously," I say. "They're shutting off the water tonight."

"Yeah, I heard. Some patients said they saw a couple of water tankers coming in this afternoon. You've got a full book tomorrow. A lot of them want tests done, and I can't say I blame them."

"Yeah, it's understandable. They're sending up some nurses in a few days to take the bloods, and we have priority with the pathologists. Anyway, let's get out of here."

"Good idea."

Later, at home, I heat up a frozen lasagne, and there's a knock at the door. I groan, hoping it's not another worried patient. There was one only ten minutes earlier asking me to look at a rash.

I open the door anyway, surprised and pleased that it's Herb. His customary Hawaiian shirt and shorts are crumpled as if he's thrown them on. "Come in," I say.

He takes a couple of steps back from the door, his face stern and businesslike, as usual. "I'll take a quick look at the torn lino if that's okay," he says, turning to go down the stairs.

"Do you need any help?" I call out. Should I tell him it can wait? But then, it is his house. Maybe he wants to organise the repairs.

He shakes his head as if he can't get away quick enough. "I'll be right. Won't be long." He disappears down the side of the house.

While eating, I read Steve's article in the paper about the missing ex-soldiers. It's chilling and sad. There's nothing about the whereabouts of the bodies, and the authorities aren't commenting. I clean up and wonder if I should take a glass of water or something down there. It's been quiet for a long time. I glance at the clock. Over an hour has passed. How long should it take?

I step onto the back verandah and into the cool night air. The crickets have started up, joining an orchestra of sounds in the nearby rainforest. Down the stairs, moths throw themselves against the window, trying to get at the light inside. Could he have left and forgotten to turn the light off? I'm a little hurt that he might have gone without saying goodbye. I go down and open the door, surprised to see him cross-legged on the bare floorboards, reading a book.

"Reading on the job?" I laugh until he lifts his pale, drawn face. "What's the matter? What's wrong?"

There's a roll of torn lino to the side, and a square of floorboard has been lifted, revealing a tiny cubby hole. A baby's bunny rug is draped over his leg. I sit down next to him.

He looks at me, tears in his eyes, and hands me the book. It looks like a diary, dusty with yellowed pages. Inside the cover is a note from a man called Billy to his sweetheart, Ellen: *So you don't forget me – April 2nd 1948.* I freeze.

He sighs. "It's all there. The baby she was carrying was my father. According to her, my grandparents stole him, which means she's my real grandmother."

I gently touch his arm. "I'm so sorry you had to find out like this."

He lifts his head and stares at me. "You knew?"

"Only about the adoption. I didn't know it was Billy and Ellen's child until last night."

"Last night?"

"Mavis told us what happened after you left."

He looks confused. "How does Mavis know?"

"Come on." I hold out my hand to help him up. "Upstairs. I'll get us a drink and tell you what she said."

The kitchen chair snarls across the floor as he pulls it out and slumps into it. He sits quietly, running his fingers over the diary, while I get some beer. I worry how he'll take the news about his grandparents. Once seated opposite him, I begin.

He's silent while I relay Mavis's story. When I've finished, I sip my beer and wait, watching him trying to process what I've said. He stares at the diary, then runs a hand over it and opens it in the middle. "She wrote this on the day she disappeared. My grandfather … It's hard to believe he could do something like that. Yet …" He narrows his eyes. "I sort of can. I was scared of him when I was little. He didn't do anything that I can remember, but I never liked to be in the same room."

I'm overcome by his anguish and maybe everything else that's happened.

"You're crying?"

I quickly wipe my eyes. "No. Well, just a little. It's so sad." I think of what might have been. "And so unfair for Ellen and Billy."

He closes his eyes for a second, then sighs. "My life might have turned out very differently. I probably wouldn't be mayor."

"Or maybe you would have anyway."

He gets up. "Maybe. I suppose I better go."

I put my hand on his arm to stop him from leaving. Or for assurance, I'm not sure which. "If you need anything, anything at all, I'm here."

He nods. "I know."

Something comes over me, and I put my arms around him. This bulk of a man lets me pull him in close, and he clings to me. We stay like that for a while. Then he pulls back and touches my cheek, his lips parted, and leans forward to kiss me. His mouth is tentative against mine at first, then soft and tender. I taste the beer on his lips and feel a hint of bristle. His lips move to my neck, my ear, and then my mouth again, considerate and slow. His hands are in my hair, my arms around his neck – the opposite of Daniel's roughness. I can't help but make the comparison. A loud knock at the door breaks the moment, and we spring apart like caught teenagers.

"God," I say, touching my hair.

He looks down the hallway towards the front door. "This used to happen when I lived here, too. Sorry."

"That's the life of a GP in a small country town with poisoned water," I say ruefully.

He half-smiles. "I better go."

"Don't forget the diary." I hand it to him, our hands briefly touching.

"See you soon," he says.

I open the door to the school principal. He looks from me to Herb and back to me again.

"I saw the light was still on. I hope you don't mind, but I just wanted to check something with you," he says as Herb slips past him down the stairs.

"Of course, come in," I say, hoping I can get rid of him quickly.

43

A week later, I walk to the pub to meet Steve, who's back in town and wants a catch-up. It's eerily quiet. No cars, no people, and shops closed for the day. The palm trees down the middle of Main St stand guard. Cigarette smoke fills the air as I reach the pub, and the murmur of voices gets louder. That's where everyone is this hot evening.

Just before I step inside, I'm stopped by Anita, the gallery owner.

"I'm glad I caught you," she says. "Look, I don't think there's much point holding the exhibition next month." She waves her arm around. "I mean, no-one's going to come."

It hadn't occurred to me that the exhibition wouldn't go ahead. "I understand."

"But I have arranged something else. I hope you don't mind."

"Yes?" I nod at two people going into the pub who yell out g'day.

"I've got a friend with a gallery in Cairns, and well, provided you and your sister are okay with it, she can exhibit there. It will probably be sold out, what with all the tourists. What do you think?"

"That sounds wonderful. Should I arrange for the paintings to be sent there?"

"No. Goodness, no. I'll organise it all. I'm going to close the gallery and work with my friend." She looks around. More people are walking into the pub. "You know? Until everything settles down."

"I understand. I'll let Lily know. She'll be delighted."

"Great. I'll get it organised. And thanks," she says. "I better fly."

I walk into the pub. Herb's on the television screen behind the bar. "A chardonnay, thanks," I say to Crystal.

"Sure," Crystal says, bringing down a wineglass. "He comes across well on the telly, doesn't he?" She pours the wine.

"Yeah," I say. "I guess he does."

"They asked me what I thought." She slides the drink across the bar to me.

"Oh, really? And what did you say?"

"I said it stinks that this has happened to such a lovely community, and there are a lot of people making plans to move and that the government should compensate us all." She smiles. "Eight dollars, thanks."

I hand over the money and glance at the screen, half expecting her to pop up on it. "Right."

"Anyway, you missed it. I was just on."

"Looking good, Crystal," a man says behind me. "Just saw you."

"Thanks, Teddy," Crystal says, smiling. "What'll it be?"

Teddy takes my place at the bar, and I glance back at the screen. Our story's been replaced by a light plane crash survivor interview. I look around, hoping to see Herb. There's Wally in a corner, holding court with a few people. Apparently, he'd been on television, too.

I spoke to Herb on the phone once since the kiss, but it was all business. I wonder if he's avoiding me. I spy an empty table and head through the noisy crowd, nodding greetings and hearing snippets of conversations on the way.

Jack and his grandmother, Joan, are at a table nearby. They glance at me, then turn away. Then I notice Herb in a crisp white shirt, dark slacks, and even a tie. He makes his way to the bar and looks so different, so official, that I can't take my eyes off him. He turns, smiles, and gives someone a reassuring nod, but the dark circles under his eyes don't hide anything from me.

Someone raises their voice. "Thought you'd be here with your snivelling grandson."

Every head swivels. It's Mavis, standing in front of Joan's table.

"Excuse me," Joan says.

"Hey," Jack says. "What's the big idea?"

Mavis raises her voice even further. "Your grandmother is an evil person, Jack, and it's time you know the truth." A hush settles across the room. She has the look of someone who's not going to waste time now that she has everyone's attention. "Did you see that article in the paper? Your grandmother was good friends with the man who ran those experiments. Did you know that, Jack?"

"So were you, Mavis." Joan protests as if this is a court, and maybe it is, in a rudimentary way.

"You made that woman give up her child to Bert Hipworth." Mavis steps back and points at Joan with her walking stick. "And you knew he was bashing Carolyn."

There's a murmur of confusion across the room. I doubt anyone knows what she's talking about, but I do, and so does Herb, who's turned pale. He catches my eye and moves towards me.

"I didn't know what they were doing," Joan says.

"Joan Babcock, you've spent your life lying and manipulating this town. You even knew about the spraying, and don't you deny it."

"Well, I never," Joan says, her hand fluttering across her chest.

"This is preposterous. Jack, I need to go home. I've never been spoken to by anyone like this."

"You don't get off that easy, Joan. Stay right there, Jack." She glares at Jack, who sits back down like the coward he is. "You've fed everyone lies for years. Told them Wally was a crackpot. Told them he was wrong. And now we find out he was *always* right. A lot of people died because no-one took him seriously. You, Joan Babcock, are a lying, opportunistic bitch." Mavis looks around at her captive and entranced audience. "If you want to know who to blame for the debacle today, you can blame this woman here. And *only* this woman." Mavis's voice is surprisingly strong, and she points her walking stick at Joan again. "The town would have been cleaned up thirty-five years ago if not for this woman."

"That's enough," Jack says, his face thunderous. "Wally is a nutter. Always has been." He glances around. "Everyone knows it."

"Only because of the lies your grandmother has spun. And don't you dare have a go at me, Jack Babcock. I know you've been buying up the land of dead and sick people so you could develop it, you greedy little man. It satisfies me no end that your scheme has now finished." Mavis raises her walking stick and slams it hard onto the table. Joan jumps, as does everyone else. "And it stops right here."

We all watch as Mavis gives Joan a final stare, then shuffles away towards the bar. Someone begins a slow clap and then another until Mavis nods ever so slightly.

Jack looks around and yells out, "Another nut case. See how she is? Why would anyone believe that old bag?"

"You bought up those places, mate," Teddy yells. "Some had hardly turned cold in their graves."

"Wally was right," another man yells from near the bar. "He tried to warn us all."

"Hear, hear," more people say.

Joan frowns and reaches for Jack's arm, whispering something to him. He looks uncertain. Then he helps his grandmother stand, and they walk away, leaving the food on their plates untouched.

"The food here is shit anyway. We won't be back," Jack says.

There's murmuring from the crowd.

As they head to the door, someone yells, "Good riddance."

After they've left, the room erupts. Herb and I look at each other, not quite believing what happened.

"Never seen that side of Mavis before," he says, sliding into the chair opposite me.

I turn the stem of my glass around and around. "She's got a loud voice when she wants to use it."

"Not as quietly spoken as we all thought." He sips his beer, leaving a thin film of froth on his top lip. I want to lean across and kiss it.

Teddy comes up to our table. His brow is furrowed with worry, and he asks Herb if he can still use tank water. Herb assures him he can, and he nods and drifts away.

"Anyway, how are you going?" I ask.

"Had better weeks," he says, drumming his fingers on the table. He glances around the room. The noise seems louder than before as people cluster in groups, talking.

"I'm really sorry about the other night," I say.

He looks at me as if he's trying to work out what I'm talking about. I wonder if he thinks I'm referring to the kiss.

"Mavis's story," I say quickly. "You had to deal with that as well as everything else."

He shrugs. "I've hardly had time to think about it. It's – "

"Looks like a lot of history between those two," Steve says, standing at our table with a beer in his hand. He pulls out a seat next to me and plonks his beer glass on the table. "Nice tie, mate. You scrub up well."

Herb pulls his tie loose. "My professional garb."

"Multimedia megastar now," Steve says to me. "Probably need to get an appointment."

"Get in line," Herb says. "By the way, great article about the missing men, mate. And thanks for holding off on the contamination angle."

"It was very well received," Steve says modestly. "The government is scrambling for answers now. Don't know if you know, but they're out at the base looking for remains. Hell of a job, but my guess is they've buried them in the cane field they owned or even the one right next door. They deliberately took single men."

"It's mind-blowing," Herb says.

I shudder.

"What brings you back to town?" Herb asks. "You wanted to meet?"

Steve looks over at Mavis, who's now seated with Anita, Wally, and two teachers from the school. "I might have to chat with Mavis. Sounds like there's a really good story between those two."

People are approaching Mavis, and there are two glasses of champagne in front of her. She seems to be enjoying the attention. Wally looks proud of her.

"Wondered if I could get a quote from you?" Steve says to me.

I grimace. "I don't know."

"Come on, doc. Give me a quote with some medical advice. Like, what people should look out for."

"I guess I could do that. It might slow down all the enquiries."

He turns to Herb. "Hoping for a quote from you about progress on the clean-up."

"Sure," Herb says. "You could come along to the town meetings. I'm holding them every Tuesday night now."

"Sorry, mate, no can do. Gotta head back to Sydney tomorrow."

"You know, I've always wondered why you came here to investigate those men," I say. "It happened so long ago. Why now?"

Steve runs his finger down the side of the glass, wiping away the condensation. "Well, I actually have a family connection."

"What sort of family connection?" Herb asks.

"My grandmother was engaged to one of the missing men. He lost his life because he wanted her to have an engagement ring."

Herb's mouth has fallen open. "Is your grandmother Ellen?"

Goosebumps spread down my arm.

"Yes," Steve says, looking from Herb to me. "Why?"

"I'm Ellen's grandson, too," Herb says, breaking into a grin.

Steve looks incredulous. "You're shitting me."

Herb leans forward, now animated. "She and Billy had a son who was adopted by Bert and Carolyn Hipworth. His name was Herbie, and I'm Herbie's son."

"The paperwork was in the medical files I found," I say. "That was who Mavis was talking about. Joan forced Ellen to give up her child."

"Bloody hell," Steve says. "So, we're related?"

"Cousins, I reckon."

It's good to see a smile on Herb's face.

They start talking over the top of each other. According to Steve, Ellen moved to Sydney and married an Italian immigrant, Lou. They had three children: Maria, Stephanie, and Lou Junior.

"Lou's my father," Steve adds.

"Is Ellen alive?" I ask.

"We found her diary under my house," Herb says. "I'd really like to meet her."

Steve's face falls. "Sorry, mate. She told me the story just before she died. I promised her I'd investigate it."

We sit in silence. I sense Herb's disappointment.

"You know," Steve says, "I was sceptical about the whole thing. I just said it to humour her, but she got so agitated that I had to promise. When I started looking into it, I found a newspaper article about her and Billy. I thought there might be something in it, and there was, but I had no idea there was a baby. She never said a word. Took that to her grave."

I think about what an amazing woman she must have been. "There's a sad history of babies being removed from single mothers. They had no choice back then."

Steve spreads his hands on the table. "I just never thought it had happened in my family."

"That military base and those who ran it ruined a lot of lives," Herb says. "Someone's got to pay for that."

"Mate, the town deserves restitution. I hope you're ready for a very long fight," Steve says.

Herb reaches for my hand across the table and smiles at Steve. "With a powerful media ally in the family, how could we not win?"

*

The Evening Sun

Senior Investigative Reporter Stephen Romano

October 23, 2024

The High Court of Australia released their landmark decision in the case Sugar Creek versus the Commonwealth Government, ruling in favour of the residents of Sugar Creek with a $50 million compensation package. The case, which has dragged on since 2008, now sets a legal precedent for all other instances where land and water have been polluted. The decision is expected to precipitate a slew of lawsuits.

The government has continuously denied allegations that Agent Orange was sprayed. However, files uncovered at the Sugar Creek military base were produced as conclusive evidence.

A joint mission by Australia, Britain, and the USA was formed to open a medical research facility at the Sugar Creek military base in 1948, where experiments were conducted on ex-soldiers. After four died, it was closed until 1961, when Agent Orange experimentation was undertaken on rainforest surrounding Sugar Creek. Testing was done by aerial spraying across an area in the hills beyond the town.

"We're ecstatic that the case is finally over, and that compensation can begin to flow to those who've lost loved ones," said Herb Hipworth, President of the National Environment Preservation Society. "It's taken years to win justice for those who died because of environmental pollution." Mr Hipworth lost his grandparents and father due to Agent Orange spraying in the early 1960s around Sugar Creek. Together with his wife, Dr Dana Janssen, State Chief Medical Officer, they fought to have the case heard first in the Federal Court and then the High Court.

Acknowledgements and Notes

It is no secret that pesticides are a common source of pollution affecting the land, fauna, and flora, as well as human health. In my research, I discovered a website where individuals associated with The Friends of the Earth have carefully documented decades of pesticide contamination and accidents across Australia. It's an eye-opening display of widespread pollution in remote and populated areas which led me to think about environmental degradation created by the storage and use of pesticides.

I was also inspired by the work of Jean Williams, a researcher who claimed that the Australian military sprayed Agent Orange near Innisfail in the early sixties. The allegations were denied by the Australian government.

The research done while I was writing *The Good Child* inspired me to write this work of fiction. I also wanted to shine a light on the real struggles of mothers who were so cruelly forced to give up their children and the ramifications it has on families even today.

The characters in *Sugar Creek* are, of course, all a figment of my imagination, as is the town of Sugar Creek and the Sugar Creek Military base. Any resemblance to real people and events is purely coincidental.

I was extremely privileged to receive wise counsel and advice about the life of a GP and medical ailments from my generous friend, Kaye Ferguson. She pointed out inconsistencies and inaccuracies and put me on the right path. Any errors are mine alone.

This novel was also workshopped and discussed at length with AJ Collins, whose guidance and thoughtful observations helped bring this story to life. Special thanks for their critical feedback also to Eleni Hale, Ara Sarafian, Mia Witherspoon and Nikki Bielinski. My appreciation also goes to my Beta readers Sally and Beth who provided valuable feedback. And a special thank you to Adam vanLangenberg for his editing prowess in taking this novel to the next level. Thank you Colin Denovan for your sharp eyes. A special thanks to Pauline and Ron who brainstormed a germ of an idea not knowing where I'd take it.

To my family and friends, thank you for your interest and encouragement and for urging me on.

Thank you also to my supportive husband, Con who plied me with food and cups of tea and was my sounding board. To my daughters, Georgia and Eva, and my mother, Yolande thank you for your feedback and counsel.

And finally, thank you, dear reader for your support in buying and reading my work. That is the real inspiration for getting the words out of my head and onto the page.

Also by S.C. Karakaltsas
Climbing the Coconut Tree
Out of Nowhere
A Perfect Stone
The Good Child

About the Author

After many years in the corporate world, S.C. Karakaltsas found a passion for writing about little known times and places. Sugar Creek is her fourth historical fiction novel. She has also written a number of short stories some of which may be found in various anthologies, including her own collection, Out of Nowhere. An avid reader, she enjoys blogging about the many books she reads.

She lives in Melbourne, Australia with her husband.

Would you like to know more? Drop by and say hello at sckarakaltsas.com